WELL WITH MY SOUL

Well With My Soul

A NOVEL BY

Gregory G. Allen

ASD PUBLISHING

Published by ASD Publishing
ISBN: 978-0-9836049-0-7
Library of Congress Control Number: 2011906770

Book design by Brion Sausser: www.bookcreatives.com
Manufactured in the United States of America

PART I

Whatever my lot, Thou hast taught me to say, It is well, it is well with my soul.

~HORATIO G. SPAFFORD

(1828-1888)

CHAPTER ONE

JACOB

REO Speedwagon played on the radio as I got dressed in my grey pinstripe suit that Halston himself had designed for me. My ashtray was full of cigarette butts, because my lover Gary, whom I had dubbed Hazel, hadn't been home to do any cleaning this evening. It had nothing to do with the fact that I had been smoking nonstop while running around the apartment preparing for this big night. Studio 54 had reopened and many of the regulars were making their way back there to relish in the festivities. Rubell and Schrager made it the place to be in the late 70s and my friends and I were certain to keep it the place to be now. Everyone loved the fact that ordinary people could dance and mingle with the famous and the notorious. But I liked the fact that I was treated like a true celebrity from the moment I walked in.

The Jack and Coke in my hand was running low, so I replenished it, since I had to blast my manager on the phone.

"I don't give a shit about the cost ... see what you can do to make this happen," I said, as I chomped on a piece of ice.

I had grown tired of other's incompetence.

"Come on, Rachel. I need that money to afford this great space, the vacations that Gary and I take, my other habits," I said. "You've been my manager for years. Are you getting tired of the job?"

As predicted, the Upper West Side had become the place to live. The area that people were afraid to live in the mid 70s was now beginning to burst with young, hip people. We had gotten in just in time before rents got much more expensive in the 80s. So what that it was a rent stabilized building? I still needed money to afford it. I should have bought the place instead of buying Gary that damn hair salon back when I was feeling overly generous towards him.

Rachel was getting annoyed on the other end of the phone, but the woman was in love with me. She wouldn't want me to fire her.

"Just make it work," I said. "Love you too."

I hung up the phone and turned up the radio. Foreigner was now providing a pounding beat for me with their hit, *Urgent*. Almost dressed to head out to the club, I stopped to do a line of coke, perfectly cut on the coffee table. The bathroom door opened and out walked a very hot man wearing only my terry cloth towel.

I had forgotten he was even there.

"You better get dressed and get out of here," I said. "My lover will be home any moment."

"Aren't you getting ready to go out?" he asked.

"I'm going out, he's coming home," I said in a stern tone. "You need to go."

What the hell was wrong with him? I may have been high, but I knew that the young trick was used to people throwing him out of their apartments.

"Can you give me a lift?" he asked.

The little prick apparently wanted to stay with me a little longer.

"Sorry, can't," I said. "Here … put your cut-off shorts on and head out … and thanks. We appreciate the business."

I threw his clothes into his arms and backed him up to the front door. He let the towel fall to the floor as he started putting on his shorts. Should I go one more round? Nah, it would mess up my suit.

"So can I say I fucked the Langston Cigarette Man?" he asked.

"If you can get someone to believe you, feel free," I said.

He grabbed me to kiss me, but I had seen guys fall for me all the time and knew the routine. Before he was even aware, he was on the other side of the door and I had it closed. I grabbed my suit jacket as the phone rang.

"Hello … Felicia, yeah … I'm going to dinner and will be there by 12:30 or 1:00. See you then."

I examined myself in the mirror. I looked damn good and had managed to maintain a decent body as a model. There weren't too many men in New York who would not want to sleep with me and plenty would be waiting at the club that night. I couldn't believe I had ever questioned that I would fit so well into the skin of a gay man; that I had ever been nervous to tear out of that closet. The lifestyle suited me almost as well as the designer duds I sported on any given day in this fast-paced life of the past six years.

My mind drifted to the exact moment the decision had been made to make the trek to the Big Apple. It had been a sweltering summer in our small town of Nocona, Tennessee. Minnie Riperton blared from my eight-track. I had closed the wild orange and green striped curtains to keep the afternoon sun out and turned on the black light, which made an eerie glow on my velvet Charlie Brown poster.

Yeah, that was the way to set the mood for me and Gary. You would think that at twenty-six, I would have changed that room, but there are some things we just have to hold on from the past.

The noisy fan in my room was cranked to full blast, with the unbearable heat. Someday, I swore I'd be able to afford air condition- ing. Those stupid cooking classes I was enrolled in at the time had air conditioning, but I had already stopped attending. Ambition and drive seemed to only be in my mind and not able to manifest itself in my day-to-day living. Sitting around a dark room in the middle of a summer afternoon was about all I could muster myself up to do.

Gary had stopped by after work and wrapped himself around me on my bed. I held him and sang with Minnie into his ear, stroking his beautiful sandy-blonde hair.

"Lovin' you is easy cause you're beautiful ..."

"Don't even try and hit that last note, babe," Gary laughed.

"Shut your face and give me some of that lip," I joked as I kissed him wildly.

"Jacob. You have to stop," Gary said. "Your mother's in the next room."

"So. We're grown men."

"In the room you grew up in ... and it's too hot in here."

Gary stood. He towered over me as he tried to get away from the sweat dripping down my back. "We have to think about getting our own place."

"Funny you should bring that up," I said. "I was just thinking the same thing."

"Really?" he asked, as he combed through my eight-track collection.

"But not in Nocona," I said.

"Jacob, not this again. You bring this up every three months. I know we're not going anywhere."

"I'm ready. I really want to do it this time," I said as I jumped off the bed.

I meant it.

I was a ticking bomb in that small town. Like I wanted to explode and do something crazy. Maybe it was just me escaping into the romance of movies. Gary had recently taken me to the new Pacino flick about robbing a bank for a sex change. Or maybe it was more rooted in deeper anxieties that time. I needed to make a move. Mama had been giving me money for years (unbeknownst to Gary) and I had been storing it away, building up a nice nest egg that would allow us to make the leap. Lucky for me, Gary had a good job and would pay each time we'd go out so naturally — I never stopped him.

"I've been dying to get back to a major city," Gary said. "Just waiting on you."

Gary had grown up in Dallas, Texas and I never understood how he could go from that to our tiny town. He had moved to Nocona to live with an ailing aunt. I fell for him the moment I saw him just four years prior. He was really more than anyone could ask for, over-considerate and patient with me.

"I don't deserve you," I said, as I grabbed him from behind and kissed his neck.

"Yeah, yeah ... so where should it be?" Gary asked, as he freed himself from my grasp. He looked so hot standing in my room in his Jordache jeans and tight tank top.

"We should try the East Coast," I said, knowing that wasn't what Gary wanted to hear.

My goal was to move to New York and hit it big on Broadway or any other part of the entertainment world. The Tennessee cooking class was just a means to an end.

"You know I don't like the cold," he said, turning around to face me. "L.A. would be a great place to live."

"I think I have a better chance at making something of myself in New York."

"And what about me?" Gary asked.

"Honey, you can cut those northern bitches' hair just as same as you do it here."

I needed him to see things my way so I kissed him hard, his lips soft and inviting.

"Guess I'll just have to study up on those northern hair-dos," Gary said. "I wouldn't want to insult them with some big southern do."

I could feel him giving in. I could usually get him to do whatever I wanted.

Mama interrupted my time with my man by hollering my name from the kitchen.

"Why does she always need me near her all the time?" I asked.

"Don't talk like that … at least she's still alive," he said.

I had momentarily forgotten that Gary really had no family to speak of back in his home state. He had been raised by a grandmother after his dad had split and mother died. The jolt of guilt sent the conversation in a different direction.

"So do we want to go to The Doghouse for dinner on Friday?" I asked.

"Don't change the subject," he said. "When do you want to move?"

"Let's just set a date and make it happen," I said. "I say we finish up stuff here. You give the shop a month's notice and then we just go."

"Shit. Are you sure?"

"More than sure, Gar. I feel it in my bones," I said. "We're meant to be northern boys."

Gary pulled me into his arms. The smell of his Grey Flannel cologne mixed with his natural musk and sweat was intoxicating. It made me shiver.

"As long as I'm with you," he said, "I don't care where we live."

With a final kiss, I pushed Gary out of my bedroom door, down the hall and out the front door into the blazing heat, as Mama yelled my name again. I adjusted the growing bulge in my pants, and thought about sneaking back into my bedroom for a quickie with myself while thinking about my man.

"Jacob!" Mama yelled again from the kitchen.

The guilt of skipping those cooking classes she was paying for guided me towards her to see what she needed.

"What's up?" I asked.

She was up on a small ladder, removing all the dishes from the cupboard. It must be one of her cleaning spurts, I thought. Dishes covered all the counters in her yellow country kitchen.

"I wanted to see if you could do me a favor and run to the Safeway," she said. "We need a few items for supper."

"I was sort of busy … in my room."

"I'm sure you were," Mama said in a tone that reeked of non approval.

Mama and I didn't discuss mine and Gary's relationship all that much, but she knew who he was to me and why he was always around.

"I just need a little help today because I want to get these cupboards clean," she continued. "Your brother is at work and I figured with you learning to be a chef and all … you could help me out."

"A chef cooks. He doesn't shop," I informed her. "He has people to do that for him."

"We are the people around here."

"Fine … let me change my clothes."

"How is your cooking class coming by the way?" she asked, as she took vinegar and water and scrubbed one of the shelves.

Did she know I was skipping?

"Great! I think I've learned a lot about the dos and don'ts of a kitchen."

"I'm sure some famous place in Nashville or something will soon swoop you up, and you'll have to move away from here," she said as I walked out of the room.

It was as if Mama always knew what I was thinking back then, even before I sometimes did. She knew I had no intentions of growing old in that small town. Nocona had a population of less than 12,000 people, one grocery store, a few strip malls, two elementary schools, one junior high and one high school … but several churches. We were one step removed from the dirt road town on *Little House on the Prairie* with Half-Pint running around in a gingham dress.

At least that's the way it always felt to me.

But that was then and this was now. Now I was one of the largest male models on the island of Manhattan. Everyone knew my face and

I didn't ever have to give two thoughts to what some old bitty at the library thought of me and Gary or how I gestured or spoke in the line at the grocery store. Even picturing that time in my life made my head throb. Back then, I would never have considered cheating on Gary. He was the kind of man who would care for an aunt, give the shirt off his back to someone if he thought it was needed, and was a complete God-send to me in Tennessee — sticking around that God forsaken town waiting for me to leave.

Guilt was something of the past. Something Mama had instilled in me and I didn't appreciate it popping up on this big night out in the city. There was only one Jacob Garrett and many men wanted a piece of me — Gary had learned that was a price to pay for being with someone of my fame. I did one more line of coke before heading out on the road — a rainbow brick road that was as far away from Nocona, Tennessee as I man like me could get.

CHAPTER TWO

NOAH

The spring breeze wafted through the kitchen windows of our home in Nocona, making Mama's floral printed curtains dance and filling the room with fresh air. It looked as if the Vietnam War would end any day now and President Ford could turn his attention to Cambodia. In California, Patty Hearst had reappeared, involved in some robbery and murder. And Anwar Sadat was busy opening a passage through the Suez Canal. But none of that worldly stuff mattered to Mama. She didn't think about things that went on beyond her immediate perimeter. At the moment, her only concern was making a snack for me and my brother Jacob.

"*Promised her he'd take her for his bride,*" she sang with the portable radio, as the frequency went in and out, focused on getting the oil in the pan to the correct temperature.

She grabbed the canned biscuits from the fridge, and as always struggled to get the package open. I tried not to laugh aloud, wondering why they made those stupid things so hard for a normal person to get into. The arthritis that plagued both of Mama's hands didn't help matters.

Once freed from their tube, she laid them all out and took the top off a coke bottle. With the lid, she pushed down in the middle, creating a donut hole that would be added into the sizzling oil later. I knew she was saving those for Jacob. He loved to eat those dainty bites, and His Highness would always get what he wanted.

"Jacob! Noah! You boys are going to need to help me soon," she cried out, not knowing that one of us was standing right behind her.

Now Mama's food was not the same as our grandma's, who before her death had been the real cook in the family. She could make anything from scratch. A barbecue meatloaf and mashed potatoes with heavy cream, butter, and a hint of chives. Corn on the cob from her own garden, bathed in a homemade dill butter sauce. A Mississippi mud cake, oozing with a moist chocolate center, which did not come from Betty Crocker. But grandma had to be able to do all that, since she had once had ten kids to feed and needed to make sure money spent could go a long way.

At fifty, Mama really didn't see a need to squander all her time in a kitchen. She had single-handedly raised my brother and me and had toiled for us as long as I could remember. While there were a few sisters she would occasionally talk to on the phone and some cousins smattered about the southland, Mama hadn't remained that close to her family after Grandma died, in fact she probably had never been close in the first place. And as the baby of the bunch, she had witnessed her older siblings pass away or just pull off from her when she had needed help once Dad died. But she persevered and proved she could stand on her own two feet. She had been finally able to pay off the $22,000 mortgage on our modest three-bedroom wood-frame home just a few years before and now enjoyed her church socials, reading groups at the library and bingo games.

She placed the biscuits in the pan and the oil caressed around the sides of each causing them to puff up and splatter oil across the avocado colored stove. Mama would clean that up later.

"Instant donuts," she said. "Jacob, get in here and get ready to put some powdered sugar on these things!"

I often stood back and observed my mother when she wouldn't notice. Another favorite 'mama-ism' of mine was her laundry room ritual with the wet clothes from the washing machine. She took each garment and carefully shook it out before placing it in the dryer. It was complete overkill, I thought. It was going to tumble until dry, wasn't it? But she always did it.

I retreated into the living room, where my brother lay sprawled on the sofa watching our 1965 Sylvania color TV. Like in most homes at that time, there was some sort of tinfoil jerry-rigged around the rabbit ears to get the best reception. But we were happy to at least have a picture in color, even if it was ten years old. Our living room consisted of mismatched furniture that looked as if it had all come from the Goodwill store.

"You acting like you don't hear her?" I asked.

"I'm watching this guy named Stallone," Jacob said. "He wrote this movie script and insists on playing the lead."

My brother was obsessed with all things entertainment. Movie stars, singers on the radio, television personalities. But he couldn't name a single player on the Oilers. Maybe someday Tennessee would have a pro football team.

"I don't know why she treats us like we're twelve," I said, plopping onto the recliner.

"Just something she likes to do. Reminds her of our childhood, I guess," Jacob said.

"Our childhood? Like that's anything to remember."

"What do you mean? We had it great," Jacob exclaimed.

"You were treated like a freaking princess. I did all the work, mowing the lawn, taking out the trash —"

"Ah, don't be jealous, baby Bubba," Jacob said. "Think of me as the daughter she never had."

I laughed and pegged his head with one throw of the pillow that was sitting on the floor next to me.

Jacob was right. At twenty-six, he had the slight figure of a girl, which made him look much younger, maybe twenty — constantly getting carded at bars. Not a big, brawny southern man with a beer gut like myself, handsome in his own unique way. I had heard him described as "something from a Greek painting," or even "a beauty contest host." He had a thick head of brown hair, nothing like the straw on my head, which had started thinning my senior year of high school. He stood six feet tall, when you could get him to get off his butt and stand up, that is; and he possessed a smile that could bewitch anyone. And trust me, he used that charm every chance he got. If he didn't shave for a week, he might pass for a lanky cowboy. Until he opened his mouth.

Jacob had been gay for as long as I could remember.

The day it become very clear to me was back in high school, when I walked in on Jacob and Bryan Derbing fooling around. He was a friend both of us had shared until that moment. Seeing them in that compromising position made me sick. Jacob swore that Bryan had talked him into it, but deep down I knew Jacob had masterminded it. Bryan had gotten married right after high school and never discussed the incident with anyone, as far as I know. But Jacob always made cracks under his breath whenever we'd see Bryan at the grocery store or somewhere. He began to wear his gayness like a badge worn by a secret agent; flashing it when he felt he could use it to his benefit. It was definitely not the scarlet letter that one would assume it would be in the South. At least it didn't appear to be to Jacob. Deep down, I blamed Mama for protecting and fawning over Jacob for so many years, as part of the reason he turned out that way.

It only fueled my own fire to be as manly as I possibly could. At twenty-three, I had a job with the parks and recreation department as a maintenance man. A real man's job. This after years of mowing lawns, hauling hay and any other outside job I could take. But as I looked at Jacob, lying on the sofa like some sort of male model, it made me realize how much all those jobs had taken a toll on me. The sun had already weathered my skin so much that I looked older than my own brother. Even lazing around the house, his hair was neatly combed, while mine was unkempt. His face had no marks on it, whereas I had scars from where I had scratched myself as a child when I had chicken pox, as well as a huge one on my chin where I fell against the coffee table as a kid. I matched him in the height department, but I was much more round, which also made me look older. He definitely got the looks in the family, while I often felt as if I had been awarded the "thanks for just showing up" prize. And I'm sure if I got close enough, he would reek of some fancy cologne, while I could smell the stink of my own arm pits.

Speaking of smells, the aroma got there long before Mama entered the room with a plate of piping hot donuts, some smothered in white powdered sugar and others in chocolate syrup.

"Fizzlesnits! Do I have to do everything myself?" she asked us.

Jacob chimed in. "Smells great, Mama."

"Thank you. You boys should try some," she said as she tried to get spilled white powder off her four year old polyester dress. Between that and her premature specs of white hair, which had sprouted over 15 years before, it seemed like there had been a powder explosion in the kitchen that covered the woman.

Jacob was already grabbing two donuts and devouring one.

"I think this is your best batch yet," he said.

"Kiss up," I said.

"Hush up, Noah," Mama scolded. "Leave your brother alone."

"Why don't you let him cook?" I asked. "He *is* spending your money to learn to be a great chef."

Jacob had been in a cooking class for a year now, one of the many fads he had gone through since graduating from high school. Community college hadn't work out. I was keeping constant tabs on all of his failures, while Mama only noticed his successes.

"This isn't cooking," Mama said. "It's just fixing up biscuits to look like donuts."

"Thanks, Mama," Jacob said, shooting a huge grin towards me.

I knew there was nothing more to say on the subject. Once Mama took a verbal stand for her Jacob, that conversation was closed.

"There is a luncheon this Sunday after church," Mama said, bringing the cat-eyed glasses dangling from a chain around her neck up to her eyes so she could see what Jacob was watching on TV.

Neither of us responded. We knew we were about to be led down guilt lane.

Guilt had played a huge part in our upbringing since Dad died. How many times could we hear "raising the two of you on my own" without feeling perhaps that we were personally to blame for my mother being a single parent, perhaps even by some twisted logic that she didn't intend, for our Dad's death? Burdened with the role of the "man" in the house, her guilt trips seemed to affect me much more than it did Jacob, who had a talent for letting it slide right off his back.

"Do you think either of you can come?" she said. "People have been asking why my boys never show up."

"Tell them it's because we're not boys anymore. We're men," Jacob said.

"That's no reason to stop going," Mama said. "You two used to always be there."

"I think if I tried hard enough I could sing that song about the little man up in the tree watching Jesus pass by," I said.

"Remember when we had the contest to learn all the books of the Bible?" Jacob asked.

"Noah always had to do what you were doing, Jacob," Mama said. "Even after you were saved and baptized —"

"Let's not go there," I said. "I remember that baptism tank and the cinder block I had to stand on."

Jacob started laughing. "Your feet came off and you were flapping like a duck."

"I thought I was a goner for sure," I said.

"At least you would have gone straight to heaven," Jacob said.

"You were what? Six?" Mama said. "It was cute for you to want to be like your big brother."

Remembering the past brought a smile to my face. There were good times in the Garrett house when Dad was alive. Mama didn't have a list of things to worry about then, things that since she had to do on her own later, must have exacerbated her loneliness. Our family road trips were either to a lake or up to the mountains. It was always a blast. People would communicate and would listen to what I had to say, as well as what words of wisdom my older brother was trying to impart. I was counted as one of the Garretts and was not invisible. Plus, I didn't have to be the man. But those times were gone now — at least for me. The air in the small house always felt thick, clogging my lungs, what suffocation might feel like. I didn't know. But I knew I couldn't stay much longer in this hen coop trying to be the only rooster. It wasn't right for grown men to still be living at home.

"I don't like to go to church anymore because people gossip about me," Jacob said. "Not very Christian of them."

"They do not, son. You should come back." She rubbed his arm as if he were a six year old boy who had fallen off a bike.

"We're both a part of the birth and resurrection society now," I said. "We attend on Christmas and Easter."

"Noah Preston!" Mama said, using my middle name, which meant trouble.

I looked at the two of them, wishing I could be more a part of their world. Was she really closer to him because he was gay? I thought that as the one person who could give her a grandchild someday, she would have a closer bond with me than she could never have with him. I'm the one that can carry on the Garrett name. I was her baby. But it just never happened that way for us.

"I need to go out and be with some men," I said, heading towards the door.

"I thought that was my territory," Jacob said, but Mama shot him a glance.

"You don't like our company, Noah?" he chided.

"No, just sometimes I think if Dad were here, we could be talking about men things, the work I do at the park —"

"Sex in the back of your car with Misty Havens back in high school," Jacob said.

"Fizzlesnits!" Mama reprimanded, using one of her favorite made up curse words.

"Sorry, Mama," he said.

"Can we get back to the discussion about church please?"

"Maybe I'll be able to stop in for a moment to say hello," Jacob said, just to get one more dig in towards me.

"That would be wonderful, Jacob," Mama now gushed. "Come help me get the kitchen straightened up. There is powdered sugar everywhere."

I watched my brother following Mama down the matted orange carpet hallway that led to the kitchen. I turned and went on out to my Ford truck. I had felt like an outcast in our house for a long time. Jacob always knew what to say, when to say it and would say it first. I wanted to leave, but with the recession, there was nothing I could do but stay put. I kept working my outside jobs, listen to Mama baby

Jacob, and stood up for myself if and when I needed to. I put my foot on the pedal and revved the engine as I pulled away from those two, playing house inside the kitchen.

***

The following week, I sat in the dim living room with Mama — me in the old beat-up recliner and Mama on the couch. As usual, there wasn't much talking when Jacob wasn't around. Silence hung over our room like a heavy wet quilt drying on a clothesline. Our star-pointed clock on the wall made a loud ticking sound, making it even more obvious how little talking we were doing.

I got up and turned the TV up to drown out that reminder.

We watched *Hee Haw* together, periodically commenting on Roy Clark or something Minnie Pearl had said, but conversation was stilted and uneasy. Mama never knew how to talk to me. I think it was because of the way I had conducted my whole life. I was the troublemaker — skipping school, failing grades, doing things I'd rather not repeat.

My senior year of high school, I found myself sitting across the desk from the sheriff in our small town. I hadn't been the only one drinking behind the bleachers on the football field that night, but I had definitely been the one with the smart-ass mouth. But who came walking through the door but the pastor of our church. Mama was never told. And he got the sheriff to let me go by making God-only-knows what kind of promise. I sort of felt indebted to him for a while, but once out of school, church certainly wasn't the place I wanted to be spending my time.

I was forced to grow up and settle into adulthood in a way that

Jacob never seemed to master. I could hold a job for one, so once out of high school, my attention shifted to working to help support the family. Something my dad had instilled in me at an early age. Men take care of their families. Period. Yet although eventually I was pulling more than my own weight in the Garrett house, the damage had been done with Mama. She had spent too much time being frustrated with me and blaming the absence of a father on my 'acting out,' so she never learned how to take any interest in what I was doing with my life. In fact, I think that in some ways she feared it. I also think she secretly blamed herself for never remarrying or at least bringing a date around once in a while to show her two sons how a man acts.

Buck Owens was telling one of his jokes on the TV, when Jacob entered through the front door, reeking of cologne, like some freakin' girl.

"You boys didn't stay out late tonight," Mama said. "*Hee Haw* is still on."

Mama loved using the events on television as a time barometer.

"Gary had some stuff to do at home," Jacob said, as he settled in next to Mama as he always did. He had this strange way of using the 'extra cushion' on her hips as a pillow.

I looked at the well-groomed young man laying on that poor woman in her moo-moo, and then looked down at the raggedy clothes I had on, with my belt buckle digging into my gut. Could the three of us all be from the same family?

"This has always been one of my favorite shows," Mama said.

"The jokes are corny," Jacob said. "I could do so much better if I was on there."

"Jacob, do you think Gary wants to move in here with you?" Mama blurted, keeping her eyes focused on the television.

The air grew thicker than I had ever felt it. I wasn't sure about Jacob, but I couldn't breathe. Where the hell did that come from?

"Mama, we haven't talked about it," Jacob answered.

"Well, you two go spend so much time going back and forth between the two places and I do think of him as a son, as well," she said.

I swore I heard Mama swallow hard on the last part of that sentence.

"Mama, I don't think you want to know what those two sons are doing," I interjected.

"Noah. I'm not an old fuddy-duddy," she said. "I read. I know things."

"Ain't no amount of books that could get me to stomach that," I growled.

"Thanks, Bubba, appreciate the input," Jacob said, as he drew imaginary lines with his finger across my mother's arm, the arm that held him back like a restraint on a roller coaster.

"I support you, brother." I said. "Just not here in our house."

"Well, since Mama brought it up … we've been talking about moving," Jacob said.

The room went as quiet as it was before he had walked in. This was obviously not like any other normal night, two boys in their twenties still living at home with their Mama, chit-chatting.

Yeah, normal.

Mama looked fearful. "You two thinking of getting your own place?"

"Something like that. But not around here," Jacob said.

"I knew you'd want to move to the city," Mama continued. "Every fancy restaurant in Nashville is going to want you," she said trying not to show her pain.

The thought of my older brother going to Nashville and leaving me with Mama suddenly hit me and started to worry me. I envisioned him standing in front of the silly wooden fence on *Hee Haw* and getting a smack to his butt, like they did in the joke segment. Only in my version of it, it sent Jacob flying across the room.

"He can cook just fine here in Nocona," I added.

"I don't think I'll find what I'm looking for in Nashville," he said with conviction.

Mama's face grew even more pensive. "Jacob … what's wrong? Are you unhappy here?"

"No. But I have bigger dreams than this place. I want to be an actor, in New York City," he said.

Now it occurred to me why Mama had mentioned Gary moving in. She had sensed that Jacob was thinking of leaving. Mothers always know. She would never have suggested such a thing in her God-fearing house. My mother may have seemed like a hip mom of the seventies, but there was no way she would have allowed sex of any kind to take place under her roof.

We were all at a loss for words, and sat with the quiet for a long moment. The voices of the gospel quartet on television filled the room.

Jacob continued, "I've been thinking about it a long time. I really want to try my way there, in the big city."

"Just one more place for you to try something and fail at it," I said, true disgust in my voice.

"Tennessee has big cities," Mama said. "Nashville is just fine, if you ask me."

"It's not the same, Mama," Jacob said. "You know I've always wanted to be an actor. Remember the shows I used to put on for you as a kid?"

Those damn Christmas plays that Jacob would drag me into, directing all the neighborhood kids. Yeah, and we had no idea that he was gay.

"You were such a creative little boy," Mama said.

"So I want a chance to show that creativity beyond becoming some kitchen chef. On stage, as an actor, or maybe even a television show," Jacob said. "But I need to get away in order to do that."

I watched a signal of surrender in my mother's body, as it sunk deep into the faded mauve sofa. But she was not going to give up that handily.

"Jacob. We need to stick together," she said.

"And you're the oldest," I added in frustration.

"Come on, you'll be fine without me," Jacob said from his fortress on Mama's hip. "I do nothing but take up space around here. I feel like extra baggage."

That was bullshit. If anyone should leave this house, it was me. I had worked harder than anyone else there and was tired of how Jacob was always catered to.

"Try getting a job," I said.

"Why do you think I've been going to school?" Jacob asked.

"I've never been able to figure that one out, truthfully," I shot back, digging my finger into a hole on the arm of the recliner to keep me from punching my own brother.

"So I can get a good job," he said. "Not be a park's maintenance man, like you."

"At least someone works around here," I yelled, jumping out of my chair.

"Oh, look at Noah go," Jacob said. "Gotta use all that brawn instead of his brain."

"Jacob, I'm concerned about your spiritual well being," Mama blurted out.

Of all the things to be worrying her, where the hell was any of this coming from?

"Mama, I think God can be found in New York if you seek him out," Jacob said with a touch of sarcasm.

"Yes, but while you've lived under my roof, my relationship to God has been able to watch over you," Mama said. "You and Gary will be living in sin up there."

Now she sounded like she was falling off her rocker at this point. Even I couldn't follow the logic in that one.

"What are you talking about?" Jacob yelled, standing up. "You just offered for Gary to move in here! Wouldn't that be sinful too?"

"But God is a strong force in this house," she said. "I pray every day. I keep us safe."

"Mom, now you're starting to sound a little too nuts … even for me," Jacob said.

I suddenly felt the need to protect our crazy mother.

"Watch your mouth!" I yelled, as I shoved him into the paneled wall.

"Oh, I'm sorry, baby Bubba," Jacob said. "I didn't know you were listed as an operator on her hotline to God."

"Fizzlesnits! … I don't want to hear this. None of it," Mama said.

She hated to hear us bicker and didn't want to see her family break apart in front of her very eyes. She slowly rose from the couch and crossed to the doorway.

"Jacob … you know I will support you in your decision," she said. "I just need some time to pray on this."

With those words, she floated down the hallway towards her bedroom.

I crossed to the television and turned it off. Jacob sat back down on the sofa. We had backed off each other for a moment, perhaps still trying to decide who would pounce first. I had more weight on me and could take him in a heartbeat. But my brother had wit and a tongue that could cut like a knife, leaving invisible wounds.

Not only did I feel bad for me, but I felt bad for my poor mother. She had braved so much embarrassment all these years, with people always gossiping about her fruity son. She had poured money into wasted cooking classes. I decided to take the first punch.

"You have it made don't you?" I said. "You can always do whatever you want."

"Noah, this is really helpful to you too," Jacob said. "Once I'm gone, there will be no more comparing you to son number one."

"So you think you can just move away and leave me holding the bag? Don't even think of it."

"You'll be fine, little brother," he said. "The bag will be much lighter without me in it."

I wanted to stomp the smug look right off his face. I stood over him on the sofa to make my point.

"What makes you think you can survive New York?" I asked.

"I can survive anywhere. Instinct."

I had spent the good part of the past six years fighting with my brother, but I had never thought about him leaving home. We fought through high school about things he had permission to do and I couldn't. We fought once he got out, because I was jealous of still being in school while he got to 'start his life.' We fought — pretty much about everything.

I knew by all rights, Jacob should have moved out years ago. But I didn't want to be left alone with Mama. What would the two of us discuss without Jacob around? How could I come home from work each night to find Mama sitting alone, crying over her first born? It was all slipping away from under me. But part of me felt Jacob leaving could be the very thing that was needed for me to finally give my relationship with Mama a real shot. Without him, would she start to talk to me about my day? What I enjoyed? Would she finally notice her baby?

It wasn't a risk I wanted to take.

"Jacob, you can't go off and leave," I finally said.

"I feel too caged up," he said as he jumped up and paced around the room. "I'm so tired of it all."

"You are so fucking selfish is what it is," I said. "You could give a flying fuck what happens to Mama."

"Ahhh … don't let her catch that language in her house," Jacob chided. "You'll be spending some time in hell with me."

"Yeah, you can go there for all I care," I said.

"Noah, come on. I'm trying to lighten the mood," he said. "That's all. I don't want to fight with you anymore. We're both grown men … it's time to make some grownup decisions."

I had to chuckle within at my older brother. He was right. We hadn't made any true adult decisions in our lives … ever. Two grown men that constantly fought to have the upper hand, but had everything handed to them by the woman who had raised them. I felt slightly embarrassed that our lives had developed to this point.

I didn't know what more to say to him. Nothing was going to stop him — that much I knew. Once his mind was made up, there was no turning him around. I was done and had to get away. Out into the stifling summer night air I sat down on our front porch. I reached into my back pocket for my can of Skoal and put a pinch into the front of my gums. It was the closest thing to smoking a cigarette in this moment that I could do.

I sat on the swing thinking back about my life, wondering where it had all gone wrong. I could say it was my dad's death from a heart attack when I was in the 6th grade, but that would be too easy. Besides, Jacob was the one who cried in Mama's arms, saying he didn't want to start high school and was worried about people treating him differently. But that wasn't about being a kid with no father. It was about being gay. He knew by that age. But he went to Mama and said he'd take care of her, take care of everything if she just let him stay home. Had he known that meant he'd be home the next twelve years? I got used to him always being here, jealous in some part of my mind, but content knowing he could give Mama the relationship I never could.

So if someone held a gun to my head and demanded an answer from me, I would have to say it was a lack of having my dad around through those important years in my life, although I don't know if I was ready to even think about beyond that back then.

I spit some tobacco juice out into the hot air, listening to the crickets chirp, and watching the fireflies chase each around our front yard. If only it were simpler times again and Jacob and I were out catching those. He watched them for a while in a jar and then set them free. I smashed them and painted my arms with their glowing juice. Yes, Mama had definitely raised two very different sons.

CHAPTER THREE

JACOB

L ife was a new and exciting chronicle for me and Gary in New
York. As two men who had never gone north of Knoxville, Tennessee, it was culture shock at its most intense. Almost everything
I saw was something I had never seen before. There were people
everywhere — covering every inch of space. Coming out of sub-
ways, getting onto buses, stepping out of cabs — I was constantly
bumping into someone. If you wanted to see sky, you looked straight
upwards to get a sliver of it, not like back home, where flat acreage
was abundant and the sky would meet the land. Horizons were full
of buildings — there was no space between them, connecting one
to another, like a long row of brick and mortar. Grass was a luxury,
except in parks, and if you did see a small patch next to the street,
it was always being used by a dog on a leash as a public bathroom.
Even the concrete used on the sidewalks felt different under my feet
than the rough cobble used on sidewalks back home.

Gary provided a history lesson with everything we saw — how
the second half of that decade spawned the growth of disco, how
promiscuity was hitting new heights since the Woodstock era, and
the gay movement going strong after the raid on the Stonewall in
the previous decade. I didn't pay much attention, I just knew I was

completely blown away by how open and 'out there' everything was in New York.

Gary was in his element. He had always loved his time in Dallas before moving to Tennessee. The pace of a city. The ability to do anything at any time. And here, there were so many gays, it made him feel happy to belong to a much larger community. He adopted the groovy fashions of a man living in the Village and allowed his hair to get longer, and adorning it with his signature feathered wings. I admit it looked so hot on him. I, on the other hand, had to get used to seeing all these men like us — gay and living openly— walking around, especially in the Village where we found a nice tiny apartment. Tiny is maybe an understatement. By Tennessee standards, it would have been considered a closet with a bathroom, but for us it was heaven.

We endured the four flights of fake marble stairs up. The smell of Italian, Chinese and Greek food that penetrated our noses in the hallways, illustrating the diversity in our building, which we thought was a treat. Inside our door was one 12x15 room with a small bathroom that had those dingy subway tiles. The kitchen was no more than a hot plate, a half-size fridge and a sink that looked out a narrow window, facing south, where the five-year-old Twin Towers rose toward the heavens. That portal gave us a wonderful peek out into the world. Everything about the place felt surreal, and yet familiar at the same time. It was miles away from what we had experienced in Tennessee. And I loved every minute of it.

I was meant for something great in life and Gary and I could be openly gay in New York. Plus the city could offer me so many other possibilities I'd never be able to have back home. Gone was the stupid cooking class from my past. Replaced with acting classes and as many auditions as I could attend. I had spent a lifetime watching TV and listening to the radio and I knew I could be one of those people with my looks and voice. I had even done the kids summer theater stuff with our Parks and Recreation Department growing up (which had been the extent of my training as an actor prior to the big city). Most importantly — gone was the self loathing I felt as a closeted gay youth who could never find his niche.

I remember I had actually thought I had found a sport I could relate to other boys with back in the third grade when I ran track.

But an embarrassing moment ended that.

Prior to starting the relay race, I split my shorts down the middle, which the coach had just decided to fix with a giant safety pin. He told me to get out there and take my place as the third leg of the race. I watched as the other boys made their way around the track, passing the baton to each other. All the while, my mind was stuck on the huge pin holding my crotch intact. Ricki Childs was running towards me as I held my arm stretched out, waiting to take the stick. Suddenly it was in my hands and I was running with all my might. The next thing I knew, the safety pin broke and I was racing in a skirt around the track. My face reddened from sheer horror, but I kept going. My team didn't win and the other boys on the team never let me live it down.

That was the end of my track career, but in one way or another, I'd continue to run throughout my life.

I was walking home from one of the numerous catering jobs, thinking about how happy I was to be in New York. Car horns blasted on the street, the smell of a fragrant spring was finally in the air and I was actually glad that winter was on its way out — though I would never tell Gary that. I thought for a moment about how warm L.A. would have been throughout the past winter, but it had been exciting to get to witness so much snow.

Of course, there were times I would get homesick, but that was mostly when Gary was slacking off on chores around the house. I hated doing any kind of housework and was used to having everything taken care of for me back home. I exerted enough energy catering and auditioning. Gary didn't always see it that way.

"Sometimes I think you believe this is a hotel," Gary had said to me the night before.

"I do my share," I insisted.

"Share of what?" Gary said. "I cook. I walk down all those stairs and take our clothes to the basement laundry. I play Hazel the maid in the apartment."

"I've been meaning to ask you about the detergent you use on my shirts," I said with a smile.

"Bitch!" Gary screamed with laughter. "I'm gonna put itching powder on your clothes next time."

All I had to do was flash one of my winning smiles at Gary and I knew I had him.

"Oh stop. You know you love taking care of me," I said.

"Someone has to," he said. "Your Mama would kill me if I didn't."

My Mama.

She had been in so much pain leading up to the day Gary and I left. Her talks with me became a constant reminder list of things to do: closing bank accounts, what to pack in the car, how to pack it … anything to keep her from saying what she wanted to say. I knew she didn't want me to leave. It was clear in the way she would stare so deeply into my eyes. The amount of physical connection she needed before we left where she was constantly by my side when in the room with me. The stories she kept sharing of me as a little boy, implying absurdly how close she and I had always been. But I had to do it for myself. I couldn't stay around there taking care of her any longer. It was time to think about my life and what I wanted. And living in the Village with Gary was exactly that.

I walked in on Gary while he was busy putting clothes away in the small lacquer bureau we had picked up on the street. Nothing seemed wrong with it. Just needed some touch-up paint. Yes, Mama had rubbed off on me with my decorating. Instantly I was accosted by the heat that was still coming out of our radiators.

"Damn, Gary! Didn't you call about that?" I asked.

"They will be turned off on the 15th of this month. Everything is on a time table in New York."

"I am sick of being a catering waiter," I proclaimed. "If I see one more hokey-pokey or conga line, I may slit my wrist."

Being a cater-waiter was something that many aspiring actors in New York did. It allowed for flexible hours. It also meant going to large parties where there was a possibility of spotting casting directors and other well known clientele. Of course, meeting those people holding a tray of hors d'oeuvres was not my vision of an artist.

"Come on, Jacob, it can't be that bad," he said as he checked the boiling water on our hot plate.

"You try serving people whose toupees are falling off their heads, jewels are glittering in the light and noses are so high up in the air, they'd all drown if a rainstorm occurred."

Gary knew I wanted to play "who has the worst job."

"Oh please," Gary said. "I have to spend all day listening to women bitch about their lives. I really would like to know the person who decided the words 'hair dresser' meant therapist."

"I'm telling you, something's gotta happen soon with these auditions," I said. "I didn't come here for this. I could have been a waiter in Tennessee."

"Leaving Tennessee was the best thing we ever did," Gary said sternly.

I stopped to think about the differences. We had lived apart for all those years, and could never live the way we do now there. All my mother's friends at church always snooped on me, as if I were an alien; and people at K-Mart would talk about me after I had paid for something and left the cash register. Here, I felt safe, unnoticed, at least for that. As a matter of fact, I had never felt so open and free about being gay. It was as if I had found the end of the rainbow right here off Christopher Street.

"I do miss having your car though," I said, opening the window and wedging in the stick to let some air in the room.

"It was your idea to sell it," he said.

"I know … I know. No one keeps a car in the city."

"But we had some good memories in that car," Gary said. "But now we can make new memories."

Gary grabbed me in a bear hug and kissed me.

"Honey, let me change," I said. "I don't feel very sexy dressed as a waiter."

Of course, there was nowhere to go to in this studio apartment, so I started changing right in the room. Gary sat on our makeshift sofa and talked to me while I got comfortable.

"Ok. Trivia," Gary said. "I have been trying to think of this song all day and I can't get it."

"Which one?" I asked.

"Well if I knew, Jake, I could tell you."

I continued changing into a pair of shorts and a tank top and ignored the rude tone. I asked questions, prodded him for answers only to discover this had been nagging at Gary all day long. I finally decided to play with him.

"I know exactly what song you're thinking of," I told him.

"Tell me what it is," he begged.

I smiled and walked into the bathroom. "Not telling."

Gary thought he could get the answer from me by announcing that the name had suddenly occurred to him. I knew he had no idea what it was still. He decided we would both write down the name of the song at the same time and exchange papers. I went along with his little plan. I grabbed some scrap paper and tossed it and a pen to Gary. Both of us wrote our answers on a page and exchanged them.

"On the count of three open them," Gary said and counted dramatically.

Together we opened the paper and broke out into huge laughter as we read our answers. There on Gary's page in my hand was his confession.

I don't really know.

Gary just knew I had written the title of the song on his page, but I got the last laugh. Instead, I had written: *I know you don't really know.*

The sound of the phone ringing cut through the puny-sized room and our thunderous laughter.

"We have got to find a softer ring for that," Gary said. "Hello … no this is Gary. One second." Gary covered the receiver as he announced the caller. "It's the Tennessee hotline."

"Don't talk about my Mama like that," I said as I took the phone. "Hi, Mama."

"Hello. How are you?" came my mother's voice.

It was nice to hear that twang over the line. Mama had come up to visit us once and we really tried to play it up big. We took her to lunch at Tavern on the Green and to see the revival of *Fiddler on the Roof* at the Winter Garden Theatre, but no matter where we went, she felt like a fish out of water. I'd work hard at showing her the best time here, but she would insist it would be better if I would visit her on her southern turf. After her usual questions about work, the laundry list would begin. Stories of what this person had done at church, or how an aunt was back at the doctor for a corn on her foot, or how Mama had been done wrong by someone in her reading group. She asked about Gary, which always made me happy. These conversations were two-fold in their nature. They grounded me to my roots, but would sometimes pull me away from the life that had become ours in New York.

"Well, I better go … I have some cobbler in the oven, but wanted to say hello," she said.

Mama's cobbler.

With any other Southern lady, this meant making the crust herself, growing the peaches, making the sauce, everything from scratch. With Mama, it meant she had bought one in the frozen food section at the Safeway.

"Bye, Mama," I said. "Love you."

Gary felt the need to get in one of his digs as I hung up the phone.

"Another chapter of *southern living*?" he asked.

"Leave her alone," I said. "She wants to keep me connected to my roots. There's something noble about it."

It must have been the sight of me in my comfy shorts that got Gary all horny. "Well, come here and let me show you southern *loving*," he said.

Since there was no other room Gary could lead me into for a romantic evening, he turned off the water on the stove and pulled me down on the ugly, lumpy sofa next to him. He began kissing me as only he knew how. Ours was a love that had always been comfortable, even ideal, but after all those years of feeling like an outsider in Nocona, in New York our love felt normal. He kissed around my ear, whispering my name, while his fingers made their way down the back of my shorts. He knew the breath on my ears drove me crazy … and he loved it. He treated me like a queen as he laid me back on the sofa, making sure I was completely comfortable as he worked the tight shorts off my body.

"These didn't last long on you," he said and tossed them aside.

Off came his shirt and I traced the muscles on his torso with my hands while he lowered himself down on top of me. The radiator was blaring heat in that 4th floor walk-up, but we didn't care. Our bodies melted into one and we made love in the home that we had made together in this new exciting land.

***

Gary and I couldn't believe I had scored a meeting with a bona-fide agent, one of the top ones in the city at that. I had been going to so many auditions and had been able to book some jobs on my own, but it was not easy. This would open a new world to me. She would do the legwork, instead of me looking through the multitude of trade papers seeking a job. She would connect me to the right people at the right time.

I glanced around her waiting room, a real office in an elevator building on 23rd Street. My lover should have seen the place. The windows that overlooked the street below had floor to ceiling glass in them which allowed natural light to spill into the waiting room. Not some piece of crap fake studio, like some of the places I had run into since moving here, boarded up hole-in-the-wall places that were in alleyways or in dark, dank basements. I had heard stories about how people take advantage of unsuspecting wide-eyed wannabes who move to New York — and I had seen my share of them. Men that just wanted to get in my pants instead of getting me into a magazine. Gary had told me if I kept trying, I'd eventually make something happen. And he was right. While he took care of things at home, I was really starting to see things take off.

I had gone on cattle-calls for auditions, circled everything that I seemed right for in the papers and made sure I at least showed my face to them — and some of those had actually been working out.

An off-off Broadway showcase. A fashion show in a Jersey mall. And several photo shoots for different clothing designers. One thing I had started to do was subtract a few years from my life. Everyone thought I was some young buck, so I went along with it and kept saying I was only twenty-two. No one blinked at my white lie and many would tell me what a long career I had in store for me, at least for the next ten years. The early thirties were when all the model work would dry up, or so was the word, only a few male models had bucked that trend. But I had a nice portfolio of photos from jobs that I had done. I was proud of everything that I had accomplished in such a short time. And everything was going to be different after this meeting today, I could tell. This was going to be my next rung on the ladder in my crawl upward.

"Mr. Garrett? You can go in now," the cute young assistant said to me.

"Jacob, really great to meet you," said the round little woman in her late 40s on the other side of the desk.

Small and cherub-sized, with red hair that snuck out from under a scarf wrapped tightly around her head, and those skin tags on her neck that people try and cover when they go out. But she didn't seem to have the need to hide them. She had a 'fuck the world' attitude about her that I really was drawn to. She seemed eccentric in her vibrant colored fashion style and reminded me of an extra on *The Wizard of Oz* with bright emerald green eye shadow. Her desk was covered with calendars, magazines, folders with assorted headshots and resumes. A half-eaten pastrami sandwich was balancing on its edge. I wondered how someone was able to get anything done in that kind of environment.

"Thanks for seeing me," I said, flashing one of my winning smiles.

She pointed to the seat with her tiny fingers indicating it was time for me to sit.

"I've been seeing that smile in ads across town and I knew I needed to get you in here," she said with an accent that didn't quite sound like it came from New York.

"Glad to hear you've taken notice," I said.

"Honey, that's what I do. There are tons of people coming to this city every year, but only a few really drift to the top."

The woman didn't seem to stop. She was collecting folders, banging them on their edges and flipping them into a drawer; taking the sandwich and tossing it into the waste basket and digging for something in the middle drawer of her desk.

"I want to do more than drift," I said with a laugh.

"Trust me, you'll do just that if I take you on," she said with an authority that said she meant business.

If? I didn't like that word. I wanted to make sure she took me. I was sick and tired of the grunt jobs I had taken to stay afloat. Gary and I were not starving by any means, but I wanted more — I deserved it. I had spent enough time paying my dues. It was time to take it to the next level.

"So what do I have to do?" I asked.

"Slow down. Let me see your book to refresh my memory," she said reaching across the desk and snatching the portfolio out of my hands.

I had done my homework on her as well. Rachel Lazlo was one

of the up and coming managers, and she already handled some heavy hitters. Not only models, but actors, singers and a few television news anchors, as well. She would be perfect for my career. I handed her my portfolio and watched her flip through the pages with an urgency that said she meant business.

"Impressive. You really booked all of this on your own?" she said.

"Guess I'm often in the right place at the right time."

"One of the lucky ones, huh?" she said without looking up.

"Luck, drive, passion … I got it all," I said.

She stopped flipping and looked at me.

"And a little cockiness too, I see," she said. And after a pause, added, "I like that."

"Just a little, when I need to be," I said trying not to push too hard, but show her at the same time that I meant business.

Rachel stood and walked around her desk to where I was sitting. She was even smaller than she seemed, but a true bad-ass at the same time. She looked me up and down like a cat ready to pounce on a mouse.

"Tell you what, I'm going to send you on a few go-sees and we'll see how well you do. If you can book with some of my regulars, I'll take you on. If not, you and that smile are back on your own. Deal?"

She extended her hand for a quick shake, suggesting this would be our agreement.

"Shit yeah!" I said too quickly, shaking her hand viciously. "Sorry, I mean, absolutely."

She was already leaving my side and heading back around to her chair.

"No, you mean 'shit yeah'. Leave all your info with my assistant and we'll take it from there."

"I appreciate this, Ms. Lazlo."

"Rachel. Look forward to working with you, Jake," she said as she reached for the telephone receiver to make a call, indicating my time was up.

I liked how she shortened my name so quickly, without any hesitancy at all.

"I'm looking forward to it too."

CHAPTER FOUR

NOAH

The days ground on one into another. It took me a long while to shake being pissed at Jacob for leaving. I had wanted to leave too, but someone had to stay with our mother. I felt the small town was a noose around my neck, keeping me from experiencing the world. And the place seemed to get smaller and smaller, but I would just have to deal with it. And I was dealing with it the way I always had recently.

Work, bars, beer and girls.

Maybe I would look up Tricia Reynolds to see if she wanted to go out again. We had been a good couple back in high school. Maybe I had been meant to marry her. I needed something to keep me happy in this town. The beers just didn't seem to suffice anymore. I barely made it through the door, when I heard Mama calling to me.

"Noah, can you come in here and get this box down from the top of the closet?"

I knew it must be time to pull out Easter decorations. Though she was depressed, she still felt she needed to keep her yard decorated for each major holiday. And nothing said 'Christ has Risen' like a huge bunny on the front lawn. I carried the box to the kitchen table so she could go through everything. Mama had a thing about managing her decorations and each box was marked with exactly what was inside. I tried to leave the room as quickly as possible, but she wanted to talk.

"Where have you been?" she asked, motioning with her eyes for me to sit down.

"It's not that late."

"Your job ended hours ago."

What's this? The third degree now.

Despite the annoyed reflection on my face, Mama didn't let up. "Maryann Reynolds was talking about you at church."

Did she have a bug in my head? Why would she mention the Reynolds family?

"That's funny," I said, trying to not sound so annoyed. "I've been thinking about her daughter lately."

"Tricia didn't do well in college over in East Tennessee," she continued. "She's decided to come back here to Nocona and work at her father's office."

Tricia Reynolds in a dentist office? Something didn't seem right. Having to watch people as they were told to spit. Making sure they were given a new toothbrush before they left, reminding them of their next appointment. And that smell of decaying teeth covered up by mint air fresheners. How could she put up with that?

"Maryann was wondering if you were seeing anyone special," Mama said as she pulled a hand-painted set of chicken and ducks from the box. "I told her you hadn't dated since Tricia left."

"I can handle that myself, Mama," I said. "Thank you."

"I just want what's best for my boys. Is that so wrong?"

"No. I just don't want you trying to set me up with anyone," I responded too harshly.

"Jacob would never blow up at me like this," she said.

There it was again. Jacob's ghost haunted our kitchen, our whole house, every move I made, never letting me forget he was there.

"No, I guess he wouldn't," I said with a scowl, pushing my chair away from the Formica table and standing up. "Jacob probably would never go out for a drink with friends. Jacob would never drink ... yes, Mother ... had a beer. I'm sure God may strike me dead now, but I did."

"Fizzlesnits! Don't talk to me like that. Do not ridicule God in my home. What is wrong with you?" she questioned, digging into the Easter boxes for the next ornament. "I don't understand how I can have raised two completely different sons."

I wasn't sure where to go with that one. I felt invisible when it came to her, no matter what I did. I couldn't even get her to look at me sometimes. Had she not realized I was the son that was still here in the house? I was the son making a living and bringing home part of my paycheck to her. Years of holding back poured out of me.

"Why do you compare me to him?" I asked. "Why have you *always* compared me? I am not Jacob."

"I really don't know what you are talking about, honey. Why don't we just go to bed and we'll discuss all this tomorrow after work," she said.

I wasn't sure if I should tell her, but I did it anyways. I let it all out that I had quit my job. After a shocked pause, you would have thought the world had come to an end right there in her kitchen. I had never seen my mother worked up with such a look of fear in her eyes. She went on about how the money was needed, never giving a thought to the fact that just maybe her youngest son wanted to do something else with his life than be a maintenance man.

"I'll get another job, Mama. I promise," I said. "I just want a chance to be happy in my work. I don't know. Maybe write something."

"What are you dreaming about? You didn't even finish college."

That was a low blow. How I wished she would just nail me to a cross and slap me on the front lawn to put me out of my misery.

"To support the family!" I yelled.

"Well, what do you call quitting a job? Supportive? I don't think so … your brother would …"

"Stop! I don't want to hear his name."

I couldn't stand listening to her praise the son that had left her, hearing her excuses about how he needed to be in New York to be an actor. I knew there was no way she would ever see Jacob as anything but perfect. No matter what decisions he had made, they were always ok in her eyes.

"You have no idea what it is like to be a mother. To see your children grow up and decide to leave you."

"I didn't leave, Mama. I'm right here," I said.

"Right here making choices you have no business making. How could you quit your job?"

Backpedal … backpedal. I didn't feel like having an all out fight with Mama. And considering the Budweiser might do too much of my talking, it didn't make sense to try and reason with her either. The woman looked petrified by what I had told her. As if she would be eating cat food from now on or something. I didn't need that hanging over my head.

"I'm sorry, Mama. I'll go back in," I said. "I'll try to get it back."

Mama went on to talk about how she wanted Jacob and me to be happy. That's all she had ever wanted, she said. Then the guilt would start about her being a burden and my having to stay with her. I tried to assure her she was not a burden and gently persuaded her to go to bed to get a good night's sleep. I knew if she went to her room, she would drown herself in her Bible and things would be back to normal in the morning. There was that word again. Normal. The Garretts didn't even know what the word meant.

Finally, she decided to go to bed. The terrible experiment had come to end. So much for the two of us trying to speak to each other. Even when Jacob wasn't here ... he still *was* here. My older brother was more powerful than I had imagined. But just as I believed I had seen it all, my mother walked towards me and kissed me on the cheek.

"Goodnight, son," she said.

"Goodnight, Mama."

And with that, the evening was over. I watched as she walked down the hall towards her room. I heard the click of the lamp next to her bed, a full with a twenty year faded bedspread on it that she had slept alone in for all those years. I knew she would be reading God's word and then praying for my soul. And I knew the evening would end with a letter to Jacob.

CHAPTER FIVE

JACOB

"One bedroom with a view," I told Gary as I read the Village Voice that was opened up on the table in front of me in the greasy-spoon diner that we had adopted as our favorite place. "That's what we need," I said trying to drown out the Commodores piping through the speakers in the background.

"I told you not to read that paper. They haven't been kind to our people," Gary said, attempting to snatch the paper away from me, causing the corner to slide into the syrup on his plate.

"Our people? Okay, Cleopatra, step away from your throne," I said.

Gary wanted to believe he was very political in every decision he made. Had we moved to California, I'm sure he would have worked for Harvey Milk. He thought Roman Polanski should be brought from France and put on trial after he had skipped out of the country in February. And he was against the nuclear testing the government was doing out in Nevada. I, on the other hand, had no opinion on these things. But I did find the new TV show about the rich family living in Dallas, Texas to be hysterically campy for a night time soap opera.

"There are plenty of one-bedrooms that we can look at," he said. He pulled the sticky, wet paper away from his bacon.

I put more sugar into the coffee cup the waiter had just filled to the rim.

"I want to do more than look," I said. "I want to own."

"If you keep booking commercials, we'll be out of our studio before you know it," Gary said as he cut into his pancakes.

Life had been awesome since signing with Rachel. She had me booked in more print ads and commercials than I could keep up with, traveling to great locations for shoots, meeting so many people. It was all falling into place in the past few months, something Gary and I had wanted since we got here. But I wanted to conquer more. I had a drive in me that I had never been aware of back in Nocona. The lazy Jacob had been replaced by a man on a mission. And this man wanted to have things. Fancy clothes. A better apartment. More modeling jobs and ultimately, to be known everywhere I went. Each decision made was a piece of the puzzle to get me all those things.

"I wish Rachel would get me a Broadway show," I said.

"Babe, just be glad those all-American looks of yours are in demand for selling products in magazines."

Gary loved being affectionate in public by calling me 'babe'. It was starting to grow on me ... a little. I took a gulp of my coffee and looked around the diner. I loved the whole idea of a diner. 24 hour eating. Any kind of food, any time of the day. The mixture of smells of bacon frying on the grill or a hot meatball sandwich. The place could make a nose drool. We didn't have these back in Nocona.

"You know what would be great with those pancakes?" I asked, crunching into a crispy piece of bacon.

"Yes, and you can't get peanut butter in a diner," Gary said.

"Guess you can't take the southern outta this boy," I said.

Gary had taken the whole paper at this point and was looking at the listings. "Here's a one bedroom in the Village."

"I really want to end up on the upper west side," I said.

I had several friends in the business who were making their way to that area, who had told me how that neighborhood had a completely different feel from that of the Village. Where the Village was loud and rebellious, the Upper West Side offered the same kind of liberal mentality we loved, without all the noise. It was also on the verge of a revitalization, which meant cheaper prices. I wanted to be somewhere that had other gay couples, but didn't feel like an exclusive club.

"I like it down here in the Village," he said. "I feel so comfortable."

"You can be just as comfortable up there. It's still Manhattan."

Another gay couple walked in and sat at a booth near us. The two were attractive, but looked as if they had been out partying the entire night and stopped at the diner to eat breakfast before going home to sleep. Gary caught my eyes looking at them and took a gander himself.

"Cute couple," he said. "Bet you couldn't see that up town."

"I think they let gays up there too. It's not like we would need a visa or anything," I said.

Gary laughed. I was wearing him down.

"Let's keep saving and we'll see," he said.

"You just keep saving those tips, so you can match what I have."

"Oh yes … my salary is really gonna match what you bring in," he said.

The Greek waiter with a sweat gland problem came by with the check and put it on the table.

"Why don't you get this and I'll get the next one," I said.

Gary reached for his wallet.

"Oh, I forgot to give you this," I said, reaching into my own pocket.

"What is it?"

I watched Gary's face as he read the paper I gave him. I was going to make an investment in him, in his career, by buying him his own salon. I had just handed him a promissory note that he would get it before we bought an apartment. He had been giving me so much since we moved to New York, and I wanted to be able to give back to him, for once. I was thrilled that I was at a point in my career where I could actually do it.

"You don't have to do that," he said, going to pay the bill.

"I *want* to. Watch. It won't take long at all. Look how quickly I've gone from a waiter to a real model."

"You're gorgeous, that's why," he said.

"So are you, honey. And you'll be making women beautiful in your own place one day. Soon," I said.

Gary left a nice tip on the table, stopped to pay the cashier and we left the diner hand in hand. As we walked, we did some window-shopping past the fabulous stores along 7th Avenue. One thing Gary had correct, the Village did offer a wide array of stores. And it seemed as if anything was permissible on the streets there. A guy could wear a skirt with a leather vest and not even be offered the courtesy of a second look. Glam rock and drag were so huge in that part of town that you never knew what was taking place behind an unmarked door, even during the day. And come midnight; it was an entire different story. Men would blur the lines by wearing make-up like a woman on their face with a Wall Street suit.

"Let's celebrate," Gary said, eyeing a colorful shirt hanging in the window.

"Celebrate a promise?" I asked.

"Like we need an excuse to celebrate. I'll call Mitch and Steve and see if they want to go to Stonewall."

"Tell Mitch to please not show up in drag this time," I said.

"Come on. It's funny," Gary said.

Drag was not my thing. I didn't understand men who felt the need to act like women. I was gay. I didn't want to be a girl. I wanted to be a man and sleep with other men. As soon as we moved from this neighborhood, perhaps I wouldn't have to associate my being gay with that kind of freakish behavior.

"I really don't enjoy seeing men in dresses."

"All right, I'll call them before I head to the shop. Damn, babe, I can't wait until I can tell that place I'm done."

"It'll happen before long," I said. "I'm sure."

Gary kissed me right there on the street and then was running from me. Life was good. I was providing for my man and was happy with the world that New York had opened up for us. I passed a fire hydrant that had been open and two kids were playing in the water. Kids were so much more daring in this city — they seemed to have no fear in their eyes. For a split second, I thought back to me and Noah playing in the sprinkler in our backyard in the summertime. It must great to be a child with no care in the world, I thought. But that was a long time ago. Now I was an adult with a fabulous life in New York — miles and miles from Tennessee. I couldn't help but smile at people as I passed them heading back towards our soon-to-be *former* apartment.

CHAPTER SIX

NOAH

"Dinner is on me tonight," I said as I put down the take-out containers from the fish place.

"That smells wonderful, son," Mama said, as the aroma of fried seafood penetrated our nostrils.

"I know how you love your fried catfish and hush puppies!"

Mama went straight to the cupboard to pull out her corning-ware plates and set the table.

"It may be take-out, but we're going to eat like human beings," she said.

"I've been craving Dave's Fish Hut all day," I said, grabbing the ice tea pitcher from the fridge.

"I thought for sure you'd be out with Trish tonight," she said, taking a seat at the kitchen table.

"Nah … figured I could spend the night with the other lady in my life," I said.

Mama smiled and I was glad I could please her with such a small gesture. I had been giving it a go with Trish for a few months now and it seemed to be working out. She and I had made a great couple years ago, and surprisingly had been able to pick up where we had left off. Somehow, she was able to keep me sane. It was just a matter of time before the marriage nagging would start though — from her and Mama.

"I spent the day with Eloise Higgins at the church food pantry," she said. "And believe me, I worked up quite an appetite."

Mama darted into one of her stories and I tried my best to pay attention. She wanted so badly to have me as a replacement for Jacob. If I offered to wash and do her hair, I'm sure it would have made her night. But I couldn't go that far. I wasn't Jacob. Listening to these stories and adding in a few grunts here and there was our relationship — and I was fine with that.

I will admit — I enjoyed when Mama told stories about the past. Those were my favorite, her tales of being a little girl and walking to the pond to catch her own fish. Grandma cleaned it and cooked it after Mama helped Grandpa to gut it. She grew up in a different time than we did — with all those siblings. Never a sense of isolation in that house, always someone around. But money was always tight for them. A pair of shoes would see them through the entire year. Love seemed abundant, however, from those anecdotes. Brothers and sisters who got along. Everyone doing his or her part in the house. A way of life that seemed foreign to me in our small family.

"I used to love to go fishing with dad too," I said as I took a bite of coleslaw.

"You did. Early Saturday mornings. He would go in there and wake you boys up to go with him."

"I couldn't wait to get out there and sit next to that water, waiting for the fish to bite."

It was true. Those were some of my favorite times. When it

was just him and me — even if I was just a young kid, I knew the importance of Saturday mornings with my dad. He would wear his favorite fishing cap, take a cooler full of Coors, which Mama knew nothing about — and at times would give me a sip. I thought it tasted like piss-water, but I took a swallow every time. Just because he had offered. My dad was a man's man. He loved working on cars, going fishing, taking me hunting out in the woods. I was able to learn from him just from watching and interacting with him. We'd get out in the street and toss the football back and forth until the street light would come on and Mama would call us in for supper. Those were great times. Just being guys. And it was something I shared with Dad that Jacob took no part in.

"Only Jacob wanted nothing to do with fishing," I said.

"No, he's rather go do the shopping with me."

"Who would have guessed, huh?" I said.

Was that a smile on my mother's face? It was. She caught my gay joke and damn it if she didn't let a smile out, if only for an instant.

"Well now look at him," she said. "He's not in the stores … he's selling *for* the stores."

"I haven't really noticed."

"You don't read the right magazines, that's why. Your brother is everywhere." She spread her arms open, to make sure I didn't get how big he was.

But no, my brother's face wasn't popping up in the magazines I was reading, that was for sure. Let's hope she never finds that *Hustler* hidden in the crate in my bedroom closet.

"You'll have to show them to me sometime," I said.

Mama froze for a moment and looked at me with such warmth in her eyes. "That would be really nice, son. I would love to."

These small, fleeting connections were growing on me. Even if Jacob was still the washer and the bolt between us, I was finding that the older I got and the longer he had been away, I was able to deal with it much better. My life wasn't as horrendous as I had always imagined it to be. Sometimes, we just have to take what comes our way and deal with it; whatever that may be.

"You may have brought home the dinner, but I have dessert planned," she said.

She went to the freezer and pulled out one of her peanut butter and custard ice cream pies.

"I'll just put this on the counter and it'll be good for us to eat in about an hour," she said.

I laughed at my mother's gourmet sensibilities and popped a hush puppy in my mouth.

CHAPTER SEVEN

JACOB

The more auditions I went on, the more gigs I landed — commercials, print ads, everything as I had dreamed about. Still no Broadway shows or TV spots, but I was doing just fine as a model and Rachel loved the money machine I had transformed into. And as long as everyone believed I was in my early twenties, I knew I had a long career ahead of me. The last two years in New York had flown by — I didn't even know where the time had gone. Life was moving on around me with so many exciting events happening in New York that I would sometimes forget to fill Mama in on all of them during our weekly calls. We had experienced a true, city-wide blackout that summer, but even that hadn't slowed me down. Over a thousand stores had been vandalized during the several days and many riots in a town reeling from financial difficulties; but Gary and I just stayed inside and made love. I didn't even notice the money problems that others were having, because I had one thing on my mind and it was to become famous doing what I did best.

Gary and I had made our move into a great apartment on the upper west side, an area that was seeing a huge change in the late 70s. I felt as if I had really made it by moving up to this part of town. It was a brownstone building with amazing character and charm. At one time, all those houses had been single-family homes — but now had been divided by floors to create unique styled apartments. Ours was a one bedroom, separate galley kitchen with a breakfast nook. It had a great loft space where I could keep all magazines and posters that used my face to sell products. The place had four times the amount of space as our village apartment. And, most noticeably, the array of 'united nations of cooking smells' no longer filled our hallway.

New York finally felt like home … but I knew there was still more for me to achieve.

I loved walking down the cramped streets, having to finagle myself to get through and seeing people do a double take. Did they know me from a billboard? Or were they just cruising? Gay men in New York had no problem letting you know they were interested by locking eyes with you on the street. The more modeling I did, the better looking I think I was getting. I loved when men looked at me. It made me feel alive. Usually I would run home and Gary and I would screw each other's brains out, because I was so hot and bothered by all the cute men that I had seen. I was propositioned so many times, but would always smile and say 'no thanks.' Gary had no idea how lucky he was to have me. Even our friends thought I was some young stud he had whisked away to the big city. Yeah, I was still playing up that "younger than I looked" thing to a T … even within our circle of friends.

I had just pulled up to our apartment on 84th Street and was getting out of a cab as Gary came running down the front steps. I watched the cab pull down the street.

"Thanks for holding that for me," he said.

"Where's the fire?" I asked.

"I got called in. There's a problem at the salon."

"I thought we were spending tonight together," I said.

"You bought me this place. That means I'm in charge, especially when things fuck up."

"You can't tell me there is a hair emergency that those freaks you hired can't handle."

Gary took off walking down to the corner so he could grab another cab, since mine had already gone through the light.

"Those 'freaks' help me run that place," he screamed. "Something I sure could use at home."

I followed him down the street a little, sensing his aggravation with me.

"I do some things ... when I have time," I said.

Gary tried to wave down a cab.

"Yeah, that's the problem. Time."

"I'm home tonight. Where are you?"

A cab pulled up and Gary jumped in.

"Trying to keep my financial end of this relationship up."

He turned from me to give the driver directions. "See you later tonight," he hollered as the cab sped away.

These incidents began to happen more frequently. Perhaps it was the move to the new neighborhood, or the pressure of running his place — but I didn't enjoy it. Living with someone day in and day out could get a little old and monotonous.

I walked into a corner store and bought myself a Tab and a small bottle of vodka. I took a swig of the Tab, poured the vodka inside the can and went for a walk towards Central Park. It wasn't the same as walking through the Village, but there were plenty of people roaming along the park.

I entered at 79th Street and kept walking towards the part they called the Rambles. Acres and acres of trails were people could get lost, bird watching, or just forgetting they were in a large city. It was a part of New York that felt like the country. Only the more I walked, the more I noticed men standing behind trees, all by themselves, lurking and watching. The sun was just starting to set over the buildings on the west side. The joggers were making their way out of the park. No one wanted to be in Central Park after dark. I continued to drink my Tab and at first found myself a little nervous by the situation. But then I noticed — these men in the Rambles were all looking for something.

And it wasn't birds.

I saw men walking by, cruising each other, and then heading off into the bushes. I walked a little deeper to see what was happening and as I expected I came upon two men. One was on his knees pleasing the other, who was darting his eyes back and forth to see if anyone was coming. He spotted me and grabbed the other man to get up, but then he could sense I was not a cop. Nor did I budge from my spot. I continued to watch them. My eyes fixed on their every move. There was something very titillating about watching someone else's sex act. The man was back on his knees and working the standing one over, who soon motioned for me to join them. I looked around to see who was watching me. My heart began to race. Did I dare? Part of me wanted to get closer, but fear took over and I turned to get out as quickly as I could. I may have been pissed at Gary leaving me alone, but I didn't need to be involved with this type of dirty operation.

***

It had been a long day on a shoot, and the work day wasn't over. There was a party that evening. But I thought I'd help out a little at home and was busy putting away groceries I had grabbed at Gristede's, when the ringing phone echoed through the apartment.

Shit. It was Tennessee.

I wished I hadn't picked up.

"Hi. Mama! How are things back home?"

I was having trouble hiding the annoyance in my voice, maybe because the frequency of her calls had tripled in the past few months. She never quite comprehended the amount of work I had to do and always wanted to recollect the past or bother me with her present.

"Call me right back, son, as this call is so expensive."

I was used to this by now, since I had taken it upon myself to pay for the phone calls between us.

"I'm just as famous as you are," she said, once I redialed and she answered. "Everyone at church has seen your pictures all over the Sears catalog."

"I'm a walking poster boy for them," I said, moving from the kitchen to my bedroom to pick out clothes for the party.

"It's just as exciting as can be. You should hear the way the people talk," she said.

I was annoyed that people were talking about me now that I was becoming somewhat famous.

"These are the same people who used to talk behind my back, right?"

"Jacob. They are just so proud of you," she said. "We all are."

I felt a sense of accomplishment in making the churchgoers hypocrites. How could they praise me now when they used to bash me so often for being gay?

"What's Noah up to?"

"Oh … same ole, same ole," Mama said. "He and Tricia broke up. I didn't think that would last long."

"That's Noah."

Noah had never kept a girlfriend. I think he had some serious commitment issues.

"Listen, Mama, I can't stay on," I said. "I have to get to a party."

"You have such an exciting life up there."

"Not really … often a party means work," I said.

"Well, enjoy yourself … and be careful," Mama said. "I see all sorts of strange things on the news about stuff going on."

"I will."

"Love you, son."

"You too."

I went back to getting ready. I could groom myself in my sleep. I was so used to preparing for a photo shoot that had it down to minutes. But where was Gary? He knew I had to be on time for these sorts of events. I sat waiting on the sofa, in my Nik Nik print disco shirt from Italy with matching polyester pants, watching the hands on the clock. I made myself a cocktail and lit a cigarette. This wasn't like him.

The door bolted open.

"I know. I know. I'm sorry," Gary said, busting in. "It won't take me long."

"I can't be late for this one," I pleaded.

"No one goes on time." Gary noticed the cigarette dangling from my lips. "I thought we said no smoking in the apartment," he said.

"I was getting frustrated. Sorry," I said, as I put it out in the ornate astray I had brought back from a photo shoot in Germany. I followed Gary around the apartment, watching him yank off his work clothes.

"Want to make me one of those, babe?" Gary said, looking at the cocktail in my hand.

"No. You can have one at the party," I said. "Hurry."

The party was in full swing by the time we arrived. Gary didn't really care for these things much, but he knew they were important to me. And he enjoyed watching me in my work mode, when I would light up as I talked to people. I could speak to anyone on any subject. I was a well-oiled machine, discussing politics, the newest music on the radio, happenings at Studio 54 or the price of gasoline. I didn't even own a car.

This particular party was at a very private club located in the basement floor of a hotel on Central Park South. There was one large dance floor with a bar that took up one entire end of the room. The rest of the space was divided up into smaller rooms, converted into lounges. I'm sure at one point this had been a wine cellar that was used for lots of illegal activities during the Prohibition. Music vibrated the room as we walked around with cocktails in hand and talked to the eclectic mix of guests.

Many times, Gary would just stand against a wall taking it all in from across the room. I would walk past him, wink at him and he would take his place by my side. He knew the rules, even though he didn't enjoy having to play by them.

No one was to know we were a couple.

In order to get the kind of modeling jobs that I was getting, people had to believe I was straight. No one wanted to buy a pair of jeans that were being advertised by a fairy. So we always played it safe at the parties. I could sense Gary was just about to ask if it was time to go when Felicia appeared.

"Hey, Jake! What's going on?" she asked.

"Just trying to hold my own at this schmooze-fest," I said.

"I hear you," she said, looking around. "These things can be so uptight."

Felicia was a beautiful model with long straight golden hair. She looked as if she had never seen a day of sun in her life. Delicate features, striking eyes that pierced through you as she spoke and such a sensual mouth … even a gay man couldn't look away from her.

"Hi … I'm Felicia," she said to Gary. "I worked with Jake on a commercial shoot."

"This is my friend, Gary," I said.

"Nice to meet you," Gary said.

"Are you in the business?" she asked.

"No, no," Gary said. "Though I've done the hair of many, many models."

I looked to make sure no one else had heard that. I was fine for Felicia to know what Gary did for a living, but not the entire room. These were my peers, clients, the movers and shakers. I definitely didn't need them knowing about my personal business. Felicia walked off towards a handsome man across the room and Gary seized the moment to insist that we go. I tried to remind him it was important for me to make appearances at these things, but he wasn't having it.

"Well, I'm tired," Gary said. "I have to be up early tomorrow."

"Fine. Go ahead and leave," I said.

"Without you?" he asked.

I knew I was making a major rule change. Gary and I had always left parties together. This was another rule that we had set early on in our relationship, once we had moved to New York.

"Yes," I said. "I told you, I'm staying."

"Cool," he said. "I'll see you at home."

I said nothing and looked across the room.

"Jake, I'll see you at home?" he asked.

I turned to look at someone else without answering Gary, until he finally walked out. I wasn't sure why I was playing this game with him, but I was pissed that he didn't realize how important these events were to my career. I knew he would get over it. I enjoyed parties and he enjoyed TV dinners and watching *The Love Boat*. There was a Swanson at home with his name on it and I knew he couldn't wait to get to it.

Across the room, Felicia and her good-looking friend were still talking. Feeling bored, I lit a cigarette and decided to join their conversation.

"So, Felicia … Are you going to introduce me?" I asked.

"Yes," she said. "Peter Broden … this is Jake Garrett."

"Nice to meet you, Peter," I said.

"You too," he said. "Did I see you on that beer commercial?"

I loved being recognized. I lived for it. Peter quoted the lines I said in it as he touched my arm. We all laughed at him, but something made me think I was not talking to a straight friend of Felicia's.

"I've seen it a couple of times," Peter said.

He smiled as he spoke to me. And what a nice smile it was. At the same time, a stranger approached Felicia and gave a swipe to the side of his nose.

"Felicia?" said the stranger.

"I'll be right back," she said.

I watched her walk away, completely aware of what was going on. I had seen my share of drugs at all the parties.

"Felicia's still doing blow," Peter exclaimed, as if he were talking about what time the evening news started.

"I'm totally lost." I said, trying to play the innocent young country boy.

"Oh come on, Jake," Peter said. "Don't play dumb with us. Felicia, wait up!"

I found myself dragged off to the bathroom with Felicia, Peter, and the stranger. It was crowded with everyone hunched around the end of the sink, watching each time the door would open. I always knew this was going on at every party I attended, but I had never made my way into this inner sanctum, perhaps sensing something about myself.

"Hey ... party's out there," the stranger said, holding something out of my eyesight.

"Jake was interested," Peter explained.

I didn't want to be the cause of any problem, but I did want to witness what they did first hand. "I just asked what you were blowing."

Felicia cracked up. "Not blowing. Doing some blow."

The stranger was getting impatient. "Are you in?"

Felicia took the lead and said, "Here, Jake. Try this. Believe me. It will get through this crazy party."

I must admit, I had secretly wanted to try coke as much as I had heard people talk about it. Just to see what it was like. This was the perfect opportunity, no Gary here to judge me.

"What is it?" I asked, as Felicia took a snort of powder up her nose.

Peter touched my arm again … the same way he had before. "Trust us. Just try it."

"Alright," I said, hunching my shoulders.

I took the white stuff in my nostril as I had watched the others do it. It tingled and itched and I instantly wanted to blow my nose.

"I don't feel a thing," I said after a few moments.

The impatient stranger wasn't as impatient anymore. It now seemed like he wanted to help me do it correctly.

"Have a little more," he said.

What a nice guy, I thought.

I snorted so much the second time that my eyes teared up. I felt it dripping down the back of my throat. It choked me and then I felt a rush go through my body.

"Alright … alright. Party's over!" yelled the impatient one, who seemed impatient again. "Everyone back outside."

The four of us filed out of the bathroom. But the entire room seemed different to me now. Everyone and everything was enhanced. My whole body felt warm and my heart raced. I no longer thought about what time the party was coming to an end, how bored I was — I just felt the music. And I was loving it!

Love to Love You, Baby was pulsing through my ears.

"Alright, boys," Felicia said. "Let's dance. Move over Donna Summer!"

Felicia was on the dance floor within seconds dancing with three men. Peter offered to get me a drink. All I could think of was how great it was to have a strong-armed man to take care of me. How did he know I was so parched? I asked him for a screwdriver, as the music washed through my ears and into my body. But I wasn't listening to the music. I was the music. I watched Peter walk away to get drinks. He was over six feet tall, had gorgeous dark hair and long sideburns. I wished I could grow sideburns like that. The classic 70s mustache was a definite turn-on for me as well. And those hairy forearms. What a man!

Felicia bumped right into me.

"Why, Jake ... what are you doing?" she asked.

"Just waiting on a drink from that cute friend of yours," I said. "*Ohhhh ... love to love you, baby.*"

I was singing and dancing with Felicia and enjoying every minute of it. This must be what a true New York party was all about. Why had I thought they were all so blasé up until that point? Gary and I had our friends whom we would hang out with, and then there were these business functions. I would enjoy a cocktail or two to get through them, but tonight was different. Tonight, I felt free. Tonight, nothing could stop me.

"Here you go, dueling Donnas," Peter said.

Forearms was back and had drinks for both of us.

"Damn, I feel good," I said.

Peter touched me again, but this time, much firmer than he had before.

"Yeah … you do," he said.

I was unsure how to react, so I quickly downed the drink. I enjoyed the compliment and the flirting. Impatient man returned to Felicia, but this time he had something else on his mind. He grabbed her and the two danced off together onto the main floor while they made out in front of everyone in the room. I was feeling the music, feeling the drink, feeling the coke I had done in the bathroom and was longing to feel Peter.

"Maybe we should go someplace else," Peter said.

Gary.

His face flashed in front of my eyes.

"I really need to get home … to my partner," I said.

"What's the rush?" he asked. "You don't want to stumble in and wake him up … the night is still young."

Something about the logic of that made sense. Why should I wake up Gary? Gary would hardly miss me tonight.

"Let me show you where I live … a great place on the East Side. Not as noisy as it is here," Peter said.

Those arms. That mustache. This white stuff that I continued to taste as it dripped down the back of my throat. Everything that was happening had a heightened sense of urgency and yet at the same time, felt as if certain aspects were happening in slow motion. As if I didn't have a care in the world.

"Always love to see how other people live," I said. "But I'll just stay for one drink."

This time, I was the one touching, grabbing his muscular arm. Peter took the drink out of my hand and placed it on a table. "Deal. Let's go."

* * *

I stumbled out of my bed not even aware of how I had gotten home. What a night. Where was Gary? Shower? I looked at the clock radio and realized he was already at work. I made my way to the kitchen where the wonderful Mr. Coffee held a pot that Gary had left for me. What a great invention, so that people did not have to wait for a percolator to enjoy a nice cup of freshly brewed coffee.

Gary had also left a note stuck on the fridge.

Tennessee hotline called to see how the party was, babe. Guess she figured you would have been home early.

I definitely didn't feel like talking to Mama today.

What had I done last night? So many new things I wasn't used to at the party. Even though I felt like crap at the present moment, I did remember having a great time. I remembered dancing. I remembered people gathering in the bathroom.

And I remembered forearms.

It was as if I could smell him here in my kitchen right now. It must be me. I reek of the guy. Of sex. Had Gary even noticed before he left for work?

I took a gulp of coffee and made my way to the shower, stripping off clothes as I went. I turned on the water to let it heat up in the shower as I looked at myself in the mirror. At least there were no marks on my body. No evidence of the hot night I had experienced. As much as I wanted to stay bathed in Peter's scent, I knew it was time to return to some sort of normalcy.

I stepped into the shower and felt the warm water rush over my body as if it could absolve me of the sins I had committed the previous night. But flashes of the events kept popping into my mind.

I was definitely seeing a new side of this city that I hadn't experienced before.

I heard the front door open in spite of the noise of the water that was splashing on my body.

"Gary?"

I turned off the water, pulled back the shower curtain and Gary was standing there in his running shorts, holding a towel.

"Nice party?" he asked as he handed me the towel.

"You know," I said as I began to dry off. "Same ol' same ol."

Gary smacked my ass and walked into the other room. He knew. I could tell. There was a distant cordiality about him. But he wasn't saying anything for some reason.

"I thought you had to work," I said, following him towards the living room.

"You're getting water all over the floor," he said, testily. I could hear him in the kitchen getting a glass and running the water for a drink.

I decided to try again. "Are you off today?"

The awkwardness of our stilted conversation was beginning to irk me. I was trying to fill in those moments with images of what he must know, or at least suspect.

He came back into the living room and stared at my naked body.

"I decided to go for a run and thought I'd surprise you and take the day off, so we could spend it together."

The gulping as he drank his water was deafening. Was he going to ask more questions? Did he want to drill me?

I smiled at him. "Great, babe."

Gary peeled off the sweaty Ramones T-shirt and threw it past me towards the bedroom floor. He was a few years older than me, but kept his body in great shape. The next thing I knew, he was yanking the towel from my hand and forcing me to kiss his pecs.

"You just got finished running, and I'm clean," I said.

"Lick them," he commanded. "You've always liked the smell of my body."

I did as I was told. I knew he could tell now. This was his way of reclaiming me. His body was smooth in all the places that Peter was covered in hair. Gary removed his shorts and forced me down on him while he towered over me. My mind kept going back to how Peter's body had felt. That was new. Fresh. Exciting. Standing in front of me was a body I had known for years and years.

I looked up at Gary's face and I could see the hurt in his eyes, but he was not about to ask me what had happened. His oblique silence was enough. I wasn't used to him dominating me in this fashion, and I was not about to start now. I stood, stared him squarely in the eyes.

We didn't speak. We let our eyes do all the talking.

And then I decided I had had enough of his game. I pushed Gary to the floor and showed him who was really the one in charge in this relationship. And he enjoyed pleasing me more that day than he ever had before.

CHAPTER EIGHT

NOAH

M y infatuation with the Sunday crossword puzzle had grown the past two years, since Jacob had left. It was a small part of my day, but it lifted me in an intellectual way that I wasn't used to. I would still hide it from Mama when I came in the door, since I didn't want anyone thinking I was trying to be highfalutin or something. It was a hidden personal joy that was just for me — something to aid in my continued education, since school was nowhere in my plan. Usually, the crossword would be sandwiched between a car magazine and something else.

I was creeping down the hall that Saturday evening when I heard my mother's voice from her bedroom.

"Noah?"

I walked to her doorway and stood there looking at her. Barbara Mandrell was quietly *sleeping single in a double bed* from Mama's bedside radio. Mama wasn't looking as vibrant as usual. Someone from her book club must have annoyed her.

"Did you have a nice night?" she asked.

"Yeah, just went to play pool with some of the guys," I said. "Yours?"

"Fine ... fine. Minnie Pearl kept me company on TV."

"Sorry I wasn't around, Mama-"

"Oh no, no," she said. "I didn't mean anything by that. I'm fine by myself."

I looked down on my mother's lap where her Bible always rested at this time of the evening. Tonight there was a crossword puzzle book.

"Crosswords?" I asked.

"I needed a break in my routine," she said.

It made me chuckle. Guess Mama was a woman of secrets too.

"Well, sleep well, Mama."

I turned to walk towards my bedroom, the Sunday newspaper tucked safely under my arm, when she called out again.

"Noah … do you want to move into your own place?" she said.

"What? Where did that come from?" I stopped and asked.

"I was thinking … you're getting older, probably tired of staying here with your old Mama."

The catch in her voice propelled me back into her room, where I sat on the edge of her bed. I felt like a little boy. I remember crawling up on this very bed when I fell and cut my knee chasing the neighbor dog down the block. But I was a tough kid who wouldn't allow Mama to see any tears because that was the kind of person I had decided to be.

"Mama, I am fine here," I said with a smile. "I think we're doing ok, don't you?"

Mama reached up to touch my face. She returned my smile with one of her own that seemed as if her heart was melting.

"I think we're good too," she said. "I just needed to check."

I stood and the newspaper fell onto the bed next to her.

"Doing some midnight reading?" she asked.

"I enjoy the crossword puzzles too," I shared.

"The apple doesn't fall too far," she said pointing to her own.

I kissed Mama on the forehead before walking towards her door.

"Good night."

"Good night, son. I love you."

"You too," I said.

With that, I was down the hall and going off into my own room. I knew she loved me and I knew I loved her. But I also sensed that there would always be an obstacle between us. I could say it was Jacob, but perhaps it was me. I didn't know how to talk to Mama any more than she knew how to talk to me. We didn't have the same interests. We didn't know how to bring the other into each of our worlds. Thoughts of my childhood raced through my mind. I tried to pinpoint the moment when we had lost our connection. I know I curled up into myself once dad was gone — I should have made more of an attempt to be there for her then. But I was a young kid. What could I have known?

I yanked my shirt over my head and threw it on the pile of clothes on the floor, then lay back in bed thinking.

Why was she asking if I wanted to move? Something was going on I wasn't sure what it was — but I knew she was hiding something from me.

CHAPTER NINE

JACOB

I ran into the apartment only to change my shirt and run right out the door again. As I peeled off one shirt, I looked down at the notes that Gary had left for me from phone calls. Too many notes that said, *Call your mama — Noah checked in — Don't forget your roots* were piled up on the kitchen counter. I just didn't have time to sit through those calls right now. My life was moving at a pace that even I had a problem keeping up with it. New York was a never-sleeping, always-churning source of energy that kept me buzzing. And it was used to presenting its number one son in all the best places. A huge billboard in Times Square, the cover of the newly revamped *Look Magazine*, things that never could have occurred in Nocona or even Nashville for that matter. I was a model superstar and it felt amazing.

"Damn, I need an assistant," I said aloud.

I washed under my arms, put on some Jovan Musk and a fresh shirt to head back out the door. I had another audition waiting in midtown. I dashed out my building, turned the corner and bumped right into Peter.

"Slow down, you mother ... oh, Jake," he said.

"Forearms? What are you doing on my side of town?" I asked.

The last time I had seen Peter was a wild night after yet another party. Peter had brought along a third guy to add to the mix. Our meetings had become more frequent for several months — and not only after a late night of partying. Sometimes it was an afternoon quickie between jobs, or a morning after the gym. More often than not, it included some white powder to sniff up my nose. The original guilt I had over him had been replaced by an excitement of trying not to get caught. And besides, it felt good, I enjoyed it, and I told myself that I deserved it. I worked damn hard and everyone had a right to a little 'pick me up' now and again. And in some strange way, it was intensifying mine and Gary's love-making. Peter was hot, wild sex. Gary was a man desperately trying to hold on to me and it showed in his sexual passion. Truth was he had nothing to worry about. I wasn't going anywhere.

"I was just visiting a friend over here … but I had no idea I could get a bonus by seeing you," Peter said moving in closer.

"Yeah well, keep that bonus in your pants," I said. "I have an audition."

"So you live on this street?" he said. "Wow. So close. You really should show me what it looks like."

"Later, I have to get to this audition. My manager will kill me if I don't make it on time."

"Come on!" he said, getting close enough so that I could smell his intoxicating scent. "We can make it a quickie … just show me your place and I'll be out in no time. I promise."

I looked at this fucking gorgeous guy smiling at me and began to think with the wrong part of my anatomy.

"Five minutes, that's it, and then I have to get on the road," I said.

We turned to walk back towards my apartment. As I walked through the door, the phone was ringing. I assumed it was my mother calling. I had no time to even think about it as Peter was already undressing me and pushing me towards the sofa. The phone stopped. He was down on his knees placing himself between my legs as my phone started ringing again.

"Fuck!" I called out.

"Let it go," he said.

Peter continued kissing my stomach and down the inside of my legs, as the insistent phone rang and rang. What if it was Rachel? What if it was a job? Or something could be wrong. I needed to get one of those phone services. I had to answer.

"Hello," I said.

"Jacob, it's Noah," came the voice on the other end.

I looked down at the man between my legs and felt like a child who had just been nabbed.

Noah spoke again. "Jacob, can you hear me? It's Mama."

This was the call I had dreaded. The reason I hadn't wanted to answer the phone and the real reason I actually did. I hadn't been returning calls to Tennessee lately because they had found a spot on Mama's lung six months earlier, though she had kept it from Noah for a few months. Once he knew, he would fill me in during our long phone calls, but I hated hearing the news. Recently there had been a campaign to blame lung cancer on smoking, but the woman had never smoked a day in her life. I remembered as a child my dad had smoked non-stop. Even on road trips in the car, he would smoke with all the windows shut. I had hated that smell. Why her? I pushed Peter away and reached for a cigarette and lit it.

"Yes?" I said.

"She's gone, Jacob," Noah said. "It happened quickly."

I watched the smoke from my cigarette curl into the air. Peter stared at me with a questioning look on his face. I was stone cold, couldn't even move or speak.

"Jacob? You there?" Noah asked.

I didn't know what to say. I hadn't even seen my mother since she got sick. Never had time to travel South due to my hectic work schedule. Or at least that's what I told Noah. Gary had wanted us to go down there to visit while she was ill. He knew what it was like to have no parents. He had watched his aunt die while he cared for her. But I put up endless objections and excuses. There was always something keeping me away from Nocona. Deep down, I knew Noah could handle it better than I could. I would have fallen apart seeing that woman sick. I didn't want to face it and the best thing I could do was throw myself into my work — the very work that had made her so proud of me. Why hadn't I seen her one last time? We used to be so close. I wanted to take time to cry, to mourn her properly, but I couldn't allow myself. The guilt set in, but I couldn't let it show.

"I'm needed at an audition, Bubba," I said. "Thanks for calling me."

"Thanks for calling you?" he asked. "That's all you can say about the woman who did everything in her life for you?"

I couldn't even talk to my brother about it. And I didn't want Peter to see me get upset.

"I'm going to have Rachel, my manager, give you a call to get the details," I said.

"Why don't you just do that," Noah said. "You have your people call mine."

He slammed the receiver in my ear.

I was still unable to move. Peter was unsure what was going on.

"What's wrong?" he asked.

"My mother," I said as I put out the cigarette in the ashtray.

Peter must have understood. He moved to hug me, but I didn't want comfort now. Not from him. Not here. Not this way. I pulled away and walked over to the window that looked down onto the concrete sidewalks and busy street, this fucking street that looked nothing like the one I had grown up on. I couldn't recognize anything through that looking glass that made me feel close to home. To my past. To her.

"I'll call you later, man," he said as I heard the door shut behind him.

A pain grew from deep in my gut that wanted to cry out, but I wouldn't allow it.

I wished that Gary were there with me. To tell me what to do. To help me through this rough time. He was the strong one in our relationship. He even helped me deal with my issues on sexuality those years before and advised me on coming out to Mama. I recall how the fear pounded the heart out of my chest as I had thought she was going to toss me right out of her southern, Christian home — but she didn't.

No, she had just stood at that worn down ironing board, and continued ironing my clothes ... the outfit I would actually be wearing to go see *The Way We Were* at the movies with Gary that same night.

"There is something we need to discuss," I had said to her to open the conversation.

She had heard all the nasty rumors about me and knew where they came from. However, she pretended it was nothing and instead carefully ran the iron up and down the sleeve of the shirt I had purchased from the JC Penny catalog. Working out the creases and concentrating on each stroke, so as not to scorch the silk.

"Miss Rogers was talking about her nephew the other day," she said. "He moved to Nashville with another guy. Apparently, this other boy is more like his girlfriend than anything else."

She had whispered the word 'girlfriend.'

She turned the shirt over to get the wide collar, as she went on, "I told her she shouldn't worry about him. As long as he was happy and not hurting anyone, right?"

"Mama. I know what you're doing," I said.

"As long as they don't hurt anyone, Jacob," she repeated, raising the iron and looking at me in a defiant tone.

I needed to test her. "But don't you think he's going to hell?"

"Fizzlesnits! The God I know is a God of love," she said, resuming her work, pretending to focus on the task, nodding to herself. "I do think we should pray for him daily, that he makes the right decisions, but God does not send souls to the eternal fire for this."

I had studied my mama's face, the age lines that circled her mouth and sprawled out from the corner of her eyes behind her glasses. Was I somehow responsible for putting those there because of her worries about my lifestyle? I knew she was hurting on the inside from the fact she was really talking about her son and not Miss Rogers' nephew, but she was trying to comfort me with her words all the same.

"Mama? Do you think *I'm* going to hell?" I asked her.

She stopped ironing again and looked me straight in the eyes. "No, I don't."

That was who my Mama was. She could disapprove all she wanted of anything that went on in her home, but she didn't want to hear someone else talking about her son. That was simply not allowed.

And now she was gone.

And I had let her slip away from me when I moved to New York. There was no getting that time back now. No going back. I would have to live with the guilt of not being there for her while she was dying.

Then it occurred to me. The funeral. What the fuck was I supposed to do? I knew I was flying to London for a photo shoot, but I would be expected to be in Tennessee. But for who? Going there now would not bring Mama back. The people of Nocona could care less about me. They would just make a big deal about my success, which would piss Noah off and who needed that at a funeral? No. It was best for everyone if I went to London, did my job and mourned Mama in my own way. I'd have Rachel give Noah the news that I wouldn't be able to make it.

I picked up the phone and called my agent.

"Rachel, it's me," I said. "I need you to call my brother. My mother just passed away."

CHAPTER TEN

NOAH

I couldn't believe Jacob's reaction. We had had many bad times, but now we only had each other. Didn't he get that? Couldn't he show some emotion, even if he was half a country away? Couldn't he tell his little brother everything would be ok? Did he have a clue what it had been like for me … and how lost I felt right then?

The isolation was unbearable. I was alone in the house where Mama had reared two very different boys. Alone to wait for Williamson Funeral Home to come and take her body from her bed. Alone to settle her affairs and make sure she was put to rest in the right way. At least she had been at home, to die like she had asked me. I was busy listing things I needed to do when the phone rang.

"Hello. Noah?" came a voice that I couldn't quite place.

"This is Noah," I said.

"This is Jacob's manager, Rachel. We're very sorry to hear about your loss," she said. "I'm assuming the funeral will be on Thursday, correct?"

"Yes … I'm not sure yet. I believe so," I said coldly.

"We'll be sending a huge bouquet to the funeral home," she said. "I already checked and saw there is only one in Nocona."

"Right. Not much need for competition in that area," I said.

"You're really very witty," she said. "Listen, I'm really sorry, but Jacob won't be able to attend on Thursday. He is flying to London Wednesday evening, but he sends his best wishes to you."

I was stunned. There was nothing I could say that could even try to refute such a comment.

"Did you hear what I said?" she asked.

Did I hear her? Of course I heard her. My own brother was missing his mother's funeral. What else was there to say? Jacob did what Jacob wanted to do.

"Yes, Rachel. I heard you," I said. "Tell the asshole to have a nice trip."

I didn't want to hear anymore and hung up the phone.

What a fucking day.

I had hung up twice on people within five minutes time. Guess I could keep up with the fancy movers and shakers up North after all. Jacob wasn't the only Garrett that could show people what he thought.

I pictured Mama sitting on the corner spot of the sofa the way she loved to do before she got sick. I felt proud that I had her for the past two years to myself. And the old woman wasn't so bad.

Not really.

I actually enjoyed how she would plan her evening around her favorite TV shows. Or watching her separate the plastic cups from the Mason jar mugs in the kitchen cabinet, because she felt they shouldn't be on the same shelf. Or even the advice she gave, especially when I really didn't want it, but she felt had to impart.

I suddenly became very aware of the mess in the house and the thought of strangers traipsing through it. Like some sort of nut, I started picking up piles of junk lying around the living room, straightening sofa pillows, and trying to make Mama's house presentable to those she left behind. While I worked, my mind continued to wander.

When she found out she was sick, she became a stronger woman. I had never seen fortitude like that. It was something I would have as an example for the rest of my life.

"My sweet, baby boy," she would say as I fed her beef broth, after propping her up in her bed.

"Now we promised there would be no sadness," I reminded her.

"No tears here," she said. "Can't a mother smile at something she has created and is proud of?"

She had me there. And I was glad she had pride in me.

"Tell me what you want me to buy for you tomorrow?"

"I'm the mother. I should be up cooking for you," she said, as she took her finger and traced the scar on my chin in a loving way.

"Are you crazy! It's my turn to care for you," I said. "You did enough for us."

I would have to remind her of that often.

"You know …" she would say with a smile, "I think I am a little crazy."

"It's a Garrett trait, Mama. Don't sweat it."

I remembered how I had broken down so uncontrollably. I had cried myself to sleep when the doctor told us that there was nothing they could do. I had watched her wither away to a small, frail woman instead of the big, vibrant person she had been. But her spirit never waned. She never stopped talking about all the big plans she had for me and for Jacob, the dreams she hoped we would both achieve.

"The Garrett boys are going to be people to reckon with in this world," she said.

"Jacob seems to be doing just fine bringing fame to our name," I told her, as I held her delicate hand in mine.

"I don't mean just Jacob, Noah. I mean both of my boys," she said. "You have so much to offer the world. I know you are going to do it."

Did you really, Mama? Or is that something you just say to a son as you find yourself at the end of the world?

With her passing, I knew a period in my life was over. There was nothing for me here in this town now that Mama was gone. I too would leave Nocona and head to Nashville, not across the country as Jacob had done. But like Jacob, I wanted a clean start in my life. The difference was I'd be taking my roots with me.

First things first.

I would make sure the woman whose body lay in the other room, who had cared for me my entire life, would have a proper burial, even if her first born would be nowhere in sight.

I opened her bedroom and the smell of musty carpet and Chantilly Lace filled my nose. Tears filled my eyes. There was so much to do, but for now I would wait by her side until the funeral director arrived to take her away from Peachmont Street.

CHAPTER ELEVEN

JACOB

Rachel was a great manager. I may have been her largest client, but I was not the only big name on her list. She continued to grow her business and become even more successful. She had a fabulous apartment on West End Avenue; one of those pre-war buildings with amazing architecture, thick walls and high ceilings. She lived there with her mother's brother who was an elderly decrepit little man. The last thing she promised her mother before she passed away was that she would take care of the guy and he would not want for a home. That was the kind of person she was. The concept was lost on me, but I appreciated that about her. She had actually tried to push me to go to Mama's funeral, but I had fought her on it and insisted that I was doing my job instead. I didn't need those church people trying to make me feel guilty. But Gary did go. Gary loved Mama too and he represented us both at the service. How was I so lucky to have both Gary and Rachel in my life? Two people who were both kind and generous? Just don't ever tell anyone else that Rachel was or she'd smack you down for it. She lived it, but she didn't talk about it.

Our small gang had grown used to meeting at her place to smoke pot before heading out for a night on the town. We would hit Studio 54, making our way right past the velvet rope, or head down to the

Bottom Line for drinks and a show. Everything was done in cabs or car services. Tonight, Felicia had talked us into going down to the Tribeca Gallery Artist Space to catch one of those new "punk-funk" bands that were popping up all over the downtown scene. I thought I had gotten away from that by moving uptown, but at times our group acted like a bunch of college kids. I didn't mind as much about being identified in one of those places anymore, since my career was now top-notch. But I still didn't care for that whole androgynous scene.

"So I said, 'What the hell am I supposed to do with that?'" Rachel exclaimed in that voice that I had grown to love. Her accent was a cross between British royalty, a New Orleans madam, and a hint of New England charm. Her excuse for it: army brat.

Everyone laughed, as Rachel held court in her house. The joint made its way around the circle. This group was a crazy mix of people who were in a perennial state of merriment — laughing, drinking, and doing occasional drugs. It was a life. We all had become inseparable. Gary was used to my friends by now and knew Peter was becoming a permanent fixture, along with Rachel and Felicia. Felicia made some comment and I saw Peter lean into Gary and put his hand on his crotch. Because of the pot, Gary didn't seem to mind.

Peter spoke up, through bouts of laughter.

"Rachel, you have got to be the finest manager in New York. Not only do you get this man some of the best jobs around, but you score the sweetest pot too."

"Where did you get this shit?" Gary asked, after taking another hit.

"My uncle," Rachel said. "Don't ask. I have no idea how he gets it."

We all broke out into laughter again with thoughts of this dear old man making his way to a park for a drug deal. I jumped to my feet and ran over to the window. Rachel's apartment was on the tenth floor. The window went from the crown molding to the wood floors and looked down over the avenue.

"I want to be the biggest male model in New York," I said.

Peter joined me at the window. He wrapped his arms around me from behind as we looked out onto the street and he whispered in my ear that I *was* the biggest. I loved how Peter felt when he held me. It was different with Gary. Gary had always been there. He knew every inch of my body. But I was still discovering parts of Peter every time we got together. I turned, held Peter in my arms and kissed him. I looked back into the circle and witnessed Felicia taking Gary in her arms and hugging him. Perhaps it was the pot — perhaps that was the point, to make these moments less awkward. Gary pretended not to notice the exchange between me and Peter.

Felicia broke the moment with a jab towards me. "I'm tired of seeing your shirtless body on every billboard. What the hell are you selling?"

"What won't he sell with that 'young' body?" Gary said. He looked at me as if he was just about to expose the secret about my age. Maybe I was just being paranoid from the pot.

Peter moved towards Gary.

"Now that's a supportive boyfriend," Peter said. "Great comeback!"

"Leave Jake alone," Rachel said. "I'm making lots of money off my golden boy."

I went to Rachel's side and sat on the arm of the chair. I held her in my arms. A place I knew that Rachel enjoyed, that she had longed for the moment she first laid eyes on me. I knew I could always hold that over her. How my hag wished I were not gay.

"Thanks for protecting me, beautiful lady," I said.

Peter took one last toke on the joint and put it out.

"Who else is ready for food?" he asked.

Felicia grabbed her coat and my coat and headed towards the front door.

"Come on, Jake … let's go flag down a cab," she said.

"The skinniest bitch in the room and you're the one ready for food," Rachel jabbed at Felicia as she followed us out the door. She hollered back to Peter and Gary.

"Are you two coming?" she asked.

"Right behind you," Peter said.

But Peter wasn't behind her. He was watching Gary go for his coat and was behind him. I looked back from the doorway just in time to catch Peter lock Gary into his large arms and kiss him. A smile came across my face as I watched. I guess the pot wasn't enough to allow Gary to do this, as he stopped Peter right away.

"No … stop … I'm not Jake," Gary said.

Ouch. Slam against me.

"Figured we could all have some fun," Peter said.

"I think you two have enough of that for all of us," Gary said.

After the initial guilt, I had never given much thought to how Gary felt about my romps. He was the one that had told me what New York had to offer. He knew what it had spawned since the free loving

60s. But he didn't know there was no dealing with a man like Peter who was high, hungry, and horny and was grabbing for him again.

"Come on, everybody is waiting," Gary said.

"Gary … you better loosen up if you don't want to lose your prize possession," Peter said.

Gary looked up and saw me standing in the door. I may have been stoned, but it was as if his eyes were asking me if this was really the life we had planned so long ago when we left Tennessee.

"Don't you love that we can all be openly gay men in this city?" Peter said as he grabbed both of us arm in arm.

"I didn't know openly gay meant promiscuous," Gary said as we neared the elevator.

"Are you hoping something will change?" I asked him, as the doors opened and we all walked inside.

Gary looked at me through the haze of the pot. "Right now, I'm just hoping for a cheeseburger," he said with a smile. And the elevator doors shut.

CHAPTER TWELVE

NOAH

In Nashville, I was living a life I never knew I could have. I didn't answer to anyone. I had a great one-bedroom apartment, the perfect size, in a complex that I could come and go from anytime I wanted. Nashville was a city that still had a down-home feel. It had great neighborhoods, a rocking downtown scene and a beautiful skyline on the water. So while it wasn't a small town like Nocona, I didn't feel the need to constantly be on the go, trying to escape something all the time. I felt much calmer in my own skin.

I suppose something about Mama's last days had rubbed off on me.

For one thing, I hated cooking and always preferred to go out. There were other twenty-something's that lived near me and we would find ourselves out at The Whiskey Shack, shooting pool, eating Tennessee smoked barbeque and just talking about our days. There were people here who shared my views on the world. That agreed with me that President Carter really wasn't doing as great of a job in the White House as others wanted us to believe.

C-SPAN began to run live feeds from the House of Representatives so Americans could actually see what was happening behind those long closed doors. I watched that channel more and more as I learned about what was going on in our government and all over the world. Egypt and Israel had signed a peace treaty, and each country had agreed to recognize the other, but I wasn't certain our president had much to do with that. I was thrilled that the Oilers had made their way into the NHL.

Another change I was working on stared back at me from the mirror each day. Ever since that movie *Pumping Iron* with Arnold Schwarzenegger and Lou Ferrigno had come out, more and more people were talking about gyms and working out. I was one of them. My mornings would start by heading to the gym, lifting weights — which was like hauling hay — and working on getting rid of the gut I'd had for several years. And it was paying off. The gals in Nashville looked at me differently than the ones back in Nocona. I'm not saying I had turned into Jacob or anything, but I could hold my own.

I had already dated a few girls in Nashville, but nothing seemed to stick. I wasn't sure what I was looking for, but I knew I hadn't found it yet. Something else Mama had said was also true. I was looking older than my years working outside, so I made a major career change. A change that had nothing to do with working outdoors with my hands.

Moving to Nashville meant a fresh start and I did just that by getting an office job. I put on a tie, loosely, around my neck each day, and did grunt work that no one else wanted to do in a real estate office. I had only been there eight months when a friend told me about an entry level job at a music publishing house. Something about the idea of working in that business intrigued me. After all, Nashville was the country music capital of the world. Maybe I'd get to meet Kenny Rogers or Mel Tillis.

Clearwater Publishing was a small publishing house, but a busy one. My job was to assist an agent by working directly with the writers after the agent had approved their songs. I was fascinated by the many people who came to Nashville with so many dreams. Everyone wanted to be a country singer or a songwriter for a singer. I heard them all. From the low down cheatin' songs to the "my pick-up truck is churnin' its motor for you."

I was also harboring my own dream.

Writing short stories.

Stories of Jacob and me as children. Stories Mama had shared with me for all those years. Stories of the South and what it meant to be a southerner. I discovered this secret desire shortly after Mama died. I wanted to remember everything about her and began to jot down notes as a personal reminder, notes I figured I'd share with my children someday. But I couldn't stop myself. The notes became longer and turned into pages. The pages began to take on structure all by themselves. My nights were spent at my desk. The words came into my head and went right on the paper.

The two small boys in the story had just caught their first fish and the youngest was upset when the older one threw it back in the water. The older was trying to teach a lesson about allowing the fish to seek its full potential. But the youngest could already taste the tartar sauce slathered across the fried fish and was hungry. He cared more about the moment at hand and less about what the fish could become, a theme that I played up to ground the story in larger issues. I noticed that even though these were stories of my childhood, the lines between who was Jacob and who was me would sometimes get blurred.

I looked down at the pile of pages in front of me. The clock said five a.m. I had been writing all night long.

I guess Jacob had been right. You should always pursue your dreams.

Jacob.

I hadn't talked to him in months. I hated to admit it, but I missed my big brother. There was a time when we had been able to talk. Before I discovered he was gay and began to pick on him. But if he had to be gay, at least he picked a good guy with Gary. I couldn't believe when I saw Gary walk in to mama's funeral. It had to have been one of the nicest displays of kindness I had seen in a long time. I had to move the weekly crossword puzzle to try and find the number in order to make the call.

"Hey there. It's me," I said.

"Hello … Noah?" came Jacob's groggy voice on the other end.

"I know it's early in the morning, but figured it's the only time I would catch you."

"This isn't a voice I was expecting to hear," he said.

"Guess I can't hide the Southern drawl, huh?" I asked.

"No," Jacob snorted. "I've just gotten used to not hearing from you."

"Can we not do this?" I said.

I had never realized growing up that perhaps Jacob had harbored his own resentment against me. I always thought it was a one-sided thing. But as an adult, I understood that I had become the man of the house after dad had died, even though I was the baby. I knew that didn't sit well with Jacob. I also knew that in some way, I held that over him. Like I was truly a man while being gay diminished his manhood.

"So, Bubba … how's the South treating you?" Jacob asked.

"Things are good. Lovin' life in Nashville," I said.

I couldn't believe that I had so little to say to my older brother, yet there I was, waking him up early in the morning.

"It would be good to see you again," I said.

"You can come up anytime you like," Jacob said. "Gary and I would love to see you. Of course, I do travel a lot for work, so make sure I know when you're coming."

This felt even more awkward than I had feared.

"Okay, will do," I said. "Just wanted to say hello. I better go so I can get ready for work. Take care of yourself."

"You too, little Bubba," he said.

I hung up the phone.

Is this really what adult life becomes? You turn into an island once your family is gone? Nothing to hold on to. Nothing to make you smile. When we were kids, we were as close as two brothers can be. Jacob would hover over me like a mama-bird, protecting me from the kids in the neighborhood. Looking back now, it all seems so strange to think that he was ever that way with me. To see what he became. To witness his selfishness. How could someone like that have come from something so normal as the kid I knew? I realized I needed to remember more of those good times, put that into my writing, in order to find a connection to my brother that at some point in our life we had lost. This is not what I wanted the rest of my life to be.

I knew it was time. Time to use some of the contacts I had made through my job to find ways to get my short stories published. This was my connection to my family. To my past. This would be something I could give back to Mama.

CHAPTER THIRTEEN

JACOB

Rachel had finally done it and gotten me on Broadway, a role as an understudy cowboy in the musical *The Best Little Whorehouse in Texas*. I really thought I deserved the role of the sheriff or the role of Ché in the musical *Evita* that was soon coming to Broadway from London. I had loved that show when I caught it on a visit there. I thought I could carry a lead simply because of my notoriety as a well known model. But there was no such luck; I felt I was barely noticed at the audition for the South American revolutionary narrator. Instead, I was stuck here in Aggie-ville working my ass off to get the gymnastic dance steps that Tommy Tune had imparted on this cast.

These rehearsals were not what I had expected. Everything was on overdrive, and I had to get up to speed to match the cast who was doing the show nightly. Plus, I didn't even get to rehearse with the whole cast, just a tyrant of an assistant choreographer and stage manager barking orders that didn't sit well with me at all. I was always exhausted from staying out late at night and the daytime marathon rehearsals.

"Jake, you've got to get that leg extended more to match the rest of the guys," the skinny bitch of a choreographer yapped at me.

"I have other ways of extending my legs," I said, with a sarcastic smile.

"Save it, girl," he snapped, and had the piano player start at the top of the dance break.

With sweat dripping into crevices on my body (that should only be touched with sweat from an all night orgy with a team of hot guys), I jumped back into my place for the Aggie Song. Kicking my boots like a real shit-kicker back in Tennessee and giving it all I had.

"Damn it, Jake! Kick on two not three," he yelled.

I was getting sick and tired of the constant berating. I thought I was doing a fine job at this stupid dance. All at once, I felt a pain in my groin and halted the dance.

"Why, oh why are you stopping, damn it?" he asked.

"Because the pain around my dick tells me stop," I yelled, as I limped towards my bag to get some water.

The two of them stood near the piano player displaying looks of disgust towards me that I've never experienced on a photo shoot.

"The guy is completely out of his element," the choreographer said, loud enough for me to hear.

"He can't even sing," the fat fuck behind the piano interjected.

"He got the job because the casting director loves his manager and wants to sleep with him," the stage manager volunteered.

I'd had enough.

"Do you three queens think I can't fucking hear you?" I asked.

"We thought you were busy tending to your muscle," the skinny one said, with more attitude than I cared to hear.

I started picking up my stuff and shoving it into the bag.

"This is really insane. The amount of work isn't worth it. I can make the weekly salary in a few hours on a photo shoot," I said.

"Welcome to Broadway, baby."

I threw the bag over my shoulder.

"Keep your fucking Broadway," I said. "I'm way bigger than what you guys need."

I tried to leave in as dramatic a fashion as possible, but the ache between my legs hampered me. I had always thought doing a Broadway show was my dream, but I guess the reality was something else. I headed out of the studio and down the hall to the elevator. I could care less what they did to replace me and I knew for sure that live theatre was not for me.

***

42nd Street had rows and rows of movie theaters: theaters that in their heyday had been wonderful Vaudeville houses, places that had hosted Jimmy Durante, George Burns and Gracie Allen, the Ziegfeld Follies. But at that time, they were all 50 cent porn houses. The same stage that would have heard the words, *Say goodnight, Gracie,* now had huge screens on them showing men and women in all sorts of compromising positions.

The rooms were dark, except for the flicker of the film and the cigarettes dangling from the mouths of patrons sitting in the wet, sticky seats. The smell was a mixture of day old sex and weeks of stale cigars and cigarettes. Men scattered throughout the theatre to watch, each other as much as the film. Some rows had men sitting closer together, giving each other hand jobs underneath raincoats.

I walked into the scene, as I had on previous occasions. I went down front and took a seat. I looked at the screen. I was not interested in seeing men and women having sex, but I was interested in meeting someone.

Anyone.

The taste of Jack Daniels was on my tongue. I lit a cigarette as I took my seat. Who would I have today? An older man came and took a seat two chairs down from me. I stood and moved away to show him I was not interested.

Down the aisle came a fresh face. Yum. I didn't recognize him, but knew I would have him. He was no older than 21. He looked at me and smiled. I responded by pushing the folding seat next to me down. The kid took the seat. I kept my face on the screen, never thinking I might be recognized in such a place. That was part of the whole allure. The thrill of getting caught. I continued to smoke my cigarette as the young man started to fondle me. I reached for the kid's crotch and gave a tight squeeze. Instantly, the young man had my pants unzipped and was down on his knees on the dirty, sticky floor. I kept my gaze on the screen, the smoke from my cigarette floating up into the flickering lights of the projector.

***

I had been waiting for ten minutes for this fucking audition. I was certainly not used to waiting in a hallway. I was always called in, taken directly into the room, and asked to show my portfolio (if by some rare chance those on the other side of the table were not familiar with my work). But this was an audition for a guest spot on a television show. Rachel had worked hard to get me seen after I had quit the Broadway show, but waiting there was making me very aggravated. I knew now I should not have done the two lines before I left the house.

A beautiful woman shifted her weight in the chair at the desk. Had she been there the entire time? I hadn't even noticed someone else was in the hall with me. Any straight man would have been spending the entire time flirting with her, but her beauty was wasted on me. Two more minutes passed and my patience began to grow thin.

"Are you sure they know I'm waiting?" I asked.

"They are aware you are here, Mr. Garrett," she said.

"Because I'm not used to waiting this long."

"I'm sorry," she said.

Sorry. She should be sorry. I was one of the top models from New York to Paris by this point. I had done runways, had several magazine covers. I could walk to the corner stand and show her right now if she wanted me to.

"This job is a fucking joke anyways," I said. "Small potatoes … doing it as a favor. My face is all over Times Square."

"It shouldn't be much longer," she said.

The door finally opened. Out walked a young actor that could have been James Dean's younger brother. Damn. I smiled at the cute young man who flashed me a huge smile back as he walked down the hall to the elevator. My crotch stirred. I grabbed my bag and headed towards the audition door. Right as I was about to enter, I looked at the nice woman.

"Tell them in there that I just got a better offer," I said.

I turned in the opposite direction towards the elevator door and the man who was stepping inside.

"Hold that elevator!" I yelled.

The young man put his hand out to grab the door just in time. I stepped inside and had an incredible ride all the way down.

***

I don't know where the hell Gary's head was at lately, but it wasn't in tune with mine, as if we were experiencing two different worlds. He was constantly complaining about how dirty and unsafe New York was. You couldn't walk down the street without seeing a pimp smack his hooker across the face and people would avert their eyes and keep walking. Needles used by druggies would be thrown on the ground up near us in Harlem and news reports would tell of deaths of small children who had picked them up and played with them. There were always workers on some strike or other, fires being set in tenements, and smelly-ass bums asleep under newspapers right on the sidewalk. This bothered Gary, but I didn't get it. That wasn't his world. He didn't have to live in it. He had a nice apartment to live in. A great job that he loved. Why did he concern himself with the freaking derelicts on the street?

My world was different. My world was having someone on the set who could hand me a drink when I needed it. Make sure there were always plenty of cigarettes, preferably the brand that I was currently shooting an ad for. Lights, wardrobe and make-up people seeing to my every whim. My world was luxury hotels in Paris, London and Rome — all brimming with young men that I could do whatever I wanted with, whenever I wanted. My world was about the finest champagne waiting for me in the back of a limo when I got picked up at Heathrow or back in the States at JFK. My world was that of the rich and the famous, and I loved every minute of it.

But there were times I wanted to be normal. Anonymous. Someone other than Jake Garrett. And those times, I'd go into the other world to see what it was like. I'd venture into those back rooms for filthy, perverted sex to see what the cheap people in New York were doing. I'd walk through the rambles in Central Park and allow some nobody to blow me or fuck me, hiding in the bushes. I'd buy drugs on the streets like a common person, instead of using my connections in the city. And when I was high, naked against a wall in some sleazy dark room that smelled of piss and booze — covered in the goop that no-named men would leave on me — I felt more alone than I ever had in my life.

***

What the fuck was I doing in Alphabet City? Oh yeah, that art exhibit of some new hot Puerto Rican last night. Yup. There he was naked on the sheets next to me. And several other bodies were piled all around the room. We must have done some wild 'shrooms or something, because I didn't even remember getting there.

I somehow managed to recall how my legs worked and walked to the bathroom to relieve myself. I looked back at the naked bodies all strewn around the bedroom. It looked like a painting you would see at the Museum of Modern Art. All naked men of different ethnic backgrounds.

I found a phone in the living room, but no sign of my clothes.

"Rachel, it's me," I said.

"What the hell you calling me so early for on a Sunday," she said.

"Come on, you work every day. Listen. I need you to come and get me."

"Where are you?" she asked.

I looked around for some mail that had an address and gave it to her.

"10th and Avenue A? What the hell are you doing, my boy!" she said.

"Just get in a cab and come get me."

"You fuck me over by quitting jobs and walking off sets, but I'm supposed to come clean up your shit now?"

"Rachel, don't start preachin', please, this is serious. I just hope I can find my clothes, so wait for me if I'm not down right away."

Rachel's silence told me she was judging me on the other end of the phone.

"I don't need you to play my mother right now," I said. "Just come."

I hung up and walked around naked looking at the artwork on the wall of this man's apartment. He wasn't all that bad. I wondered what he had been like in the sack.

A voice came from behind me.

"Looks good," he said.

I turned to see a beautiful strapping black man staring down at my naked crotch.

"The painting is on the wall," I said.

"I wasn't talking about the painting," he said.

Figuring I had to give Rachel some time to get from the Upper West Side all the way down here, I needed a distraction. So me and the un-named man had our morning breakfast on the floor.

CHAPTER FOURTEEN

NOAH

Thank God that Reagan's conservative stint in the White House was going to lead the county away from the wild times of the 70s. Our country needed it. Just the thought of him heading into office opened the door for the American hostages in Iran to come home that same day. And the country lost a great newsman the night that Walter Cronkite signed off the air. I doubted that news would ever be delivered in the same way. But while the Gipper was leading Washington, there were some groups in New York who were doing everything they could to hang on to the uninhibited times of the previous decade. Jacob took no notice to the changing world around him and was still living every moment like it was his own private party — or so I'd been told by Gary each time that I called and he picked up.

I was sitting on Jacob's sofa in New York with Gary, waiting for him to get home from a photo shoot. Flying up to New York was something that was very different for me. I wasn't completely taken in with the city the way my brother was, but at the same time — there was something uniquely appealing about the grit and glamour of it.

"I don't know what's keeping him," Gary said. "He should have been here by now. It could be anything." And he threw up his arms in surrender, making it clear that he had gone through all this before.

I looked around at how they had decorated their apartment. I'm sure to Gary, I seemed like a Southern judgmental Republican, but I really had nothing to judge. There was nothing here that was yelling out, "Hey, we're two gay men!" It was really no different from a man and a woman living together. No nude posters of men on the wall or Judy Garland memorabilia.

"You sure are tan for living in New York in the winter," I said.

"Jacob and I just flew back from Hawaii last week," Gary said.

"You don't have to be so damn uncomfortable with me," I said.

While I said it to Gary, I meant it more for myself.

"Sorry, Noah. But you used to give us a lot of shit," Gary said with a chuckle.

The guilt struck me hard. Even though I was a young punk then and jealous of all the attention Jacob always got, it didn't excuse my actions. Once I put naked pictures all over Jacob's car with the words *honk for good head* written on the back. Only people didn't honk. They would throw crap at his car. But the more Gary and I would reminisce, the more tension left the room. While I was never fond of thinking of what the two of them would do in Jacob's room, Gary was always pleasant when he came to our house. He sat in the kitchen and talked to Mama in a way that I envied. I could see how much he cared for my brother. And someone needed to watch after him.

"So how do you like living in Nashville?" he asked.

"Much better than Nocona, that's for sure. And the job at the publishing place is great."

"That's so freaking weird," he said. "You were always outside working with your hands. Who would have thought ..."

"What … that I had a sensitive side?" I asked.

No one could ever picture this big straight man hunched over a typewriter, jotting down stories. I looked towards the door expecting Jacob to walk in.

"I wanted you to know that it meant so much to me that you came down for Mama's funeral."

Gary didn't respond. He just smiled as if he had recalled a wonderful memory of the lady.

"Can I get you something while you wait?" Gary asked. "A drink? Some pot?"

"Pot? You guys do that shit?" I asked.

Some tension drifted back in, as if a parent had walked in on two school boys sitting in a dark room with a bong and soft rock sounds coming from the stereo.

"Not often," he said. "Jake's manager gives it to him, and sometimes we'll have some to mellow us out."

"I worry about you guys in this big bad city," I said.

As if to punctuate the very reason that I should worry, Jacob walked through the door reeking of whiskey and obviously tweaked out on something. I could see the years beginning to show on his face. Jacob had always looked so young and fresh, but that was not the man that stumbled in. The years had caught up with him and he was looking his age — plus some. I wasn't sure how he was continuing to get the work on those looks that seemed to be vanishing. His body was still slight in build, but kept in as good of shape as a man that was obviously abusing could keep it. But Jacob didn't even notice anyone else in the room as he stumbled in, trying to peel off his coat.

"Babe, where have you been?" Gary said. "Your brother has been waiting."

Jacob finally noticed I was there. "Bubba!" he said. "You look like you've lost weight."

"We haven't seen each other in a long time," I said, glad that someone noticed the work I'd been doing at the gym.

Jacob went to hug me, but his feet did not cooperate and he landed on the floor. "What the fuck you doing up here?" he asked.

"I told you I was going to be in town," I said. "Someone has to check up on you guys."

I had never really seen my brother drunk. It wasn't a pretty sight. Growing up, I was the one who was always out too late, getting in trouble and stumbling in the house in the middle of the night. But I sensed Jacob was on much more than just liquor.

"Listen to my baby brother," Jacob said. "Playing the mother hen since the mother has left the nest."

"Jake, why don't I make you some coffee," Gary said.

"Who wants coffee? Bubba, do you want coffee?" Jacob asked.

My disdain for my brother was growing.

"I think he wants to sober you up there," I said. "You seem pretty messed up."

"I'm fine," Jacob said with a dismissive wave. "We had a few drinks after a fucking long shoot. So what?"

Jacob fumbled into his pocket to pull out his cigarettes and lit one. He went on to talk about the amount of cigarettes he smoked on camera as well as off. Those ads paid many of his bills, but he seemed to forget what had taken our mother.

"Someone's gotta keep me and Gary in our high life style," Jacob said. "Right, Gar? That's why you stay with me."

"Jacob, you're just being mean," I said.

"That's not why I stay and you know it," Gary said.

"Gary knows he has a good thing here," Jacob said. "And he knows there are plenty of others waiting in line."

"Fuck off," Gary said, picking up Jacob's coat and shuffling into the other room.

"I can't help it if I have the drive and ambition to make something of myself," Jacob said.

I couldn't let my brother's mouth get the best of me this time. I had so much drive now in my writing. By the looks of things, my life was actually going better than his.

Jacob continued. "Bubba. Do you have any idea how much money I make?"

"No. And I don't really want to know," I said. "In fact, I don't want to talk to you when you're like this."

It was only five in the afternoon and my brother was blitzed. I don't think he even knew what was going on around him. I tried to talk about other things several times, but Jacob kept bringing the conversation back around to himself. Gary had come back in the room with us and couldn't seem to control Jacob either.

"You just hate me because I was the number one son, don't you? Just admit it," Jacob said.

I knew Jacob was reaching inside of his drunken stupor to pull out ammunition from the past with that one and it pissed me off.

"Jake! Shut the fuck up," Gary yelled.

"No. Let him talk, Gar," I said. "Maybe he's more honest when he's all messed up."

"I was the daughter Mama never got to have, so she did everything for me and you couldn't stand it," Jacob went on.

I hadn't gone there to fight with him, but like most times the Garrett boys got together, we were quickly heading down that road.

"You know, I always thought you just didn't care about me or Mama … what happened to us," I said. "But now I see you couldn't really care what happens to anyone. Even yourself. I guess that's why you didn't come home when Mama died. Why you let me handle everything."

Jacob got very quiet and sat down next to the window on the floor. His high felt as if it were starting to fade. Tears started to fill his eyes. Gary moved to me and put his hand on my arm.

"Noah, you better get back to your hotel," he said. "You probably don't want to be around to witness this."

I turned to head for the door, but stopped to look at my brother, huddled in a fetal position on the floor.

"Brother … you better slow down," I said. "You'll be joining Mama and Daddy real soon if you don't. Premature death runs rampant in our family."

Jacob started to cry as I walked out of the apartment. I knew the mention of Mama had to have set him off. I stood at the door and could hear what sounded like Gary moving towards him and then I heard singing.

"*Lovin you is easy cause you're beautiful.* Remember that song?" Gary asked.

"Gary. Why do you love me?" Jacob said.

"Don't talk now, babe. Just bring yourself down."

"I've been such an ass," he said.

"Shhhhhh. It's ok," I said.

I knew Jacob was crashing from his high, but I never expected to hear him attempt at an apology.

"I miss my Mama," Jacob cried out.

There it was. He was a real person. He could actually feel something. And right now, seeing me only made him think of family and Mama. I hadn't done it on purpose, but at least I had gotten through to him. I walked down their stairwell and outside. I decided to head back to my hotel and have dinner alone in this big, overgrown city. Maybe on my next visit, I could actually get to speak to my brother and not to his drugs and alcohol.

....

CHAPTER FIFTEEN

JACOB

Studio 54 looked much the same as it did before it shut down two years earlier. Many of the same stars were there — Andy, Calvin, a teenage Brooke, who was doing quite well for herself the past two years in movies. The dance floor was full of people dancing to the beat of not only current music, but some of the old disco music we used to get down to before the place closed. I saw many people sitting along the wall in the booths that I had spent several evenings having sex with up in the balcony. Some of those people were still doing all the illegal things that had made the place so infamous; but now taking their drugs to a more secluded place instead of doing them right out in the open.

Forget the cocaine spoon that hung from the ceiling. I'm sure people thought I was a walking cliché myself with two young, shirtless men under each arm. But I didn't give a shit.

I was stopped before I could get to the booth where my friends waited. The music started for *The Hustle* and the crowd went wild for those that had loved it the previous decade. Fuck those who said disco was dead. Inside this huge sanctuary, that era was celebrated and revered. I could see Rachel and Felicia and the others waiting for me, but partiers always stopped to give me a kiss, or slip something into my pocket. Life felt the same as a few years before, only every move was now done with the sleight of hand. I could see Rachel with a fabulous new scarf around her head looking at me standing so close to her, but I pretended to be engulfed in a conversation with Liza. I couldn't hear their voices yet, but I did notice the two men at the table with them, busy checking each other's orifices for foreign objects. I smiled as I got closer to the table.

"Go upstairs you two. We don't need to see any of that!" Felicia yelled at them.

The men pushed past others to get out of the booth. "Hag!" one snarled at Rachel as he took his friend up the staircase.

"Bitch!" she yelled back at him. "Ah ... it's Jake, the pain in my ass!"

"Hello everyone!" I yelled. "Happy New Year!"

Felicia laughed at me. "What the hell are you talking about? New Year's?"

"Then what the fuck have I been celebrating all night?" I asked.

The entire table laughed and passed around some pills. I looked at the two men under my arms. "Guess we shot our streamers too soon," I said.

I pushed the two men away into the crowd and took a seat at the table. Felicia was now busy kissing the impatient man who at last had a name after all these years.

"Wayne, whatcha got for me?" I asked him.

"Thought you'd never make it," he said.

Wayne opened up his pill bottle and put a few onto my tongue and was back to making out with Felicia. I chased them down with the concoction of Tab and about four different kinds of alcohol that had been handed to me.

"I didn't expect to see Rachel here," I said.

Felicia came up for air. "Leave her alone. She's off the clock."

"I'm always on the clock," I said.

Rachel knew this banter meant nothing with us. We had gone through too much together, through so many years. Not only did she get me some great jobs, she also was there to get me out of many tight spots. She also knew she could never stay mad at me long.

"Shut up, whore, and give me a kiss," Rachel said.

We made up with a wet smooch. Felicia pushed her way out of the booth. Popping one more pill she asked, "Anyone feel like hitting the floor?"

"Hit me with a couple of those," I said. I needed to catch up. She slipped me a couple of pills and I chugged them down with whatever booze was handy.

"Okay. Ready," I said.

Wayne must have had other ideas for me and grabbed me by the arm, pulling me away from the table.

"Men's room first," he said.

"And Gary puts up with this shit," Rachel said.

"Rachel … Gary is a saint," Felicia replied.

"Not really, but he enjoys our apartment on the Upper West Side and all the other perks," I said as Wayne dragged me away from the table.

I heard Felicia yell. "And to think … I've let Wayne make out with me several times!"

"We're all whores in one way or another," Rachel said.

He whisked me past the dancing revelers and up the grand staircase. I saw couples having a good time in the balcony, but Wayne was dead-set on getting to the bathroom. We had barely made it through the bathroom door, when he grabbed another man who was just trying to leave and shoved him into a stall with the two of us.

Wayne pushed me to my knees and pulled out a bottle of poppers. He shoved the bottle under the stranger's nose along with mine. I inhaled the medicinal aroma that made my head rush, as I unzipped the pants of the stranger and started working on him. Wayne wanted to get in the action as well and forced me onto his, while he made out with the stranger. I worked my way back and forth between them, sniffing poppers until I dropped the bottle.

"Shit," I said.

"Come on, man. Don't stop!" the stranger yelled. He was very close and wanted me to finish what I had started. The stranger shot all over me, grabbed a piece of toilet paper to wipe himself off and disappeared. I then turned all of my attention to Wayne. We were both gasping and grunting until Wayne couldn't take it.

"Stop! I'm not ready yet … the night's too young," he said.

My face was covered in sweat and spit and some cum. I was still on my knees and my face was fire-red from the poppers and the drugs.

"Do you have any blow?" I asked.

Wayne seemed to want to get out of the room, perhaps for air or maybe just to get away from me. He threw the vile of cocaine down to me and walked out of the stall to the sink. He wet his face and walked out.

"Catch you outside," he said.

I couldn't wait to get the blow in me. I opened the vile and poured it out on the toilet bowl lid. I went for my wallet to get a credit card. Too messed up to even cut it, I lowered my nose onto the lid and began sniffing.

"Shit!" I yelled.

I was breathing hard and still had not caught my breath from working on the two men.

"Oh fuck."

I tried to stand to get out of the stall for some air, but fell down hard against the cold tile floor.

Did the outside door open?

"Someone there?" I asked.

I was panting.

"Stop spinning!"

As fast as I could, I pulled the toilet paper off the roll to wipe my head. Sweat was beading up and dripping on my face as quickly as I could wipe it away.

"Oh shit. Oh God. Help me! I don't want to die."

I couldn't hold back from all the pills and liquor in my system. My head was over the toilet with the dry heaves. I tried to stop them, but the buildup in my stomach was too great. I knew I should have put some food in there. An urge was growing and growing inside me, so I just hung my head over the toilet hoping I could release what was inside me.

So much was flooding my mind. What I ate for breakfast. How I was going to get out of the bathroom. The time I had the flu when

I was seven and puked all over my aunt's chenille rug. Then the time in 6th grade when my friend Eddie and I were playing show and tell with each other's bodies. I continued to gag over the toilet bowl, but then the water reminded me of my baptism when I was seven. Suddenly, I was in church and all the old goons I had grown up with were pointing at me and calling me a sinner.

Like a good Christian boy, I reached into the deepest part of my past to find my faith. The faith that had aided me through my life when I had guilty thoughts of men. The faith that helped a teenage boy deal with the death of his father. The faith that had been seared into my brain from the moment I could understand it.

"God … God are you there? Please help me. I promise … promise to change my life."

The room continued to spin. Someone was there. I was sure. Was it God? Had He come into the bathroom to save me from my misery?

I drifted back to my childhood. All those years in the church memorizing the books of the Bible, the day I accepted the Lord as my savior and walked down to the front of the church. Going under the water as I was baptized. The comfort I felt at church singing in the choir. Why were these thoughts playing in my head now? Was this the fucking end? Is this how it is when you die?

"My sweet, little boy." I swore I heard Mama's voice.

"Mama! I don't want to die!" I cried out.

"Jacob, what are you boys doing in there?" I continued hearing her voice.

"God help me! Please!" I said.

My mother's voice was like a ghost calling from the past, catching me in the horrible act.

"Eddie's mother called and wants him to come home now," she said. "Jacob! I hear you two moving around. I know you're in there. Eddie! You better get home, dear, before it gets too late."

My world was spinning on the same orbit as the bathroom. The lights in the bathroom seemed to be pulsating the beat of the music. I saw shadows in the corner of the stall. Mama. God. Satan. I wasn't sure who.

"Never again. I don't want this. Take it away. GOD!" I yelled.

And as I shouted out God's name one last time, I threw up all over my $500 suit and passed out on the men's room floor.

CHAPTER SIXTEEN

NOAH

"I don't want you to freak out," Gary said. "The doctors say he's going to pull through."

I had personally seen how fast my brother's life had been moving and had been expecting this call. And here it was. Bottomed out. My brother, the addict. I tried to warn him, but there was no listening to me.

"What's the next step?" I asked. "Is he going to go right back to his old ways again?"

"I don't want to give myself false hope," Gary said. "But I think this one really scared him."

It sure as hell should have. I can't imagine waking up in my own vomit staring at the floor of a public restroom. But there were many things about Jacob's life that were beyond what I could fathom. No one in their right mind could keep up with the fast paced world that he had made his life.

I thanked Gary for the call, for keeping me up to date and offered my help. Gary did so much for my brother and I was very aware of it. He was a good guy; and I knew that he had tried to get Jacob to stop his destructive ways for a long time — but maybe this was what Jacob needed. He had to hit rock bottom in order to come back out of it.

I hung up, grabbed my Skoal and a stir foam cup as my spittoon and went to my desk. I took a sheet of paper, rolled it into the typewriter and my fingers began moving. A fable about addiction came pouring out of my soul. Not just Jacob's addiction, but addiction in general — what it does to people, how it affects everything we do. And I do say *we* — because in one way or another, I think everyone has something they believe they cannot live without.

In my story, addiction was a wild animal. It had the cunning attitude of a fox, with the quickness of a panther, and claws like a mountain lion. Nightly, it would come to the backdoor of a lone cabin in a desolated mountainside where a man lived all by himself. The animal would ask the man if he wanted to come out. Each visit, he would bring a gift to the man: food he had found on another part of the mountain, a sled so that he could slide down the mountain and join the rest of society, a radio to make contact with the outside world. On each succeeding night, the gift caused the man to step outside the door a little bit more — edging towards the animal closer and closer. Until finally — one night, the man sat and talked to the animal. The man decided he didn't need to leave the old house, since all he needed was right there. Food, shelter and now, a nightly friend in the animal. He felt he could be king of the mountain and use the animal to go out and forage for him what he needed to survive. Soon, the animal had moved inside the house with the man and the two were living as a family. The man became greedy and wanted more gifts from the animal and would make him work harder and harder each day, almost like a personal slave. One night, the animal had taken enough abuse from the man and while the man slept, he devoured him whole.

I spit out some of the tobacco into the cup and looked down at the paper.

I had never written a story such as that before. It was not one of my usual southern tales, but it obviously was something eating away at me about Jacob. Or was it about me? What was my addiction? What was it that I could not live without?

It was becoming clear to me the older I got, that for me, it was family. In Tennessee, Mama's family was dying off around me, and the only other connection I had on this earth was to a man who didn't think highly of himself at all. He surrounded himself with people who would say yes to anything he wanted, those who needed him for one reason or another: to sell a product, make money off of him — use him as a commodity. But for me, he was the only brother I had. And as many problems as we had, as much grief that he had brought me through the years, he was the only family I was going to get. Until the day a woman stepped into my life that I chose to make my wife — if I ever did — Jacob was all I would have. And though many miles separated us, I was so happy he hadn't left me alone in this world on that October night.

CHAPTER SEVENTEEN

JACOB

Rachel studied me from across the table at the Jewish deli on Broadway and 63rd. I'm not sure if she were looking at just my face or trying to peer inside to see how I had recouped. I knew I looked like a new man. The lines from years of abuse were still there on my face, and would always be there as a symbol of what I had gone through ... but I had a very fresh look about me now that had to be pleasing to the eye, even if I no longer looked twenty five.

"I really can't believe how fast these three months went by," she said, smearing some butter onto a bagel.

"Maybe for you."

"It was only ninety days," she said, doing her usual whirlwind of movements grabbing and moving everything on the table as quickly as she could.

"Sheer hell ... at least the first two weeks were," I said.

I remembered waking up in that place — that place for addicts like me who couldn't handle coming clean on his own. There were numerous hours of dry heaves as I gave up the ghost of every substance I had grown addicted to. Ridding my body of the poison that had taken control. Then they force me to take other drugs to make me forget the ones I really wanted. There were nights when I thought

I'd be better off if I died. I thought it over and over again, praying to God to go ahead and take me. But I'd see Gary's face in my mind, waiting patiently for me on the other side. Then by the end of the second week, I began to question why I was praying to God. How had He made His way back into my life? I hadn't thought about religion or church in years and as soon as I thought I was on my death bed, He makes a cameo appearance. None of it made any sense.

"Ok, Mary Martyr. At least you're here now," Rachel said.

"Yup, I'm still here."

"I think it's time to start sending you back out on auditions," Rachel said. "Spring shows will be starting soon."

"Rachel. Don't you think I'm starting to look too old?" I asked.

"You look great. Everyone will want you more than before. Distinguished gentlemen are the rave for the 80s."

"I'm not sure I can do it."

"What?" she said.

I couldn't exactly give her an answer as to why; I wasn't sure myself. I recall making a promise to God on that bathroom floor, but that was just a stupid means to an end.

"Do you know the kind of press we could get from this?" she asked.

"Just … give me some time," I said. "To breathe. Decide what I want."

"You're really fucked up in the head, you know that, Jake."

"Yeah well … it's a lot saner in here now than it used to be."

Rachel didn't understand. Our relationship was built around me making money for her, but Gary understood. He had been wonderful through it all. I had put him through so much shit for so long, and he was still right there by my side. He hated the life I had been leading. He even decided to go clean with me and give up drinking and smoking pot. Anything to give our relationship a new start.

I looked into Rachel's eyes. I knew she was wondering where this would all leave our small family of partiers. I was the glue and this glue was done with all of that. I wasn't sure that we had anything else in common. I guess it would take a while to figure that one out.

"Ok, kiddo," she said. "I'm outta here. Gotta get to work."

"But it's Sunday," I said.

"Some of us still have to work on the Lord's day. Me. Gary."

Rachel kissed my head and grabbed the check. "This one is on me."

I watched her pay the cashier. He was a very attractive man and I felt he was looking at me.

Get that out of your head, Jake.

I knew clean and sober also meant staying true to Gary. And that was something I was determined to do.

I left the restaurant and walked down Broadway. It was a mild day for February, so I thought I'd walk for a while. My life didn't quite feel like my life anymore. It was all new and different. Even talking with Rachel felt odd to me and I couldn't put my finger on the difference. I went across the lower end of Central Park, reliving my old life. I recalled wild times in some of the bushes in this park. Anonymous sex, scoring drugs when I couldn't get them in other places. It was as if I could see it all happening again, but this time, I was looking through a movie lens. I could see the people taunting me from behind the bushes to come and join them for one more time. I passed a man who smiled as he walked into the park and I knew where he was heading. Even on this February day. That didn't keep an addict away from what they wanted. Now my counseling from rehab was starting to work. Like a tape recorder stuck in my brain.

Try and do things as normal as possible. Don't make too many rash decisions to alter your life.

I don't think my counselor wanted me to relive the past in such vivid details, because we both knew that would mean I'd be right back where I was before. All of it was so good. So strong. The drugs. The sex. The booze. I craved it all.

I wanted to get off this memory merry-go-round and headed out of the park, walking down 6th Avenue. Maybe I would pop into Gary's salon to surprise him. Seeing his face would help me forget about the parts of my life I was missing. I decided to stop at a phone booth and make a call.

"Hello," came the voice on the other end.

"Noah. It's me."

"Big brother?" Noah said. "So they finally let you out?"

"Yeah, I didn't play well with others."

"Haha … you never did," he said. "So what are you doing now?"

"Waiting. To see if God sends some sort of sign," I said in a joking manner.

"Oh," he said. "You made a deal with the casino man in the sky."

"Don't make it sound like that," I said.

"Hey, we both grew up with it and watched deals get made all the time," he said. "Just be sure you cash those chips in for something really good."

"I just want to be happy right now that I feel good about myself, life, and Gary."

"Well, tell Gary I said hello. I need to get back to work."

"Is everything going well, Bubba?" I asked.

"I'm working on some things," he said. "Might have some good news to share soon."

"I look forward to hearing it." I said. "Take care."

"You too."

"I love you, Bubba."

Silence. I could tell my brother was stunned. But then he spoke.

"Yeah, you too," he said. I hung up the phone and continued walking towards Gary's place. There I knew I would be loved, not judged and some of these demons would let go of me.

***

Finding something to do during the day was proving to be harder than I had thought. Gary would leave me and go to work, so usually I'd go do some of our shopping. Or I'd go to the gym. But no matter where I went, the past was there. I had sex several times in the showers of the gym where I worked out back during my former life. Even the streets near Columbia made me think of college students that I had befriended for sex or for drugs. Today I decided to hit a completely different area of town.

I was in midtown walking down the block towards Radio City Music Hall, wishing someone would tell me what the hell I was supposed to do with my life now. In front of the music hall, stood a couple in their mid thirties holding a Bible. They looked like two lost Southern tourists. The man was busy praying to God about their purpose for being in the city — that God had called them there for a reason and they asked God to keep them strong in their faith and convictions. No one joined them as I listened to the wife try and console the husband for their lack of any followers. The man then caught me looking at them.

"Excuse me," he said. "Have you accepted Christ as your personal savior?"

This was something I hadn't thought about in years.

"Many, many moons ago in Tennessee," I said.

"Praise the Lord," the street minister said. "There is another person in New York City who believes in God."

I explained that God had recently pulled me out of a dark place and that I was in debt to the Lord now. This caused the woman to ask what church I went to and since I didn't have one, I was invited to join theirs.

"Where is that?" I asked.

"Right here. We meet every Sunday in front of Radio City Music Hall," he said.

The thought of me, Jacob Garrett, standing on the street in front of Radio City each Sunday morning brought a chuckle that I couldn't hold back.

"Ahhh, but don't you think you should find a building somewhere?" I asked.

"Church is state of mind," the man said.

I was starting to wonder if these two were not some loonies.

"Where you from?" I asked.

"Texas," she said.

"Now I get it," I said, pleased to slam that overgrown state that had given me my lover. "Well, why don't we go somewhere and talk indoors. I've been walking a while and it's getting cold out here."

"Come join us at our house," she said. "I'll be making lunch and we can chat. We live around the corner, just on the east side."

The woman's face looked sweet. Innocent. Familiar. Something about it reminded me of home. The peace you get when speaking to people of faith. The warmth exuded from the two and a peace that I knew was divine.

"I'm just crazy enough to do that," I said.

"My name is Bill and this is my wife, Judy."

"Jacob. Jacob Garrett."

With that, the three of us walked off as I told the Texans the Reader's Digest version of my life, to get them up to speed where I was now. I'm not sure why, but I was compelled to share all my dark secrets. Almost like a Catholic who goes to confession. That's what it was. These people were sent for me to confess all my sins.

We made it to their beautiful doorman building apartment and Judy headed straight to the kitchen to finish a stew that she had left cooking in a crock pot. The best invention of the past ten years that would allow women to spend less time in the kitchen and more time with their busy lives.

"You have had a fascinating life," Bill said after he finished the prayer to bless the food.

"I guess that's what you could call it," I said.

It really must seem fascinating to regular folks who didn't live through it.

"Do you believe the rehab helped?" Judy asked as she passed me some tasteful cornbread.

"I really do. It got all those toxins out of my body."

"But what about your mind?" Bill asked.

He was right. The toxins still plagued my mind. It was a constant battle against them. The two talked about their lives, how God sent them to New York to preach His word and how they believed God had a true purpose for them.

"How do you know?" I asked.

"You can tell," he said. "It's a calling to do God's work."

I know everyone in my life thinks that rehab brought me back to life, gave me a new lease — but it didn't. Looking at these two people. Being in a place that I would never be nor have a reason to be. I knew it was God. I know had it not been for Him, I would have died on that bathroom floor.

"I know that He pulled me right out of the mess on that bathroom floor," I said.

"Amen," Judy said.

"He saw me teetering on the edge and grabbed hold of me. I owe Him."

As if a flash went off in my brain, I believed what I had just said out loud. I did owe God. The God that Mama had prayed to for all those years for my soul. Who had watched over me in every bad thing I had ever done in this city. He still loved me and He took me out of where I had been. I wasn't sure how I would repay Him, but I knew that I owed Him.

***

Rachel didn't want to hear anything I had to say on the phone.

"I made a promise," I said.

"To give up your career?" she asked.

"To give it all up. I don't want to surround myself with that now," I said. "I told God I'd make a change in my life."

"You are not thinking straight, Jake, This isn't you."

"It is me. That's what I'm trying to tell you."

I took a cigarette out, opened the window to my apartment and sucked in the nicotine while talking to Rachel.

"Some people are given a second chance and they decide to use that chance to make a difference," I said.

"But modeling is what you know."

"I'll do something else."

"Call me later, Jake. I gotta run."

Rachel hung up on me and I knew she was annoyed. But I meant it. Whatever it was that I said in that haze on that bathroom floor pulled me back into life. I was going to do it. I know that a lot of people make deals with God when they think they've hit the bottom, but now that I was sober, I wanted to make good on my word.

I couldn't help but think what my Mama would be saying to me right now. She had banged religion and the Bible into my head my entire childhood. And I had run as far away from that for so many years. But perhaps that was the one thing that had been a constant in my life — and now I couldn't let go of it. Maybe without knowing it, Mama had been setting me up for the biggest part of my life that was yet to come. Who knew?

How I wished I would have seen her before she died. How I could have spent a few more moments with her before she was taken from this world. I should have gone with Gary to her funeral, but I had more excuses in me that was always wrapped up in that selfish career. The main thing was it was time to move away from the sinful career that had caused such bad problems in my life and to continue to surround myself with people like Bill and Judy. People that would set me on a better path in this city that was full of paths of sin.

CHAPTER EIGHTEEN

JACOB

There is nothing like New York in spring, the feel of the cold leaving the air when you wake in the morning. Take a walk down 5th Avenue and hum a Judy Garland tune in your head. Go up to the Cloisters and walk through the beautiful gardens located on four acres of gorgeous land in a park in northern Manhattan. The whole thing was donated by Rockefeller and is part of the Metropolitan Museum. That was exactly what Gary and I decided to do. It felt like the country and the city all rolled into one. Gary reminisced about Tennessee, but both of us knew New York was our home — even through all the rough times we had shared.

As we walked along, my mind drifted to the moment I first laid eyes on my gorgeous man — to what felt like another lifetime. I had walked into the Doghouse — a local burger joint back in Nocona.

He sat at the counter, enjoying a greasy burger deluxe, while I stood waiting for my order to go. My eyes constantly floated back to him, watching him dip his French fries into the ketchup and bring it to those beautiful lips. I was in my early twenties and had already experimented with guys, but still had not talked about it with many people. But something about Gary made me want to shout out that I was a man willing to do anything he wanted.

"Here's your food, Jacob," Harvey said, handing me my to-go bag.

Gary looked up at me and smiled. And then I felt as if there was no one else in the place except for us, wondering what that smile was about. I gave him a smile back and walked towards the front door. As I looked back, he caught my eye again and winked. This man had to be like me.

Once outside, I was frozen. I didn't want to leave for fear of not seeing him again. I waited a good ten minutes and then the front door opened and out he came. He wasn't someone you would automatically assume was gay. He was tall and big-boned. His soft innocent face and baby blue eyes were not hard for me to fall for either.

"Hey, what's up?" he said.

I'm sure I looked stupid (and obvious) just hanging out there for no reason, with the food in my bag getting cold.

"Good," was all I could get out.

"Your food," he said pointing to the paper bag that was now oozing grease in my hands.

"Yeah, I thought I forgot something inside," I said. "Just trying to figure out what it was."

"I'm Gary," he said, extending his hand.

That handshake spoke volumes, the way he held my hand a beat too long, the gleam in his eyes.

"Jacob," I smiled. I felt my hand go moist in his strong grip.

We walked from the Doghouse to the park across the street where the locals didn't give a shit about two good looking men walking and talking. I thought people had to sense what was going on, but his demeanor somehow comforted me. Gary had always been so open about his life and so nurturing when it came to mine.

I looked at that man who had grown older with years, but the same twinkle shined in his youthful eyes as he talked about the gardens in the Cloisters. How was it that I had let so much hurt and pain come between us?

"I haven't said thank you," I said.

"Yes you have," Gary said. "Many times."

"How about I'm sorry."

"You don't need to apologize, babe," he said. "We both did a lot of bad shit in our days."

"Most people would have left years ago over what I put you through."

"I'm no saint either."

"I was just too messed up to ever know what was going on," I said, smelling the fresh bloom of a dog rose.

"And now you're clean. That's what matters," he said.

"You got that right."

"And I'm so glad to have you back near my age so people don't think I'm after some young kid," he said. "I like the thirty three year old lines on your face."

"You just like me getting old," I teased.

"I just like you being with me," he softly said.

"You are too good to me."

Gary grabbed me in his arms and started singing a song from a new cast album that he played non-stop in the house. *And I'm telling you, I'm not going,* he sang at the top of his lungs as he held me. I felt odd by the public display and pulled back. After all, there were families with children running all around the lush garden setting. What would they think at two men holding each other?

"I love you," I said.

"I know you do … even when you pull away."

Gary smiled, tugged at my shirt and we continued walking through the grounds towards the main museum building.

***

Rachel had stopped by our house to check in on me. She tended to overdo the mothering thing. She listened as Gary and I shared how in love we felt again, and drank her lemon tea.

"Would it really kill you to offer me a cocktail?" she asked, sounding like an Irish barmaid.

"Not in this house, sweetie," Gary said as he walked into the kitchen.

Rachel was upset that I wasn't going on any auditions she had set up for me. But I couldn't bring myself to do it. The world was full of things I knew I needed to stay away from. I wasn't ready. Even though the bank account was depleting, we still had some savings. So I was in no hurry to get a stay-alive job again in the city.

"You mean you didn't blow it all on cocaine?" Rachel asked, standing up to leave.

"Ha ha," I grunted, smacking her on the butt to punctuate the moment.

Rachel went towards the kitchen door to thank Gary for the tea and tried to whisper about some party she was going to, but I heard her. I invited her to come to a Bible study with me, but she wasn't having any of that.

I lit a cigarette. "I can't do all of that old life stuff anymore," I told Rachel.

"You must miss it," she said as she grabbed her coat. "You can't just quit cold turkey, can you?"

"I'm not. God is helping me."

I could sense Rachel was uneasy with the new me, but this was something I needed to do.

"Well, when God decides to make you straight, you call me," she said.

She kissed me on the forehead and headed to the door.

"You know you're my number one gal," I chuckled. "But I'm way too happy with men to give that up."

"Have fun at the Bible study," she said.

Rachel was out the door to go to a fabulous New York party. I got a twinge deep inside of me, thinking about the old days and the fun she would have tonight. At moments, the past gnawed at me until it caused a physical ache inside my body. But I shook the feeling by thinking of something else. I got up to get ready to head to Bill and Judy's apartment. Gary came back in from the kitchen.

"So, you want to go to the movies, babe?" he asked. "That new movie version of *Annie* is playing."

"What a gay cliché we'd be," I said.

"That's true. Let's stick to seeing Broadway shows instead. Then no one would know."

"I'm still upset *Ain't Misbehavin'* closed while I was in rehab."

Gary laughed and kissed me.

"Let's go do something," he said.

"I have to go to Bill and Judy's."

"Between AA meetings and Bill and Judy's, I never see you."

"That's not true." I went to my AA meetings while he was work-ing. "I like the people at the Bible study. They make me feel safe."

"Do I make you feel safe?" he asked.

I grabbed him hard in my arms. "Of course you do. I'm just get-ting help from these people. That's all. Don't feel threatened."

"I'm not," he said. "Believe me. Go. Get out of here. I'll just watch some TV."

He kissed me and sent me out into the New York night with a sense of trust I know he had never known with me before.

I walked down the street to catch the cross-town bus, stepping over a man asleep on our front stoop. The poor guy must have hit his bottom too. I kept walking to get to the friends that would understand me. I didn't dare ask Gary to go with me. Not that he would. Not that the group didn't know I was gay. But I also knew it wasn't something I wanted to share with Gary. This was a part of my life that gave me a different kind of comfort than what Gary could offer, a comfort that comes from being around God-fearing people.

Like Mama had been.

These people accepted me without wanting something in return the way so many of my other friends had. They enjoyed my clever banter, but never came back with cheap shots like people in the business did.

I was deep in thought when a man walked past me. We caught eyes and held the gaze a little too long. We passed and I knew the man had turned around to look at me, but I fought the urge to turn and look back. Some old habits were very hard to break.

But I kept walking.

I got to the bus station and looked down at the ground until the bus came.

"Sorry I'm late," I said walking into the gathering at Bill and Judy's apartment. "Couldn't get away from the ball and chain."

"Hello, Jacob," Bill said.

"Any new auditions this week?" asked a guy on the sofa.

"Nah, Randall. Still waiting for that Christian soap opera pilot. Then I know I'll get my foot in the door."

"God may shut some doors, but he always opens a window," Judy interjected as she handed me a Bible.

"Straight from *The Sound of Music*," I said.

Judy laughed. "Jacob … don't poke fun at my simplicity."

"Darling, I was merely pointing out a musical theatre reference," I said. "You can take the man out of the theatre, but can't take the theatre out of the man."

I enjoyed the Bible study, not so much because of the material we went over, but because it felt safe. It reminded me of my childhood and it kept me from doing things I would regret.

"This is Samantha," Judy said. "She volunteers at the hospital. We've been talking about this group and she wanted to join."

Samantha was a beautiful woman, high cheekbones like a French model, her auburn hair pulled back into a twist, floating on her head like a cherry on the top of a perfect sundae.

"Hi, I'm Jacob. And if I were a betting man, I'd have said you were a model," I said.

"I have modeled," she answered.

"Ok, Jacob. We're not here to bet. We're here for God's word," Bill said. "Are we ready to start?"

Everyone took a seat in the living room as Bill led us in a prayer.

"Heavenly father, we come here this evening for you to shed light on the darkness."

I looked around the room. These people were my new family. No more Felicia, Peter, Wayne and Rachel, but the God-loving people in this room. Samantha opened her eyes during the prayer and caught my eye. I smiled and bowed my head. There was something angelic about her, yet very real. I knew I wanted to get to know her better. Hopefully, she'd be returning.

CHAPTER NINETEEN

NOAH

Thirty years old. Here I was starting another decade of my life and taking stock. Perhaps 1982 would be my year. I looked at my face in the mirror that morning and saw my father staring back. The thought of him made me smile. My Dad's smile. Dad would have liked the man that I had grown into. Of course, I wasn't thrilled with what age was doing to my appearance. My thin hair had receded even more, the leathery skin I had in my early twenties had begun to crack with age lines, but that scar on my chin seemed to add character to my face now.

I brushed my teeth and the end of the toothbrush hit my gums at the front of my mouth, causing me to winch in pain. I pulled down my bottom lip and saw white sores on the inside of my mouth. Great. At thirty I guess my body was going to start giving out on me. I made a mental note to pick up some Anbesol for it.

I picked a shirt out of the closet that I knew I would be comfortable to wear all day and into the evening. A few work folks wanted to take me out to celebrate tonight. They were a good group of friends, but something still seemed to be missing in my life. I looked down at the letter from the publishing house in New York. Maybe that was going to fill my constant need for a purpose in my life.

I knew I wanted to share my news with my big brother. I should call and wake his ass up. God knows there were plenty of times he had called me in a drunken stupor in the middle of the night. But we were on the mends now that he was sober. I had managed to let go of the pain and anger I had felt after Mama died. We now had a fresh, clean slate to begin again as a family. And maybe Jacob would be a little wiser with age and sobriety.

His phone was ringing.

"Hello?"

"Hey, big brother," I said.

"Noah. What time is it?' he asked.

"It's 8:30 your time. I've called you earlier than this before. Why are you still in bed?"

"No reason to get up today," he said.

"Well you need to be up next week, because I'll be in New York on Friday."

"What? Why?"

"One of the many publishing companies I've been talking to … something about my story grabbed them," I said. "They want to meet with me!"

"Noah, shit! That's wonderful," he said.

It really was. But working in the music publishing industry, seeing how often dreams were shattered, I knew how to keep myself firmly planted on the ground. A meeting was just that — a meeting. But maybe something would come of it. It had taken me a while to find my passion, but once I had … it had changed the way I viewed the world.

"Who would think a big New York place would want a good 'ol

boy's southern story," I said.

"There are tons of transplants in this town," he said. "And though I haven't read anything of yours, I'm sure it's good."

"You want to read something?"

"Once it's all done, then I will," he said.

Why did Jacob not want to read the stories about our past? Was he afraid of visiting that time in his life? How was he so sure that he was prominent in them?

I could hear the lighter and the sucking sound of a new cigarette on the other end.

"Well, I figure while I'm there … I could see you," I said.

"Of course. Call me when you're done with your meeting. And good luck."

"Thanks brother. Now about that cancer stick you have in your mouth—"

"I do not —" he said.

"I know, I know … can't expect you to give up booze, drugs and cigs," I said with a laugh.

I could hear the exhale on the other end. "Allow me some pleasure."

"You take care of yourself and say hello to Gary," I said.

"Will do," he said. "And Bubba, happy thirtieth birthday."

I was shocked that Jacob would remember my birthday. Much less that it was a milestone one.

"Thanks, brother."

"Don't get too wild tonight," he said.

I laughed, said goodbye and hung up the phone.

I was very excited about the possibilities with this book. And I was also excited about seeing Jacob and his new renewal of life. Everyone should have a second chance. I was pleased he was getting his. Now if I could just get the rest of my life together and find a woman for longer than two months. Then the nagging voice of Mama would grow silent in my head. I smiled, thinking of Mama, the new brother I had up North, and grabbed my gym bag to head out my apartment door.

....

CHAPTER TWENTY

JACOB

I had been talking to Bill for about an hour. I was glad he had agreed to meet me for breakfast. It's funny. In New York, all people do is get together to eat and talk. You can walk down any street in Manhattan and see some sort of meeting occurring in every single restaurant. When they make the movie of my life, I sure hope the director comes up with better locales for me to converse with my friends.

I had nothing to do today since Noah woke me with his exciting news and Gary was out jogging in the park. It was nice to have some time for just Bill and me, without Judy or the others. I liked how I felt around him. I felt closer to God when I talked to him, like a great Jesus fix.

"Jacob, I know it's been really hard for you, but I think you've done an incredible job," Bill said. "Temptation will always be everywhere. I deal with it every day."

"What are you tempted by?" I asked.

"I've had my demons to deal with. Addictions."

"Mind me asking what your addiction is?"

Bill knew all about my past and only paused for a moment.

"Porn."

I was completely blown away by Bill's answer. Never in a million years would I think he would have had to deal with something like that. The man was the godliest person I had ever met — next to Mama, of course. We discussed how that particular addiction haunted him on every street corner newsstand in the city, how the devil could grab hold of any of us and hold on for dear life.

I played with the packets of sugar and thought about my days visiting different porn shops on 42nd Street. I told Bill that I knew the power of that addiction very well.

"There is no addiction that's too big that God can't help with," he said.

"Well, I can keep myself away from drugs and wild sex. I just keep substituting."

Speaking of substitutes. I fondled the new product of NutraSweet that was there on the table with the sugar. I wondered if I should start trying that. Again, too many conversations happening in my head.

"There's another area you need to consider," Bill said. "You know the Bible says a man should not lie with another man as he does a woman. It's an abomination."

I had been waiting for this to come up. I knew Bill was going to bring it up — it was just a matter of time.

"You know everyone in the church loves you, despite the affliction you have," he said.

"I've never seen it as an affliction," I said, turned off by the word.

"Oh, it is. God is very clear on this subject. Judy and Samantha have been praying for you regularly about it."

"I didn't know I was getting special prayer treatment," I joked.

"Be serious for a moment, Jacob. Tell me what God is telling you."

"I can't believe it's wrong when I love Gary so much," I said.

"Do you truly love him, or do you think he has just been safe for you … since you moved here together?"

"I've never thought about it like that. I never knew any other love except Gary's, Mama's and my brother's."

And that was the truth. Sometimes it's a matter of what we know. But Bill asked me if I thought I would have treated Gary the way I had if I truly loved him. The dangerous question flopped around in my brain. I had never been faithful to Gary and I wondered if being with a woman could make that different. But being gay was all I had ever known. And Gary was such a part of that. Perhaps, on some level, I reasoned to give Bill the benefit of a doubt. Gary had pulled me into this world back in Tennessee, but I had never seen it that way. So many thoughts were now rushing through my head.

"If you had a wife, you'd want to be faithful to her," Bill said. "Sharing my life with Judy has lessened my need for porn and now that she's pregnant, we're going to have a wonderful family together."

"I need to think about this," I said.

"Treat it like a band aid … or like your addiction to drugs … just wipe it out quickly and then let God help you with picking up the pieces and putting together a much fuller life with Him."

"Thanks, Bill. I really appreciate you caring enough to talk to me about this," I said.

"That's what family is for," he replied.

We walked out of the restaurant and went our separate ways.

Bill had called himself family. I liked that. Mama was the only family that I had where we could discuss things. She and I used to talk about so much. What would she say about Bill's advice about Gary? I couldn't get the thought out of my head. Was this really part of the deal I had made a year earlier on the bathroom floor?

Was I supposed to leave Gary?

I liked the relationship Bill and Judy had. I liked watching how Judy played the role of a pastor's wife. I wanted that. I wanted the family and the whole thing. And if they could have a baby in their thirties, so could I … with someone. Gary and I would never be able to have that. But could I really do this to Gary?

***

I lay in bed that night thinking about what Bill had said. Gone were the satin sheets and water bed we had slept on during what I now referred to as my crazy days. Gary had always hated that bed, but always did whatever I wanted back then. He was next to me reading one of Stephen King's new novels, completely engrossed in it. He still looked attractive in his reading glasses and premature spots of grey on his temples. I wasn't sure where to start with all of the information that Bill had given me. I had only been out of rehab for eight months and had been dealing with an entirely new life. No career. No drugs. No anonymous sex. Haven't I given up enough? I felt like a newborn baby looking at life for the first time. The city seemed different. Not the carefree world we had moved to, but a place to display responsibility. Perhaps the fact that we were on a conservative swing in the country was a good thing for me in the coming decade. It eased the pain of letting go of that old life some.

Gary looked over at me as I stared at the wall.

"What are you doing?" he asked.

"Praying."

Gary let out a heavy sigh and went back to his book.

This was something I wasn't sure I was ready for … letting go of this man I had loved for so long.

I began to ask God in my mind what He wanted of me. As a child, I was taught to go to God in prayer and He would answer. But I wasn't hearing any answers. Or perhaps they weren't the answers I wanted to hear.

"Are you done praying?" he asked as he placed his book and glasses on the night table.

"Sure."

Gary turned off the bedside lamp and rolled over to put his arm around me. I was still sitting up in the bed with his arm across my lap. I felt frozen. I needed to slide down and go to sleep, but he started to reach for my crotch to massage it. I couldn't do this. Not now. I leaned over and kissed him on the head, rolled over and kept my back to him. I felt him spooning me and trying to get me aroused, but it wouldn't work. I lay perfectly still, as if I were falling to sleep. Finally, he rolled over away from me to sleep back-to-back.

I couldn't help but wonder what was going through his mind, the dread he must be feeling as he witnessed me changing. And I was. Something was definitely happening in my brain.

***

I had never been inside of a Catholic church, but everyone talked about St. Patrick's Cathedral and I wanted to see if I could come closer to God inside there. The place was beautiful, tall pillars topped off with pointed arches, with ornate, colorful stain-glass windows that displayed different times in Christ's life and statues everywhere you turned. It felt completely different than what I had in the southern church I had grown up in. I almost felt as if I had stepped back in time when I walked through those huge iron doors. There were rows of small candles that people lit and knelt by to offer a prayer. Now I had seen plenty of movies and knew how people would go into the confessional to talk to a priest, a screen separating you from him, so you did not have to see him.

People were sitting in the pews praying and then I saw someone come out of the confessional box. Did I really want to go in and talk to some strange priest? Did I believe he could help me in dealing with my relationship?

I slowly walked towards the box, opened the wooden door and went inside. There was a small bench for me to sit on with a mesh screen for us to speak through. I sat for the longest time. Finally the preacher coughed to signal that I could speak.

"Forgive me — I'm not sure what to say."

"Do you have something you need to confess, my child?" he asked.

"Yes."

It suddenly occurred to me what it was I needed to confess. I hated myself. I hated the fact that I had always been gay. I was ashamed of it. I was embarrassed to tell him. I was mad that I never had the life that Bill and Judy have. Words came pouring out of my mouth as I shared these feelings with him. That I lived with a man for all these years, but had secretly hated myself for it.

I think I completely scared the shit out of this priest. He wasn't expecting something like that in the middle of the afternoon, I'm sure. But he did tell me that everything was possible through God. That God could help me to remove the cancer that was this sin. That God would stand by me while I made the choice. I felt like a boulder had been lifted from between my shoulder blades. This man I didn't know — that I couldn't even see for God's sake, listened to me share something I had never told a soul and helped me feel better about myself in the end.

I was out the front of the Cathedral and found the first pay phone on 5th Avenue that I could get to. I dialed the number and waited for an answer.

"Bill, I'm ready. Can you help me decide what to say?"

***

It's a wonder the neighbors did not call the police on us. The noises coming out of our apartment on 84th and Amsterdam were enough to wake the dead. I hadn't meant to blind-side Gary with it, but there was no other way to do it. I caught him sitting at our kitchen table as he was trying to plan a dinner party for our friends.

"You're fucking kidding me," Gary said.

"Gary, I know you're upset," I said. "But this is God's will in my life."

"I knew I should have pulled you away from those Jesus freaks. They are brainwashing you, Jake!"

"No. They are not," I said. "I know this is what I need to do, what is right for me."

"Right? What makes this right?" he asked. "What in the name of God —"

"Please don't use God's name like that," I said, turning to face the sink.

Gary stood up from the table.

"What about all the years we've been together?' he asked. "Does that mean nothing to you now?"

"I didn't say it didn't mean nothing. We've had our ups and downs … like —"

"Like any normal couple," Gary added in a pleading tone.

"This is far from normal," I said, trying to keep my composure.

Gary reached into the back of a cabinet and pulled out a small bottle of tequila.

"Yes, babe, I had this hidden here … from you. Because of your problems," he said. "But tonight, I think I deserve a shot."

Gary took a swig from the bottle and kept speaking.

"Think about your sweet mother. She loved God more than anyone I have ever met. And she had no problem with us being together."

Gary was wrong there. Mama had plenty of problems with us, but was too much of a lady or too good a mother to bring it up. I knew she had prayed for us daily. That she was worried about us moving to New York and living in sin. And to think back on my sinful life was an ache in my heart. I could finally see that everything I had done was a huge mistake.

Gary stared at me as I left the room and headed back towards the living room. He was quick on my heels.

"So after all these years … I'm … I'm to just leave?" he asked.

"You can take a week or so to get another place, but we should do this soon."

"I can't believe this is happening?" he asked. "How can you be so cold?"

I could see the tears gathering in Gary's eyes, but his anger was winning out.

"I'm not trying to be cold," I said. "I'm just being honest."

"Honest? What the hell do you know about honesty?" Gary asked.

"Honest to myself. It's what I need, what I had never done before."

I was finally releasing the hatred I had for myself for so many years. I didn't want to take it out on Gary, but something was right about the way I was doing this. I knew it.

"I stood by you during the drug problem. I looked the other way every time you fucked around ... and I know there were plenty of times," he said.

"You're just talking out of anger and hurt now."

"To think, I was even happy to see you turning from the drugs, as crazy as your methods were ... but this is who you are. You're a gay man."

I knew this was killing him. Part of me was dying as well. But I had to stick to the script I had memorized, the script that Bill had painstakingly helped me to write so that I could get through this moment.

"Homosexuality isn't right," I said. "God does not want this for you or for me."

"Don't even think of dragging me into your little twisted God-land on this one."

How I wish I could save Gary in the same way I was saving myself.

"Don't you think I want you to be as happy as I am? Don't you think I want you to experience the same peace and contentment that I have found?"

"So while you were out finding this, who was home taking care of things?" he asked. "Who was keeping this place up and doing your laundry and cleaning your house?"

Gary was reaching for anything he could throw at me now. But how much was I supposed to share with him? He had to know that my turning from homosexuality would mean finding a woman to tend to my needs. It was time to tell him.

"Those are all thing a wife can do," I said.

"Are you listening to yourself!!! Women, barefoot and pregnant in the kitchen darning your fucking socks?"

"There is a definite plan that God has and women should be submissive to their husbands ..."

"Are you going to start dating women?" Gary sighed.

I had to take a moment. I felt like I was reaching the point of no return. I knew what I was saying was right, but my heart was still not quite certain it was ready to go there. At times I wanted to scream that it was all a joke, but I had to go forward. In the long run, I would be a much happier person for it.

"I'm sure I'll get married some day," I answered.

Gary grabbed me and threw me down on the sofa, holding me down.

"Jacob where are you! Where the fuck are you inside of that brain?" he screamed.

"I understand you're upset," I said in the calmest tone I could muster.

"Jacob, I love you," Gary said. "I've loved you for as long as I can remember. And you love me."

"We moved here together. We were comfortable to each other, like brothers."

Gary jumped up to get away from me. "I can't listen to this shit anymore. You're not Jacob. I have no idea who you are."

"Be happy that I'm discovering who I was meant to be," I said.

"Be happy? You're breaking my heart, but you want me to be happy?"

Gary had no more to say to me. He grabbed his jacket and walked out the door. I couldn't move. I was stunned that I had done it, shocked by the things that had come out of my mouth as well as his. We had spent the last seven years living together and now they would be history. Had I just thrown away everything I knew and loved? For what? I needed someone to talk to. To be with. I picked up the phone and dialed.

"Samantha. It's Jacob. Want to grab a cup of coffee? Columbus & 72nd. See you in half an hour."

CHAPTER TWENTY-ONE

NOAH

I called Jacob as soon as my meeting was over and told him all about it. How it was exciting and intimidating all at the same time. I felt like the biggest country ass sitting in that office. All those Yankees around me; talking about my novel — like they totally understood the South. Throwing ideas and thoughts at me. It was overwhelming, but I appreciated everything they said. One thing was certain; I don't think I could ever do what Jacob did and move to this city. I would feel so out of place. But I had grown to enjoy my small visits here more and more.

I walked up Broadway from the midtown office, looking at all the overdone, ornate Christmas decorations along the way. This city really knew how to do Christmas. It looked different than on the Thanksgiving parade on television. I loved noticing the places like Columbus Circle which I had seen so many times with large balloon floats heading down from Central Park West. Now I was waiting at a diner for Jacob in the exact same location. Where was he? I was just about to get up to call him, when he ran in the door.

"Hey, brother," I said. "Was getting worried."

"Sorry ... still have a little problem with time after all these years."

"You look great," I said, happy to see the body of a completely drug free man sitting in front of me. This was not the man I had seen on previous visits.

"So do you," he said. "Nashville has obviously been treating you well."

"It's so much better living in a larger city. You know, I always thought I wanted to leave Tennessee, but … I just needed to leave Nocona. Nashville has everything a city could offer. Well, maybe not this one."

"I can't believe you got called to New York for your meeting today," he said. "Very exciting stuff happening for you."

"Yeah, it really is. Even though I work in a music publishing place, it is nothing compared to a New York office. I felt like such a duck out of water in that fancy place. Everything was crisp and clean while I sat there in my wrinkled shirt from a suitcase and my cowboy boots."

"I'm sure you were fine, Bubba," he said. "They probably loved the fact that you played into the whole southern stereotype."

"This is something I've always wanted to do my whole life, but was too scared to even admit to myself … but these people actually like my work."

I couldn't believe I had never confided in my big brother about my secret desire to write, and yet I just blurted out those words like a gushing dork. I'm sure the small talks we had on the phone made it seem like some sort of hobby. But it wasn't. It was real and it was a part of me — a part of me that involved my brain. At one point in the past, my family had never acknowledged that I even knew how to use my brain. That was the reason I hid the crossword puzzles and the newspapers from them all those years. I never wanted to hear

Jacob giving me a hard time about it. But now we were two adults who could discuss it without fear of attack.

"What do you write about?" he asked.

"Me. You. Mama. Life. I change all our names, of course."

Jacob laughed at me. "Name me Skipper."

I laughed back. It felt good to be laughing with my brother.

"Do you ever talk about our religious upbringing?" he said.

That was an odd question coming from Jacob. He had always hated the idea of religion, and barely tolerated it with Mama. Must have something to do with his rehab and his AA meetings.

"I have used some of the things that went on in the church," I said. "Miss Potters Sunday school class, the smell of her perfume that would knock you out when we came through the door. How she would correct us on the proper way to say the books of the Bible."

"I always had a problem with the Old Testament names. Why couldn't people just call themselves David or Steve back then?" Jacob said with a laugh.

I loved this easy relationship we were having.

"Remember when we were kids and we'd go on those road trips?" I said. "We'd get so bored you'd have us put our feet up in the back window of the station wagon and do feet shows for the other passengers."

"And you didn't know I was gay? Who else would come up with a foot show?" he asked.

I laughed again "Dad would get so mad at us and make us sit on opposite sides of the car totally quiet."

We looked at each other and said "mummy face" in unison. I was glad that I had discovered some of the good memories that Jacob had always seemed to have. It had certainly helped me in my writing.

"I'm proud of you, little brother. I think it's important to go after what you want in life," Jacob said. "Follow your heart."

"What? You yanking my chain?" I asked, gulping down some water.

"No. I came here in search of something. Maybe I didn't find it on TV or as a model, but I think I found it."

"Yeah, you and Gary do pretty well," I said.

"Noah, Gary and I broke up."

I felt terrible. I had gone on about my book, my visit to New York and never even asked about Gary.

"Oh, man, I'm sorry," I said. "Shit, I had no idea. I thought things were good now. What happened?"

"We're just in very different places —"

"They say that can happen when one person stops drinking or doing drugs in a relationship. Maybe you just need to talk to someone, together. You have been together for over ten years now. Don't you want to try and work it out?"

"Bubba, so much is going on in my life. More than I can tell you. But I'm changing … every day."

"We all are. That's the great thing about growing up," I said.

There seemed to be more that Jacob wanted to say, but I wasn't sure what it was. He changed the subject after he grabbed the menu.

"So what are we eating in this joint?" he asked.

After that, we talked about day-to-day things in our life, but seemed to be staying clear of an important issue to Jacob. What could have prompted his breakup with Gary? I couldn't believe he was blaming Gary in any way. It had always seemed to me that Gary was the one helping him and pulling him back each time. He wasn't going to tell me now, but eventually I'd learn what was really going on.

***

At first, Gary did not want to see me, but I persisted and stopped into his shop. He told me that Jacob's friend Rachel was walking him home and that I could join them on the walk through the park. It was so freaking cold out, but I wanted to show him that I did care about him. Besides, maybe I could get some information from him and Rachel about how Jacob was doing since rehab. Rachel wasn't the blood hound that I had pictured in my mind when I spoke to her on the phone after Mama's passing. She was actually a rather nice motherly figure for the guys.

We rambled through the park, bundled up like Eskimos in the cold — and it was cold. I wasn't sure how much more of this weather I could take. I wanted to get inside somewhere with a big cup of coffee. Gary and Rachel were pressed up against each other like two girlfriends, with me walking along side of them.

"I miss him, guys," Gary said. "I really do."

"I'm sure you do, honey," Rachel said. "I do too."

"I've tried to call him. I've even waited outside the apartment on the stoop to talk to him. He just keeps avoiding me."

"We hardly talk anymore either," Rachel said.

"It's all because of that damn church," Gary added.

I didn't know much about Jacob's church and never really thought of him even being part of any church. Was this why he was asking me about our religion as kids? We passed children making snow angels on the large field, painted a white canvas instead of its normal green. Their laughter had to be refreshing to Gary.

"You know you just have to let him go," Rachel said.

"I can't eat. I can't sleep. It's killing me," he said. "It was so long, our life together."

"Have you thought about going home?" Rachel asked, looking towards me.

Why would she look at me? Gary wasn't moving in with me in Nashville.

"He is my home," Gary said.

"You stood by that man through thick and thin," I interjected.

Gary nodded. "I can't get over him."

"It doesn't seem right … Jake sober now and you don't get to enjoy it," she said.

Who was this new Jake? I had only seen glimpses of it at the diner, and I liked the kinder man that I saw. Booze and drugs were no longer dictating every word that came out of his mouth.

"At this point, I'd even be happy with the old Jake," Gary said.

"Honey, you don't mean that," Rachel said.

I decided to change the subject. "How are things at the salon?"

"I've added two more people. We're very busy," he said. "But I don't even feel like going in most of the time."

My change of subject wasn't helping. Gary was a walking mess of despair and loneliness.

"Maybe you just reminded Jacob too much of his past," I said.

"His past with men," Gary said.

"What do you mean?" Rachel asked.

I wondered the same thing. I had given in to the reality when talking to Jacob and Gary. I had to switch my pronouns and thoughts to adjust them to a male couple. So why the obvious statement? Was there more to this story that Rachel and I didn't know about?

"He didn't tell you guys why we broke up," Gary said. "The man wants to get married someday. He doesn't want to be gay anymore."

"Jesus, Mary and Joseph," Rachel said. "What the hell does that mean?"

"Fuck if I know," Gary said. "He certainly didn't give me the details."

This was a shock to my very core. None of it made any sense. My relationship with my brother, for good or bad, always orbited around his gayness. It's how he defined himself. It's how I defined our relationship since we had never done anything that normal brothers would do.

I noted Rachel trying to make sense of it as well. Here I was with two people who were both dealing with losing someone and none of us understood what was happening.

"You need to go out more," Rachel finally said. "You guys had other friends, didn't you? Don't you see them?"

"I've seen them more than Jake has," Gary said. "He's cut himself off from anyone from his past."

"I have to tell you both, I'm completely blown away," I said.

Jacob had told me none of this when I had lunch with him.

And why not? Was he afraid of my reaction? The truth was — I didn't know how to react.

"Our friend Felicia said he wouldn't even take her calls." Rachel said. "He lumps all of us into that part of his life that now hates."

"If he hated it so much, why did he spend so much time getting so damn good at it?" Gary asked.

Images of my brother "getting good at it" flashed through my head and I needed them to leave my mind as quickly as possible.

We reached Central Park West and started walking across 72nd Street. I looked up at the Dakota, where just two years prior, at the entrance, Yoko lost the great love of her life. My mind thought how Gary must be relating to that about now.

"This whole neighborhood makes me think of him," Gary said.

"But this is what baffles me, Gar," I said. "I can understand him wanting to … needing to get off the drugs, of course. But how do you just decide you're not gay?"

"I sure couldn't do it," he said. "Although I've done nothing recently that anyone would even know I'm a gay man."

Gary was right. In my haste to always be judgmental about anything that didn't fit into my normal world, I often forgot what it was like for these men to live their lives. Yeah, I can go to the gym and change my appearance. I can change my career path and try something different. But could I just decide I wanted to date men? Hell no. And I don't see how a gay man could decide to switch what was such a core part of him and date women.

I looked at the snow starting to fall around us. There was something poetic about the grieving man standing in the snow, pining for his love.

"I hate the damn cold! Why did he make me move here?" Gary asked.

Buzz kill to the romantic story throbbing in my head. It was time for me to grab a taxi and leave them alone, so they could talk about my family without me hovering. Plus I had already heard more new information than I ever had imagined.

"I need to get back to my hotel, guys," I said.

I gave Gary a bear hug to show him that one of the Garrett boys was still a loving, caring person. And I patted Rachel on the back to say goodbye.

"Thanks, Noah ... for caring," Gary said.

"I'll talk to you next time I'm in town," I said.

Rachel took his arm and they walked off at a hurried pace.

"Come on, love. It's time you get a drink in you ... and fast," she said. "I think it's time both of us did."

I watched and wondered if I would ever see either of them again. New York was a big city and who knew what direction my brother's life would take by the next time I visited him.

***

Being back in Nashville was like heading back to the country after returning from New York. I had pulled into the Sonic for a quick foot long and tater tots. Not the meal of a famous writer, but I was nowhere near that point ... yet.

In the seat next to me were papers and note cards with ideas, jumbled up thoughts about what I would be writing on next. The floorboard was full of remnants of previous meals that I had eaten on the go.

If I ever got into an accident and someone discovered me in this truck, they would think I was a rat breeder or something for all the garbage in there.

I was very lucky to have the kind of job in the creative world that I did, so my boss understood when I had to run off to New York, and also left me time at night to write. Or times like this on a lunch break, sitting in my car pouring out my heart onto a piece of paper.

"Here ya, go," came the perky voice outside my window.

I looked up to see the cutest little blonde thing standing there with my food and lime cream slush. I'd pay for this later at the gym.

"That was quick," I said as I reached into my wallet for the money.

"We're trained on punctuality here at the Sonic," she said with a smile.

"Keep the change, darling," I said, reaching out the bills to her.

"You gonna sit here and write while you eat?" she asked, peering through my window.

"At least you can tell I'm writing — and not just think I'm living out of my truck."

"I've seen you here before," she said. "You're always busy writing away, too busy to look up and notice me."

She smiled and went back in and got her next order. I wondered if she was right. Was I too busy to even see the world around me? My mind was always on someone's song at work, or whatever story I was working on. Mama would have called this girl back and had me going out with her tonight. But I'm not sure the gum-chewing gal would completely understand the madness that is me and my writing.

One hand fed my face while the other kept busy scribbling on the pad sitting on the passenger seat. Perhaps the next story would be about a cowboy who meets his love at the Drive-In. I could set it in the 50s, when they roller-skated out to the car to serve the customers.

I scratched through the stupid ideas I had written down and instead of throwing the food wrappers in the floorboard, I put them back on the tray still sitting on my window and pressed the call button again.

"Welcome to Sonic. May I take your order?"

"I'm just finished and wanted someone to take the tray back," I said.

Not five seconds passed and the bubbly blonde was at my side removing the tray.

"That was a record," she said. "You must really have to get back to work."

I thought about asking for her number, what she liked to do on the weekends, if she wanted to get together.

"Yeah … the boss really cracks a whip," I said with a smile.

I put the truck in reverse and pulled out, looking back through my side mirror to get a last glimpse of her. How was I supposed to find the right girl if I couldn't even talk to them?

Noah, you need to get your head out of books and back into the game of life.

Not now. Now there was a songwriter waiting for me at the office to see what kind of great deal I could help his group get on their newest song. And someday, someone would be on the other side of the table, someone helping me in the very same way. Maybe this deal would go through in New York and my novel would be published — and maybe it really wasn't about anyone reading the stories — it was just about writing them. Great Noah, you've found a way to turn a hobby into therapy. Just what you needed!

I reached for the can of Skoal on my dashboard for my habitual after meal ritual. I stopped and wondered what girl would want to kiss a man with this stuff in his mouth. Were the sores I've seen in my mouth from packing this in there three times a day? I decided to see if I could give up one of my addictions and tossed the small can out the window as I headed back towards my office.

CHAPTER TWENTY-TWO

JACOB

I was slowly growing more and more bored with my day to day life. I needed a challenge again, something to fulfill me. While my life was changing quickly with my new friends from the church, there was nothing for me to do by way of a job. I knew the entertainment world was a place I needed to stay away from. My days in those venues had come to a close. So it seemed as if I had to create a job — something I felt I could do better than anyone else, something new to master and conquer.

I would spend most of my time meeting with Bill and discussing religion. I found it easy, since Mama had versed us on the Bible for so many years growing up. While I looked up to Bill, at times I believed I knew more than he did about what he was preaching. Sure, he had his own past that he could draw on when talking to others, but his story was nowhere as radical as mine. He hadn't lived with the sinners of this city like me. I thought he could use me in his church in a much deeper way.

I had been praying about what God wanted me to do with my life and I knew that He meant for me to climb mountains. Going after something that was difficult and accomplishing it was what I was good at. And now God expected those same large cojones from me as I planned for this next endeavor. Finally, I figured out what it was I was supposed to do.

I thought of who I wanted to share this news with and the only person that I came up with was Rachel. It had been a while since I told her about the breakup with Gary and we weren't talking much any longer. But today, I needed to see her face-to-face to describe what God had in store for my life.

"Thanks for coming, Rachel," I said, as I greeted her at my front door.

"I've missed you, Jake. Life is very different without you," she said, grabbing me with those small arms of hers.

"I've missed you too … hearing that voice of yours."

"You can call anytime, you know," she said.

"Please, sit down," I said.

I noticed Rachel looking around the apartment at the photos of me and Gary that I had never taken down. I hadn't even thought about that prior to seeing her face now. I just found comfort in keeping them up and no one needed to see it. The crackle and pops from the wood in the fireplace filled the gaps in our conversation.

"There is so much happening to me and I want you to be there," I said.

"I understand … we've gone through so much, Jake."

"Rachel. How did you grow up? Religion-wise."

"Catholic. When I wasn't on an army base, I was in Catholic school. The little dress and everything," she said.

"Why have you given up on God?"

"I didn't really give up. I just, I don't know, turned away," she said.

"He didn't fit into my lifestyle."

"That's because you sensed your lifestyle was wrong," I said.

Rachel's face squished up like a prune.

"Did you really call me here to talk about my religion?" she asked.

I told myself to slow it down. I was coming on way too strong.

"No. To talk about mine," I said. "I'm really changing. I know what I've been called to do."

"What?"

Could I just come out and say it to her? I knew the words would freak her out. Hell, somewhere inside the idea of it was freaking me out, but it was the right thing. It was a way to pay back God for what He had done for me. To thank Him for the new people He had brought in my life. And to still make a mark on this city like it had never seen before.

"I want to be a preacher," I said.

More crackles from the fireplace. It was as if I could read her mind. She was reliving our history together. In her eyes, I was the man who had done just about everything the Bible tells you not to do. I had lived out Sodom and Gomorrah several times over.

"What?" she finally said.

"God has called me to lead people here in this city and I want to answer that call," I said.

"Now, I know this has to be a joke. You?"

"It's no joke," I said.

"How many times did I have to play your alibi with Gary?"

"That's the old me."

Suddenly I had a flash of the old me and new me speaking face to face. The old me kept saying he wanted to come out and play, but the new me was stronger and wiser.

"Oh, my God, Jake. I still remember the time I had to go down to Alphabet City on a Sunday morning to pull you out of an all night orgy."

"That was wrong —"

"And you never found your clothes, so I had to give you my coat," she laughed.

"I admit those dark days were bad, Rachel. I know that," I said.

"A preacher!"

"Yes."

"But Jake, you're gay," she said.

Was I to tell her everything at once? Could she take all of this new information at once? I had to get it all out to her. I felt I had no choice.

"God is working on that too," I said.

I remembered how Rachel had told me for years if I ever went straight she wanted to be there. I just hoped she wasn't thinking that now. I wasn't looking for her to stand beside me as a wife. I just wanted her to be there as a friend.

"This is all getting way too freaky, Jake. I don't get it."

"It's too much to take in at once, I know, I can tell," I said. "But look, I'm happy in my life ... finally. And God is going to see to it that I get all I deserve as I follow His will."

"I ... I don't even know what to say, Jake," she said, and folded her hands on her lap.

It must really be bad for her when the woman who always talked with her hands had suddenly gone limp.

"Say you want to be there with me," I said. "Say you want to be in my life. I want to know you are my friend. I want to have you as a friend. But I can't condone what you do."

I saw through her expression, both empathy and pity, that Rachel got what I was saying. I didn't need to beat her up with it. I knew she missed me and wanted nothing more than to be close to me again. But she knew a preacher could not hang out with the people who frequented the clubs and bars as she had done for so long. She was a lonely person and needed me in her life. And I could make good use of our relationship in my quest to do God's will. This could be so much more fulfilling for her life than anything we had done in the past.

"I really need to think about all of this," she said, tucking some of her red locks underneath a new scarf she was wearing on her head.

"That's fine. Take your time. I believe God is going to bring you through this," I said.

God had a plan for Rachel the same as He had for me, as He has for everyone. And together, we'd be able to move mountains in this town.

***

This new life fit well, like a suit that had long been hanging in the back of my closet that now screamed to be worn. I was living off my savings in my rent-controlled apartment, immersing myself daily in the Bible to help me change, attending some courses at the Bible Institute up town, and dating someone for about four months.

A woman.

Samantha and I had become very close during all of our talks. It started with me walking her home from the Bible study one night.

"I never thanked you for being there for me during my breakup with Gary," I said, as I put a piece of gum in my mouth.

"We all need people to talk to," she said. "I was glad you felt you could trust me to lean on."

"You are so easy to talk to, Sam. I feel I can be myself."

"People shouldn't think they have to put on airs for others. I don't like that. If I'm with someone who doesn't like me …"

I looked at her as she stopped.

"You do what?" I asked.

"I retreat into myself and don't add to the conversation," she said.

"You don't do that with me."

"No, you don't make me want to retreat, Jacob. You challenge me. That's good."

I smiled.

"So I'm a challenge, huh?" I asked.

"No. I said you challenge me," she said. "You make me think about myself, what I want from life … why I'm even in this city. Not that many make the time to do that."

"As Bill tells us, there is a plan for everything," I said. "God brought me here for a reason. I'm sure of that."

We often discussed our upbringing, and family life. She came from an upscale Connecticut family that kept all their emotions bottled up tight. I told her how Mama had taught us to take care of ourselves and not rely on others. As a child, I was very protective of my brother and my family, but as I aged — I began to look out more for number one, realizing that everyone around me seemed to be doing the same thing. She moved to New York as an escape from her home life. She needed a place she could blend into. I had seen it more as a place that I could conquer and had done a great job of that in my previous profession. Both of us had found a niche in the city and had decided to make it our home; even against any odds that had come our way.

The more we spoke to each other, the more in harmony I felt with her. There was a something that felt good, felt right. While she did not grow up in the South, she did grow up out in the country; away from city life — and we could relate to that slower lifestyle. While grabbing a quick slice of pizza one day at lunch, she told me that she loved horses and was a champion rider by the time she was fourteen years old.

Another night, I took her to my favorite place in Chinatown. There she told me that by sixteen, she was entering beauty pageants and her mother got her an agent to do some modeling. She had stayed with that, even while attending Vassar, through her early twenties, but then felt she should be doing more with her life.

"I knew you had been a model, the moment I laid eyes on you," I said, as I tasted the sweet and sour chicken on her plate.

"But I never had a billboard in Time Square, Mr. New York," she teased.

We both laughed, enjoying the scallion pancakes that had just arrived on the table.

As we continued to spend time together and work our way through all the nationalities that made up the Manhattan restaurant scene, we sensed more and more walls tumbling down between us. I was fascinated by her diverse background. She had worked at the U.N.

as a consultant for a gender equality project, while volunteering at as many different organizations as she could. But we both realized our largest common denominator was our constant search for something in New York that we couldn't find through work or careers.

So we had kept searching.

I loved that Samantha wasn't shy and quiet with me, but did notice it around others and I was drawn to that. In part, I saw her as a self-improvement project. I wanted to get her out of that mindset.

"Why did you agree to go to Judy and Bill's apartment that first night?" I asked.

Samantha looked at me, knowing I would continue to dig deeper and deeper into her private life.

"I was tired," she said. "Tired of looking for answers in the wrong places. Judy told me at the hospital how much studying the Bible had helped her, even before she had met Bill. I guess I was willing to try it."

"Lucky for all of us I guess."

I smiled at her. How happy Mama would be if she could see me right now.

"Sometimes, God sends small angels to help you though a regular day," she said. "Judy was one of those for me."

"I know about angels," I said, as I took her hand.

Samantha never judged me about my previous life, though she knew plenty about it after a while.

"I don't think you being gay in your past should be an issue for your future," she said.

Could this woman be for real? What person in their right mind wouldn't have an issue with me living as a gay man for the past fifteen years of my life? Maybe she enjoyed being my friend and that was all this was meant to be.

"Thank you. That's an amazing thing to say."

"Why? We all have a past to deal with. It shouldn't have to be lugged around everywhere."

"I've been praying about it daily," I said.

"I know. So have I."

The way she looked at me told me she had strong feelings for me. It was not a case of simple friendship. Yet there had been no pressure from her for goodnight kisses or to go any further than what I was comfortable with. This made her all that more amazing.

The night I finally decided to kiss her, it was as if God Himself were whispering in my ear and talking me through it. We had been walking down the street after a huge rainstorm and I had just grabbed her arm to help her across one of the many puddles that formed at street intersections in New York. Before I knew what I was doing, I had her in my arms and I was kissing her. It was soft. Everything about her was tender. So different from the roughness I felt with a man. I enjoyed being the strong one when she went limp in my arms. I enjoyed finally feeling like a real man.

***

I had been working very closely with Bill on his plans for the church, where we both felt it should go and grow from here. It was hard for me to keep my thoughts to myself as I believed I had some great ideas on what we needed to be doing to grow the congregation. If God planned on using me as a beacon to wake up the sinners of New York, I needed to put this small church on the map.

"How are you doing in the seminary classes?" he asked.

It reminded me of my Mama asking about cooking classes. And just like those, it turns out, that I didn't enjoy these much either.

"They are fine. I had so much of this growing up, it's like riding a bike," I said.

"I know God has called you, Jacob, and I love having another southerner helping me to lead our congregation."

"I just wish we could move the classes along," I said.

"It takes time, but you'll get there."

"I know I have it in me to share God's plan with others," I said. If Rachel were here, she would be calling me out for being cocky with a comment like that.

"Just keep taking the classes you need to get the general overview. It will take a while to become a full-fledged pastor, but I want to have you start preaching some sermons soon," Bill said. "You know, so you can get your feet wet."

That's exactly what I wanted to do. Stand in front of a congregation and tell them what God was saying to me. Tell them what they needed to be doing to get right with the Lord. Use my disgusting past as a way to show them I was a normal, broken man who God had called to share his message.

"I've got a lot of sermons in me, I feel it," I said.

"I think it's all proceeding along very nicely," Bill said.

"Yeah. Just one more thing I knew God wants in my life."

"What's that?" Bill asked.

"A wife."

CHAPTER TWENTY-THREE

JACOB

Tonight was the night. I had been planning it for a while. Ever since I had met Samantha, I had sensed that she was the one. God told me to ask her to marry me. I knew she would say yes, since this was God's will. I planned the evening down to the last moment. It started with a carriage ride through Central Park. It always worked in the movies, so why not with Samantha? I booked The Rainbow Room three months in advance. We had just finished a great meal of steak and lobster on the 65th floor at Thirty Rockefeller Plaza. Complete with dancing, lots of laughs — and not one drop of wine. While it was a little too expensive for my dwindling bank account, the night called for it. As I walked her back to her east side apartment, my hand continued to play with the box in my pants pocket.

"I'm over this cold weather," I said. "It's time for spring. Growing up, we'd have spring by March."

"Things aren't the same up here in the North, Jake. We've had snow storms on Easter."

"God had to call me to the North, huh?"

We both laughed. We had talked many times about God's will in both our lives.

"Thank you for a wonderful night, Jake," she said as she pulled her coat closed around her neck.

I fondled the box some more. When was the right time?

"I loved how everyone stared at us tonight. The gorgeous couple on the dance floor," I said.

"Stop it. Vanity isn't a good thing," she said.

"It's true."

"You are going to make one handsome preacher," she said.

This was it.

We were standing at the corner of 5th Avenue outside Tiffany's. Every woman's dream. Or would Samantha look at the princess cut diamond in my pocket and compare it to something more glamorous in the window? I decided to go for it.

"And you'd make a wonderful preacher's wife," I said.

Samantha stopped.

"Are you … asking me to be your wife?"

"I'm not asking you to be Bill's wife," I said, a huge grin on my face.

I reached into my pocket and pulled out the box. Never in my wildest dreams did I think I'd be here at this moment in my life. I always assumed I'd be with men my whole life. I pulled her over against the building and opened the box.

"Samantha. You have made me happier than I ever thought possible. God knew I needed you and I hope you know how much I need you too. I love you and want to spend the rest of my life with you."

Had I just said that? To a woman? I had. And I knew I meant it. I loved her. Not in the way I had loved Gary, but it still felt like love just the same.

"Will you be my wife?"

Samantha made me sweat for a moment. She looked down the street, into the window, taking her sweet time.

"Absolutely, Jacob Garrett. I want to be your wife."

"Whew. I was nervous for a sec."

"Why? You knew God had ordained this."

"Yes. I did," I said. "But this just makes this year all that more special … this will be the best year of our life. Just wait and see."

I placed the ring on her finger, took her in my arms and kissed her. The kiss felt different. Not like other times, but as if it all finally made sense. Everything in life lined up. This was what I was supposed to be doing, a man proposing to a woman and holding her in his arms. Protecting her. Loving her. What a feeling.

"I want a fall wedding. October. To give you a good memory of that day when your life changed," she said.

I was very touched by her gesture. She was a remarkable woman, selfless and looking to make the day just as much about me as it was about her.

"You are incredible. That'll be two years from the day I became a new man."

"And then we'll start a life together … with God leading the way," she said.

Samantha must have noticed the tear forming in my eye and matched it with one in her own. I knew she wouldn't mind having a sensitive husband. The snow fell around us on the street as I kissed Samantha goodnight outside her apartment.

I watched her walk inside and then walked off, lighting a cigarette in the cold air. God was moving correctly in my life and I owed Him everything.

CHAPTER TWENTY-FOUR

NOAH

Sally Ride had finished her infamous space ride on the Challenger, a gay themed musical, *La Cage Aux Folles*, had opened on Broadway, and a Soviet jet fighter had shot down a plane carrying 61 Americans. The summer of '83 was a momentous one for many Americans, but for my brother — it was his coming out party — as a straight man. Jacob had planned a lunch for me to meet Samantha; and Rachel had come along as moral support.

For the most part, things went smoothly at the Unicorn Café. I learned a lot about Samantha, about what went on in these Bible studies, and caught on quickly that Rachel was able to keep Jacob in her life and gain some sort of younger sister with his fiancée. Odd as it seemed, I thought I sensed a little jealousy on her part at times, but it seemed to me she was "converting" too in order to hang on to my brother.

"I love when I can get Samantha away from Jacob for lunch or shopping, while he is at class," Rachel said.

"That reminds me, we still have a girl's shopping day for the honeymoon outfit," Samantha said with a laugh.

"Just get something beautiful," Jacob said with a smile.

I looked at my brother. I was ready for a zinger about him wanting to wear it or something, but kept it to myself.

"Rachel has helped me," Samantha said. "It's been good for me to know someone from his past — and now I can always talk to Noah as well."

"I'm not sure you'll want my stories," I said.

Everyone laughed.

The entire lunch had sort of hazy film over it, as if these people were all wearing masks and no one was really being themselves. The check came and Rachel and I both went to grab it. Jacob never even gestured for it.

"I got it, Rachel," I said.

"Well, we certainly can't," Samantha said. "My parents have been helping out with those classes that Jacob takes."

Jacob shot a look at Samantha, clearly about discussing money issues.

"I kept telling Jacob he was going to bust through all of his savings," Rachel said. "He should have taken on a few jobs that I tried to send him on."

"I think that would have been hard … to step back into that part of his life," Samantha said. "You see how much he's thrown himself into his new work."

"I didn't know this was a praise Jacob luncheon," I joked.

"I am very happy that people notice the hard work I'm doing," Jacob said. "And really glad Rachel got involved in the church."

"Between you and me, I figured I would just come and visit a few times and that would be it," Rachel said, as if giving the speech of her life. "I was sure I would never stay. But I was drawn in to the Bible studies. And then when I realized I didn't have a personal relation-ship with Christ … I had let the priest do it for me all those years … it was like a light bulb went on."

Now I knew what it felt like. Those people who used to come to the door on Saturday mornings to shove religion down your throat, but all with a smile. The lunch had that tone to it.

"Jacob and I were very involved in church when we were kids," I said. "He got a lot of practice back then."

"Jacob has really changed my life," Rachel continued. "I don't see things the same way anymore. The man has a gift. He can make anyone believe, if they just stop for a moment and hear God through him."

I looked at my brother who was sitting there beaming at the praise. I guess it was good that he had found something he believed in so much. Or that perhaps God had really helped him out of a dark place. But something felt very odd.

"I do love the seminary classes," Jacob said. "It's a far cry from our days at Studio 54, Rachel."

"I'm very glad you realized that being gay was still keeping you in that old world too," she said. "And that you found such an amaz-ing woman."

Was this the same woman that I had walked with through Central Park, who had consoled Gary after the breakup? And now she had done a complete about face. Was I the only one who felt this was an episode of *The Twilight Zone*? Where was that waiter with my change?

"Is that hard for you?" Samantha asked. "To still be a part of that world as an agent?"

"I really try and witness to my clients now, without beating them over their heads," Rachel said. "But I have my ways of letting them see the importance of God in my life. And the importance of Jacob. I owe him a lot."

Rachel placed her hand on top of Jacob's sitting on the table. I had just about enough of the love-fest. I couldn't understand how both of these people had changed so quickly. I didn't think it was possible for someone to do that.

"From what I hear, he paid you plenty … you made some good money off of him," I interjected.

"Money is money," Rachel said. "What these two have is something more."

The waiter returned, gave me my change and smiled at Jacob who returned the look. What was that? Was this marriage built on a lie?

"Well, Samantha, great meeting you," I said, as I stood to make my way out of the restaurant. "I guess the next time we meet will be a chapel in Connecticut."

"I look forward to it, brother," she said, kissing my cheek.

I said my goodbyes and walked out the door. What the hell had I just sat through? It didn't feel as if I knew anyone at that table. I hoped this nice woman knew what she was getting herself into.

CHAPTER TWENTY-FIVE

JACOB

It was uncomfortable having Gary back in the apartment. I wasn't sure how to react, but I didn't want to let him think he had any sort of power over me. It was obvious to us both there was something so familiar in the air, but something also hovering that felt uneasy to me. Maybe I was just worried one of us could do something or say something that would put us right back to where we had left off.

"Once I get these last few things out of your way, you should be fine," Gary said.

"They're not taking up any space, Gary," I said. "I don't mind holding stuff if you don't have the room."

"You've hung onto it for over a year. Besides, my sublet is working out well and I can squeeze some more stuff in there."

"You seeing anyone?" I asked.

"I didn't think you would care," he said.

"Trying to say the right thing, Gary. That's all."

"Let's try doing this without talk," he said. "I won't take long."

The pain was still there for him, I could tell. Being in this place, with me ... a place that we had picked out. It was too much for him. And I was worried it was too much for me as well. Gary's ghost was all over this apartment, and now he was here in the flesh. The sight of him. The smell of him. I couldn't stay any longer.

"I'm going to run down to the corner store," I said. "Do you want anything?"

"No. I should be gone when you get back," he said.

I walked towards Gary, unsure what I was going to do when I got there. Would I pat him on the shoulder? Give him a hug? Perhaps a kiss on the check, but that would be a little too much Judas. The old Jake was whistling our song in my ear and Jacob was trying to pray him away.

I decided a simple hug would be best. Like with a brother going off somewhere.

"Take care, Gary," I said as I hugged him.

"You too," he said, as he nuzzled into the nape of my neck.

I couldn't handle his breath on my ear and I pushed him back. We looked at each other in silence and I could tell Gary was about to speak, to say something that might ensnare me, so I opened the door and walked out.

After I closed the door behind me, I placed my ear to it, and I could hear Gary moving around as he gathered his stuff. I remembered our past in this apartment. Sitting on the sofa watching TV, endless Saturdays snuggling up in bed all day long — more memories than I cared to dredge up. I wanted to open the door and run back inside to him, but that was Satan tempting me. It wouldn't help with anything. The door opened downstairs and I heard footsteps on the staircase and humming. The perfume — I knew it.

It was Samantha.

I wasn't prepared to encounter her right now. Not with Gary in the apartment. I walked up one flight of stairs to hide from her. How embarrassing to be cowering in the stairwell of my own building. She took out the key I had given her and opened the door.

"Honey! Oh. Hello," Samantha said.

Talk about awkward. They were meeting face to face for the first time in my apartment — without me there. I wondered who felt more frazzled, who felt that this was their home court.

"Jake ran down to the store," Gary said. "I was just getting some final things and I'll be out of your way."

"No problem," she said. "I think he sort of likes having your stuff here."

"Oh?" Gary asked.

I walked down the stairs as they shut the door, so I could eavesdrop with my ear to the door. I felt like a peeping Tom in my own building. I seriously hope none of the neighbors were watching.

"I try to move things sometimes and he'll say, 'No, Gary put that there,' or 'Gary always said that goes best there.' I finally stopped trying."

I had never noticed I did that, and I felt a pang of guilt for doing that to her.

"So what are you going to do when you move in here?" Gary asked.

"I was hoping we'd start over fresh after the wedding in a new place," she said. "But Jacob likes this place too much."

More guilt. But it was a great neighborhood and apartment. Why would I give that up? I could sense Gary was moving towards the door so I stepped down a few steps from the hallway, but could still hear them.

"Of all the straight men out there," Gary asked in a placid tone. "Why are you drawn to a man you know is gay?"

"God is working in his life every day," she said.

"You don't know him."

"I met him once before," she said. "I never told him, but I was the temp at the desk of an audition he was at. I saw his rudeness. I saw what drugs were doing to him and now … now, I see a whole new man."

I didn't even recall ever meeting Samantha in my past, but that blew me away. She had seen me like that and still loved me. This made me even happier to be making her my wife.

"He's still gay," Gary said.

"He still struggles, yes. But he's going to be a wonderful husband, and a preacher and I'll be there by his side," she said.

The door was opening as Gary wished her luck. I took a few more steps down around the corner, but now I was caught. He was going to see me on the stairs.

"And maybe one day God will lead you away from that world too," Samantha said as she was about to shut the door behind him.

"Lady, I'm happy in my world … but thanks," Gary said as he walked out the door and down the steps. He turned the bend and I pretended to be coming up the steps.

"Oh, I didn't know you'd still be here," I said to him.

"You've got company," he said as he walked past me. "You really should let her decorate the way she wants."

With that, Gary was down the steps and out with his box of

things. I walked slowly up the stairs to the apartment door. I couldn't help but wonder what Samantha was thinking on the other side of the door. I opened it slowly and the first thing I noticed was a missing photo on the wall that Gary and I had bought on a vacation. Had he taken it with him?

I made my way into the living room. Samantha was waiting there.

"Hi, honey. Guess I beat you home," she said.

Over her shoulder hung the beautiful sunset photo. She must have caught my eyes.

"Oh, I thought that would look good there," she said.

"It does," I told her.

But I knew once she was gone, I would move the photo back to where it belonged. At least until she moved in here for good.

CHAPTER TWENTY-SIX

NOAH

The day had arrived. The event that would go down in history as the year my brother married a woman. I was still in shock over it. I stood outside the old Connecticut church with Rachel.

One thing you had to love about this part of the country was the history. All these New England states had a charm found in every building design, unseen anywhere else in the United States. It was a picturesque setting; the church on the meadow with the fall foliage was a beautiful sight. I was standing in front of the church with Rachel waiting for the service to begin.

"I still can't freakin believe it," I said. "My gay brother … my brother the cook, actor, model, cater waiter is getting married … to a woman!"

"Your brother has really gone through a lot the past two years. I couldn't be happier for him," Rachel scolded.

"Don't get me wrong. I'm happy too," I said. "I mean, I'm here and all, in the wedding. I'm just not sure it's the right thing for him."

"Why? Because he's no longer gay?"

"No longer gay? Come on, look around you," I said. "Have you seen the string of gay New Yorkers trying to get into this event? They drove up here to Connecticut just to witness it … like a car wreck that you can't stop yourself from watching."

"Is that how you feel about your brother?" she asked.

"That's how I feel about some of these changes in his life. Yes."

"Shame," Rachel said. "I'll remember to keep you in my prayers."

Rachel turned and walked into the church. This woman had changed so much since the day Mama had died. She was cold that day, then loving towards Gary on our walk, and then praising Jacob at our lunch. She was a midget Sybil! And now she was going to pray for me and my attitude. The whole day was befuddling and Jacob's friends just muddied the waters even more. I sure could go for some tobacco now. Why had I given up my Skoal?

I decided to walk to the back of the church to see how my big brother was doing in his room. It was a brisk October in Connecticut. I walked around the outside of the church, but the windows were open into the room where Jacob was getting ready.

Jacob was standing in front of a full-length mirror in a tux, looking as handsome as any magazine cover he had been on. He still had his same slight build, which teetered on effeminate, even if he was a newly declared straight male. No longer did he look like a young man who didn't understand the world. He had experience all across his face. He had a look of certainty in his eyes — I assume knowing this was what he wanted. I could only imagine what was going through his head. I'm sure he felt it was his big day, like he was the bride. At thirty-five years old, he was getting married to a woman. He was as shocked as I was, I'm sure.

"Lord, this is it," he said.

I made sure he couldn't see me through the open window.

"This is the day that the Lord has made," he continued. "I will gladly rejoice and will gladly sing praise to you. I can't believe I got here. What a wonderful woman you have sent me. She is everything a man could ask for. How you have turned my life around, oh Lord. Thank you. Thank you for loving such a lowly man as me. And I promise to serve you and to raise my family to serve you. I know one day, we will all go inside Radio City and it will be full with people shouting your name. No more hanging out on that sidewalk. But today … today is for Samantha and I pray she is calm and collected."

I was stunned by my brother's sincerity. Perhaps he really did believe God had changed him. I know the drugs and wild sex needed to end in his life, and for that, I was also grateful to God.

There was a knock at the door and then it opened. Holy shit. It was Gary.

"Surprise," he said.

Jacob looked shocked. "Gary."

Gary walked into the room and shut the door.

"I had to witness it," he said. "I just had to see you."

"You shouldn't have."

Jacob went back to fussing with his tie.

"Shoot, if I could walk you down the aisle myself and give you away, I would," Gary said.

This made Jacob laugh and seemed to put him a little more at ease.

"Just to get rid of me, huh?" Jacob asked.

I felt guilty peering through the window, witnessing something I had no business to see. But I couldn't walk away. It was just too good.

"We've gone through a lot together," Gary said. "And I don't regret it, Jake. Not one moment. There is no one else on earth I would have rather shared those days with."

"But it was all a sin," Jacob said.

"If there was ever a law passed that said you and I could be taking vows today, I'd do it in a heartbeat."

I was struck by his love for my brother. He had been a part of my life for so long — I couldn't help but feel bad for him. But I also knew my brother didn't want to go through this today. I could see the angst return to his face. Should I go in and stop this?

"That will never happen," Jacob said. "You know that, right? That's all of Satan."

Ok, so my brother doesn't want to be gay, but does he really think it comes from the devil?

"Then forgive me, because I am a sinner," Gary said. "I loved a man. He loved me. And we were happy. Is happiness not of God?"

"Not that kind," Jacob answered.

"Then I'm lucky I got to share a moment of it with you. Even for just a part of your life."

"Gary, I should —"

My brother couldn't even finish his sentence. Gary took him in his arms and kissed him. I saw Jacob trying to push him off then he pulled back and looked Gary in the eyes. Was he going to smack him? Throw him out? I was glued to the window like it was a television set. But I think Jacob saw it, because I know that I did.

There it was.

All the love the two had shared. All the happiness. It was all caught in Gary's eyes. Then I couldn't believe it. Jacob pulled Gary into him and kissed him even stronger. This wedding was off. The freak show that people had wanted to witness was not going to happen.

"I can feel it, Jake," Gary said as he held my big brother. "It's still in you. I'm still a part of you."

Jacob did not push him away. He just looked at him while he held the man at arm's length.

"God has wiped me clean of those sins," his mouth said, but his body shook while he spoke.

I was so confused. I wasn't sure who this person was. It was as if someone were controlling the words coming out of his mouth.

Jacob continued. "And now, I'm going in that church and marrying the woman who will bear my children one day. And who I will be with until the end of time."

Gary's eyes filled with tears of love for my brother. My heart ached for him. He was like a brother to me as well.

That was it. Gary and I both knew it.

The robot standing there had made his final proclamation. The wedding was going to start. I'm sure Samantha was in her room pulling the veil down on her face, ready to walk down that aisle to meet Jacob.

"I love you, Jake," Gary said, as a tear trailed down his cheek.

Jacob started to walk out the door to take his place at the front of the church.

"I love you too, Gary," he said, a catch in his voice that proved to me those words rang true.

He was out the door. I needed to run around to get myself into that church, but I stared at Gary who slowly fell onto the leather sofa in that small office space. Jacob shut the door to him, to the life they had shared, and was off to start a brand new one.

PART II

....

CHAPTER TWENTY-SEVEN

JACOB

Settling down and getting married forced me to pay more attention to the world. After all, I would now have a part of me, my children, living on in this morally corrupt society once I was gone. It looked as if Vice President Bush would be keeping the country on the conservative path that Reagan had laid out in the fall presidential elections. Lord knows we needed it. Jimmy Swaggart had confessed in front of the world that he had sinned against God. And porn king, John Holmes, passed away from AIDS. In my new walk with the Lord, I had my own private judgment on each of these people, as well as that terrible disease, but I knew I needed to concentrate on my own small corner of the world that was the Upper West Side of Manhattan.

So much had occurred in the five years since I had married Samantha. I couldn't believe what our lives had become. We weren't young and stupid when we got married. We were in our thirties. We knew what life was about. We knew what to expect … well, at least we thought we did. Samantha had tried again and again to get me to move into another apartment, but I had special ties to the place and didn't want to move. The East Side girl became a Westsider over night.

She began to worry about money after marriage, or lack thereof, and took a part-time job in a local bookstore. She loved surrounding herself with books. But I didn't like my wife working. It was my duty to provide for the two of us — so I saw to it that job didn't last long.

Of course, all those seminary classes I had to take were not free. I had to take a quick one-time modeling gig in Hong Kong that Rachel lined up, just to keep me and Sam afloat. It was like a shot of adrenaline, but not something I wanted to repeat too often. It felt nice that I could still demand so much money outside my own country; but stepping back into that world gave me a rush that I knew could be very dangerous. Jake would constantly rear his ugly head and taunt me the way the serpent had chided Eve in the garden.

Those classes became more of a problem beyond just money. I never knew seminary could be so boring.

Why did I need all of that?

I knew what God wanted. God spoke to me each day. I didn't need to sit through endless, tedious classes about Bible stories I had heard all in my youth. Finally, I just gave them up to save my family some money.

I sat at my church office desk, trying to prepare my sermon for that coming Sunday. The picture of my two young children caught my eye and sent my mind back to my wedding night.

We had left all the guests at the Chestnut Village Inn dining hall and went upstairs to a beautiful suite. I felt like the luckiest man in the world with this beautiful woman in my room. I had tried to get the thought of what Gary had done prior to the ceremony as far out of my mind as possible. But once the guests were gone and it was just me and Samantha — it felt as if Gary was in the room with us.

"I'm just going to go change," she said, like a young giddy woman.

I knew it was time to prove to her what a stud I could be in the bedroom, even while the thought scared me to death. Gary's ghost was watching me undress and Jake was in the mirror, telling me I couldn't go through with it. I left on my tux pants and had the shirt unbuttoned as Samantha stepped out in a beautiful off-white silk camisole with a small silk robe over it.

"You look gorgeous," I said.

Neither of us were virgins in that room. We had shared everything about our pasts. But I felt like a virgin. This was completely new territory for me. I took her in my arms and kissed her. Kissed her to remove Gary from my mind and to wipe away the last fifteen years of my life. I lifted her up and carried her to the four poster bed that had been decorated by her friends with rose petals. I kissed her neck, down to her beautiful full breasts. I opened up the robe so I could access her entire body, touching her thighs while I kissed her all over.

But the whole time, nothing was happening down below in my pants.

She removed my shirt and was clawing at my back — but it wasn't working.

I felt like a failure.

"I'm sorry," I said. "This isn't working."

I got up and crossed to the chair in the room as the moonlight came streaming in the window. Samantha followed me to the chair and took my face in her hands. I thought I was going to burst into tears. I couldn't fucking make love to my own wife.

"It's ok," she said.

Wonderful Sam. Non-pressuring Sam. She didn't make me feel

bad about it at all. She took my hand, lead me back to the bed and we lay down together. She turned her back to me and wrapped herself in my arms and we slept that way the entire evening.

The next morning, we left for the honeymoon, which was a dream on an exclusive beach in the Bahamas. So romantic. Just the thing Gary and I had done several times. Fire Island. Hawaii. Jamaica. But with Sam, it was different. And with Sam, again … I couldn't do anything sexually. I had thought it was perhaps just a mental block. I knew God wanted me with a woman, so God had to make it work. But not once on that trip did I ever make love to my wife.

It took over three months and a few glasses of merlot to get me loose enough to go there. And since it wasn't hard liquor, I didn't feel I was doing anything wrong. Of course, I know that no rehab place around would ever agree with that logic.

Michael Jacob Garrett was born on October 11th, 1985. All good things seemed to come to me in October. At thirty-six years old, I became a father. A husband who would care for my wife and son, and a man who was capable of all things other straight men were able to do.

The other smiling face in the picture was that of Veronica, my beautiful daughter who was only a year old, but already the spitting image of her mother. She kept her mother very busy. Samantha was now a stay at home mom. She chased our kids up and down the ever changing streets in our neighborhood. There were more young couples with kids our children's age popping up in that area all the time and I was pleased that we were a part of that scene. Her ability to stay on top of our home life gave me the freedom to take care of things at church.

The church.

There had been so much growth and change over five years. More and more people were brought in and the congregation's number crept higher and higher. Mornings in front of Radio City were getting old, especially as the group got larger. At first, I talked them into going to different people's apartments to worship, but even that wasn't what I wanted. I wanted our congregation to have a building. A true church.

I was walking past a building on 94th street off of Broadway that made me stop in my tracks. I had passed it many times and didn't know it had been a church. I went in, used my charm on those in charge and before I knew it, I had a place for our group to meet and for me to have an office space. We could hold services on Sunday afternoon when the building was not in use.

I didn't want to leave Bill and Judy and felt guilty about using them as our parent organization to start my own congregation. But that was what I wanted and I started Christ Redeemer Church and hardly looked back at that small group on the East Side. Most of the people followed me, and eventually Bill and Judy ended up moving down to Atlanta. I was just doing God's will and God wanted me inside a building. He was using me as a vessel in this city.

Rachel became a huge part of the church, and she brought in some of her professional clients as well. So there were always Broadway singers raising their voices to the Lord on Sundays. And since we were not far from Columbia University, college age kids from all over the country were looking for something that felt like home.

I was smart in recruiting the students from that area to attend my services. Our numbers had grown well over a hundred people on some Sundays. My goal was to grow so large that we would have to go to a space like Radio City Music Hall on the inside.

That was the apex for me.

Naturally, those numbers had gone back down over the last year — due to parishioners moving out of town, leaving to do a national tour, or college kids heading back home. But I kept working. Even with fifty people we could call full members, I was pleased. My preparation for the sermon and my thoughts on the past years were interrupted by the ringing phone.

"Christ Redeemer."

"Jacob, it's Rachel. Do we have the soup kitchen this Saturday?"

Rachel was constantly calling me to discuss church issues, get a pat on her head for her good deeds or even stroke my own ego by reminding me how great it was for getting us off the streets. Her uncle had passed the previous year and I knew she was lonely in her apartment, so Samantha and I tried to entertain her as much as we could. I was proud of the Lord's servant she had become. Most times, she didn't have much else to say and the conversations ended quickly, so that both of us could go about our business for the day.

I was just getting back into my work when there was a knock at my office door.

"Come in," I said.

Jeff Golden came through the door. He was nineteen, attending Columbia's School of the Arts and had also lived in Tennessee his whole life. A blonde haired, blue-eyed handsome young man that had those all-American boy looks that every casting director would kill for. I was very glad he had come into the church. The past year, he had done so much helping out with music, watching my kids, talking to me. I saw much of me in the boy. His wide-eyed look on New York, his eagerness to learn new things and his love of God. His Mama had raised him right.

"Jake, do you have a minute?"

"Sure, Jeff."

I was up on my feet whenever he entered my office, offering my chair and sitting on the edge of my desk. Allowing myself to be closer to him than an outsider would perceive as acceptable. However, he had an aura about him that made me want to be near to him.

"Do you know how much Samantha and I have loved having you here?"

"That's great. I was lucky to find you," he said. "I needed something that felt normal since leaving Tennessee."

"Don't know if you can call us normal, but hey, we try."

I was always trying to make jokes with Jeff. I wanted our times together to be light and fun.

"It just feels like home," Jeff said. "Singing hymns, playing with your kids …"

"They love you. It's like they have a big brother," I said, smacking the side of his leg with my own in a playful manner.

"It's just so strange in this wild city to find something so calming."

"God can do that," I said.

"Yes, he can. Especially when you're fighting so many things."

I could sense Jeff's nerves. I knew he was gay. I saw it the minute the good looking young man came through the doors of my church. New to the city. So many possibilities. So many ways of getting into trouble.

I touched Jeff's arm. "Jeff, did I ever tell you about my past?"

"No."

"Come by the apartment sometime. I'll show you great photo albums of me as a leading model in New York in the late 70s and early 80s."

"You?"

I forgot how ancient I probably seemed to the younger generation as I knocked on the door of turning forty. But I still looked good and I was sure especially to a young gay man.

"Don't sound so surprised," I said. "It wasn't that long ago."

"I just assumed you were always a minister."

I smiled. If this kid only knew the path I had taken.

"Far from it," I said. "I was a druggie, a sex addict, cheating on my boyfriend ..."

"Boyfriend?"

The last five years had proven me to be a respected minister with my congregation, but simply talking about the past made me think of Gary. I had to continue.

"Yes, I was gay before God moved in my life and brought Sam to me. She has helped."

As if God himself were directing the scene, my phone rang at that moment.

"Christ Redeemer," I said.

"Honey, it's me."

"I was just talking about you, Sam to Jeff. Are your ears ringing?"

"Tell him I say hello," Samantha said on the other end.

"Sam says hi."

I could tell Jeff was still lost in thought over the bit of information I had just shared.

"Jeff?"

"Oh. What? Yes, hello," he said.

"Jacob, I was thinking of asking Rachel to come watch Mickey and Ronnie tonight so we could get out," Samantha said. "Just us."

I smiled towards Jeff, before I let my wife down.

"We can't rely on Rachel all the time," I said. "We can spend an evening together, the four of us."

"But I thought it would be nice for us to go out … do something fun."

I covered the phone with my hand to speak to Jeff.

"Women … can't live with em …" Then I went back to the phone, smiling at Jeff the entire time. "Sam, I think you need to pray about this. I think there is a reason you're trying to run away from the kids tonight. Take out your Bible, pray and call me back."

"Ok, honey," she said. "I will."

I loved my wife. She had given me an incredible family. She cared for me. She loved me. But I had a greater calling as a pastor that superseded some of the family obligations. My congregation needed me. And right now, that meant Jeff.

I hung up. "God brought her to me, but she won't leave me alone," I said as I broke out in laughter at my own joke — allowing my arm to brush against Jeff's arm.

I could sense that Jeff was nervous and wanted to talk to me about something.

"I have been waiting for God to move in my life," Jeff said.

"I thought maybe you were. God sent you to me. I know he did. I'm going to help you get past this. Being gay can be cured."

Jeff's face lit up. I knew it was a release for the kid to have someone understand what he was going through, without judging him.

He smiled as he got ready to leave. "Thanks for talking to me. I need to get to work, but we'll talk some more later?"

"Absolutely," I said as I stood, hugging the young man in my big strong arms.

I felt like a father, or an older wiser uncle. I wanted to help this kid as much as I could. Looking into that face made me think about all the possibilities that were waiting for him. And I knew I could take part in molding his future. A short five years earlier and I would have been trying to get into the young man's pants, but those days were over for me. I had to constantly remind myself that, but they were. I had a greater purpose in my life and told God that I would stay true to being His disciple.

"Have a good day at work," I said.

Jeff was out the door and in the elevator. I was pleased with my small breakthrough. I shut the office door and went to my coat pocket. I pulled out a cigarette, went to my window and opened it. There in my church office, overlooking an alley on the upper West Side, I tasted one of my addictions that I could just not shake.

CHAPTER TWENTY-EIGHT

NOAH

I had worked hard at making a life for myself in Nashville, but it seemed fate didn't plan for me to stay there. So I had followed in my brother's footsteps and did something I never expected I'd do.

I moved to New York City the previous year.

I knew I could be a writer from anywhere in the country, but my editor and publisher were in New York and a part of me was still lonely in Nashville. Like the ghosts of the Garretts loomed over that state. And damn it if something didn't just feel right about being here in New York and near the only family I had.

At thirty-six years old, I was in the best shape of my life. The years working out had kept me fit and my body had come a long way since working as a maintenance man back in my twenties. I could officially call myself an author, with three books published. I loved writing fiction and drawing from what I had known and lived through. There was nothing like the thrill of walking into a book store and seeing a display of my books. Traveling the country for book signings and the occasional discussion on southern fiction — though, unlike my brother, I didn't love being the center of attention. I was much more content in my one bedroom apartment on the East Side and writing the books rather than talking about them. The lack of a vehicle was very strange to me for the first six months, but I had slowly gotten used to it. As a southern man, my truck had always defined me — but I guess you could say I was changing somewhat. Where my truck had looked like a junk yard on the inside, this apartment was always kept clean. Perhaps that had something to do with my traveling and being away from it.

I still had a problem keeping a girlfriend for any length of time, but I enjoyed my circle of friends, seeing my nephew, niece and sister-in-law, and having lunch now and again with my brother. We made sure the park divided us. Even though we were in the same city, we did not feel the need to be in each other's lives at every waking moment. The knowledge the other was only a bus ride away was plenty of security for us both.

I was pleased for Jacob, but I still didn't quite get the religion thing. And as much as I loved his children, I still believed they were born out of a very strange bond. I had seen my brother look at other gay men on the street. Even now, after being married for five years. I had seen him kissing Gary at his own wedding, getting into it before he realized what it might mean. God had not changed him. Jacob was still gay. But that was not my problem.

All this was going through my head as I walked out of Rizzoli's bookstore on 57th street. I had just been checking out my competition on the shelves. A small game I liked to play. I must have been walking too quickly and humming the music coming from my Walkman, and I bumped into a woman.

"Oh, I'm so sorry," I said removing the head phones.

"No. It's my fault. I wasn't paying attention," she said.

I picked up her bag and handed it to her, and then I really looked at her. She was very nice looking, not glamorous like other women I had dated, but a real natural beauty. She had long auburn hair, wonderful hazel eyes, and was around thirty. I instantly felt I wanted to get to know her.

"Here. Again, I apologize," I said.

The woman smiled.

"Good tunes?" she asked.

"The new Randy Travis tape," I said.

"Don't know him," she said as she started to walk away.

I couldn't help but continue to talk to her. "This is going to sound like such a line, but do I know you?"

"Did you grow up on Long Island?" she asked.

"No, no. I lived in Nashville for the past ten years."

The woman seemed to warm up to me with each word she spoke.

"A cowboy in New York. Explains the Randy Travis," she said.

"I thought you didn't know who he was," I said jokingly.

"I can put two and two together," she said coyly.

I couldn't let her out of my sight. I wanted to keep her there on the street talking all day.

"I'm sure there are some ranches out on Long Island," I said. "I could show you how to rope a cow or something."

The woman laughed loudly.

"Now that's a line," she said.

"Yeah, a pretty bad one, huh?"

"Do you spend a lot time trying to pick up women outside bookstores?" she asked.

"Well if you want a smart one, it's either here or lurking around NYU. And those are all too young for me," I responded.

There was that smile again. It seemed she enjoyed talking to me as much as I did to her.

"My name is Noah Garrett."

"Naomi Weisman."

Now there was a name I had not heard in Tennessee. There was poetry to it. The way it lingered in the air after she had said it. Or maybe it was the smile in her eye — something caused me to keep going.

"Do you have time to grab a cup of coffee?" I asked.

"You know, I don't usually do this … but why don't I give you my number and you call me sometime," she said. "I think I would like to hear some of your southern tales."

We exchanged numbers and made plans to meet up. I walked down the street pleased that I had taken the time to go to the book-store. And even more pleased that I was getting better at taking chances.

CHAPTER TWENTY-NINE

JACOB

I left my house and sauntered up my regular route to the church office. I had on one of my suits as I liked to do when meeting someone from the church. I had looked at myself in the mirror before I left and thought it was time for new clothes. But our money would go towards the kids now, so I'd continue wearing these suits that were a tad loose on me.

Time to put some weight on.

I walked to the corner, turned onto Broadway and headed north. Passing each corner newsstand, I adverted my eyes to not get a glimpse of the pornographic magazines. Sometimes, I admit, I just had an urge so badly.

The need for sex with men would eat at me more than the need for a drink ... though that would come and go as well. Temptation can come in many forms — sometimes, we bring it on ourselves. For instance, with Jeff. I loved how the boy idolized me, but there were times that old Jake would taunt me to try something with him. That would ruin so much of the effort I had put into converting him.

"Lord. I am your sheep," I said aloud. "Please guide me onward."

And with that, I continued walking until I got to the chapel. I had told Pamela I'd meet her at ten.

Pamela was a 20-something, high-powered attorney for a large corporation who had joined the church three months before. Like a young Tyne Daly from *Cagney & Lacey*, she didn't take any crap from anyone. I liked having her as part of my flock. It was always exciting to see the caliber of my congregation rising. It made me feel important. It made my work feel important. It validated what I was doing.

Pamela was waiting as I walked up to the building.

"I love a woman on time," I said, walking up to her.

"You and me both," she said.

I didn't let that comment go unnoticed. I made a mental note of it, since it was clearly something that I would have to deal with in the future. I knew that Pamela was a lesbian, she had the short cropped signature haircut to prove it, but she had grown up with a minister father. So she knew what was right and what was wrong. But I was careful with her. She gave too much money to the church for me to scare her away — and I was no fool when it came to funds for the church. We went into my office and chatted about the plans for Sunday school and other business.

"I can offer some legal counsel on how to run this organization, but you really need an accountant to talk about how you handle the funds," she said.

"Oh, I would never want to place you in a predicament like that," I said.

"Don't worry, I wouldn't let you."

Pamela smiled and then she dropped a huge bomb on me. She was having Jeff move in with her along with another female member of the church.

I felt as if someone had stabbed me in the stomach. Jeff was my pet project. God wanted me to stay close in the boy's life and if he moved in with Pamela, her mixed views on homosexuality and religion would definitely rub off on him. I couldn't let this happen.

"Do you believe that's the smartest thing to do?" I asked. "For all three of you to live together?"

"Why would it be an issue?" she said. "We all attend this church. There are three bedrooms in the new place —"

"But it's two women and a man."

I knew any other man would love the idea of that, but I was honestly just grabbing at straws to find something to stop her.

"A gay man," she said.

"That doesn't matter," I said. "In the eyes of the Lord, it's still wrong. Hand me that Bible."

Even with the power and money she brought into the church, I knew I needed to set her straight. I couldn't allow her to take Jeff away from my influence, my assistance.

"I don't see why it would be wrong to split rent in an expensive city like New York," she said.

"You make plenty of money, Pamela," I said.

"But they don't. I can help them."

I held the Bible in my hand and closed my eyes to pray. I opened the Bible, pointed to a verse and began reading it to her.

"Genesis 6:7. So the Lord said, 'I will wipe mankind, whom I have created, from the face of the earth — men and animals, and creatures that move along the ground, and birds of the air — for I am grieved that I have made them.' God is telling you there is wickedness and evil in a home built on non-solid ground and He is not pleased."

"What is that? Bible Weegie Board?" she said.

I was put off by the way she described my methods. I had been doing this for the past few years now and found it very helpful. Whenever I couldn't come up with the answer, I'd take it to God in prayer and allow God to speak to me directly through a verse in the Bible.

"That's the word of the Lord. Speaking to you," I said in a sober tone. "We should all hear God in whatever manner He speaks to us. God tells me many things to pass on to my congregation and I know this is one of those things."

Pamela was a tough woman. I knew she loved the Lord and she knew He loved her. She still wasn't so quick to buy into my methods.

"We will all think on this together … and go to God in prayer," she said as she stood to leave.

Maybe I was getting through to her, after all.

"I'm always praying for you, Pamela. And I'll always be here to say things people don't necessarily want to hear."

"I'm praying for you too … and this church," she said as she opened her briefcase. "So how is Sam doing?"

"She's busy planning Mikey's birthday party next week," I said.

Pamela took out her checkbook and I noticed her writing a check out to the church while she spoke. I had to love her for that.

"What day is his birthday?" she asked.

"The 11th."

"Wow. That day is being declared National Coming Out Day for gays and lesbians," she said, and handed me the check with a smile.

Pamela had to get back to work, so she excused herself and

walked out of the office. I couldn't believe they were going to make a day for people to come out of the closet. It just proved how much this city needed people like me fighting the fight of the Lord. And I didn't like how much joy she took in announcing to me that it was on my own son's birthday. I thought about the rest of our conversation.

Why had she come to me? She knew what I would say. Or was it a test? Was she thinking I would condone it because of my past? Now I wasn't sure what they were up to. I needed to speak to Jeff to talk him out of this crazy idea.

***

God was using me a vessel. I knew I had to get through to Jeff. To save him from himself. We had met at the diner on the corner of 89th and Broadway many times — discussing my sermons, the music he wanted to choose, life in New York. This time, I wanted to share my past with him. Let him know about everything I had gone through to get to this point in my life. We were through most of our meal and I had shared a lot about my past.

"I can't get over the life you've had," he said, gulping down an egg cream.

"Learn from my mistakes, then. No reason for you to go down that same path," I said.

"I would kill to have the career you had."

"That career almost killed *me*," I said.

"But that's why I'm here in New York, to experience all of the ups and downs of the arts."

"Jeff, you can be an actor without having to walk down that sinful path. Look at the actors in our church who love God and who still work in that field."

"That reminds me, I think I'm going to have a true Christmas Cantata this year, with solos, duets, trios … you name it," he said scooping up a final French fry.

I flashed back to the day I had met Gary at The Doghouse eating his fries.

Jeff continued. "We'll put the word out in a local paper to get more people in. I could also ask some more students from Columbia to come perform, as well."

The boy had such fire, such passion for what he did. Even though the church was unable to pay him, he loved my mission and what we were trying to do. He invited friends to continue to grow the church with me. I loved working with him, planning our services and functions. We made a great team. But I knew what we really needed to discuss. I had to get him to change from his ways so that God could fully use him in this city.

"So how is it going abstaining from sex?" I asked.

I could sense his embarrassment, as he responded. I'm sure he found it odd talking about sex with his pastor, but I knew plenty about gay sex.

"I haven't had sex with anyone here in New York," he said.

"Good boy. See, God is working."

The old Jake popped into my head reminding me how sweet being with a virgin could be.

"I'm not saying I don't still think I'm gay," he said. "I can't really remember a time when I wasn't."

"It'll take time."

Lord knows how long it took me — is still taking me.

"It's all I've known," he said.

That was the thing about homosexuality. If you practiced it long enough, you could really dupe yourself into believing it was who you were to the core — but deep down, you always knew it was wrong. Even Jeff admitted to hiding it for years from his family and friends; watching the Lana Turner movie, *Madam X*, with his mother and sister and crying over the ending. I tried to explain that crying at a movie doesn't make you gay.

"I know that," he said. "It's more the longing that I feel when I'm around a really attractive man."

I gulped.

"That urge that you feel in your pit, that ache of attraction doesn't always go away," I said thinking about myself.

"If they are a part of you, than why would you want them to go away?" he asked innocently.

"One has to fight it, as I do each day. Turning my head from the men I pass on the street or from the copy of *Honcho* hanging on the corner news stand."

"Wait a minute," Jeff blurted out. "I thought God changed you."

"God is always working within me," I said. "But it is still something I fight each day."

I swore the look on the boy's face changed. It no longer felt he was looking at me as a pastor or a confidant. No. This felt like someone on a date with a gleam in his eye. Or was I reading into the situation through the haze of my own temptations?

"Why do you want to fight?" he asked. "Have you ever thought …

that maybe that's just who you are?"

This poor young man was so confused about how God and Satan worked.

"No. God wouldn't make me that way," I said. "God has a purpose. Remember when you first met us? You were with Bill & his wife in front of Radio City?"

"Yeah … I thought that was pretty weird," he said.

"God has shown me a vision, Jeff. An awakening in New York City. One day before the millennium, we will be inside of that building … and it will be overflowing with people listening to God's word. I will be standing on that stage, sharing what God has told me with all the sinners of New York. And maybe, just maybe … God plans for you to be there too. Right by my side. Leading the flock in song, raising their voices to the heavens. Would you like that?"

"We'll never have that many people in our church," he said.

"We will if we keep trying."

"I'm pretty happy with our church here," he said.

"Always think big, Jeff. God doesn't want us to settle on something small. He wants us to share His word throughout the world. But to do that, you need to be right with Him. You need to give up the gay lifestyle and choose to serve only Him. I'm here for you if you need to lean on me. I've done it for myself and I can help you."

"Don't you mean God can do it?" he asked.

The door opened and two men walked in that were obviously a gay couple. Jeff and I both looked at them — probably wondering what the other was thinking. I began to question if the couple thought that Jeff and I were together.

"There is something else we need to talk about," I said. "Pamela told me about your plan to get an apartment with her."

"Isn't she wonderful?" he said. "Who else would help out a struggling student like myself and Lauren? I think God connected us through you, through your church."

Now that one hurt. Tying me into their web. This boy wasn't as innocent as he pretended to be.

"I don't think God would see it that way. He would see a man and two women living in sin, out of wedlock."

Jeff gave me a look that called me a jackass for even mentioning this. Obviously, two of them were both gay and nothing was going to happen — in his eyes.

"Even if you are gay now, if you expect God to work on that sin with you — you need to meet him on His terms," I continued.

"I'm not sure if God would be so upset about me saving a few bucks on rent," he said. "I work while I go to school; I spend so much time with you and Christ Redeemer without getting paid. I think God might understand."

The kid smiled and finished sucking every last drop of egg cream through his straw. It was playful and very sexual at once. I looked into the boy's eyes. He didn't get how God used me to do His work. He didn't understand the depth of my love for the Lord and for him, my longing to keep him from experiencing the horrors that I had experienced. I bowed my head and started a prayer, asking God to deliver this boy from his wicked ways and for Jeff to lean on me — whenever he needed me.

CHAPTER THIRTY

NOAH

I was so content since I had started dating Naomi the previous spring. I was fascinated by her life, her Jewish faith and how she had turned against her families' wishes to have her married off before thirty. I loved a rebel, and she fit the bill. She ignored the trends of the late 80s fashion and instead went more with an Annie Hall thing. But she was always very up on the times for swimwear fashion, since that was her day job. I loved that I had found someone who could express themselves creatively. I had never dated someone who completely "got" what I did.

She didn't always go to synagogue, which I could relate to. I hadn't stepped into a church since arriving in New York. She loved all kinds of music and introduced me to new artists and sounds that were completely new to me; taking me out of my country comfort zone. Who thought this big guy would have new age music in his Walkman … and enjoy it? But I would still wear my cowboy boots when we'd go out, just to keep some of the past with me, however inconsequential.

We talked as equals. I never assumed the role of a southern man trying to keep his woman in her place. While she was a few years younger than I was, she behaved older and wiser in so many ways. I always thought it had to do with her growing up in the liberal world that is the Northeast. She even made me rethink some of my conservative ways. Perhaps I didn't know everything like I thought I did.

Within our first three months of dating, she had me doing things in this city I had never done as a tourist. She was a 'do-er' and I was mostly a 'watcher', but I loved doing things with her. We took the Circle Line cruise around Manhattan, traveled out to the Statue of Liberty and Ellis Island to see where immigrants had come through when arriving in our country. Hearing stories of her ancestors that she knew came through that gateway was amazing. We ate at the top of one of the defining symbols of New York, Windows on The World in the World Trade Center. I felt like I was up in the clouds, this beautiful woman unbelievably with me — talking about everything and getting to know each better and deeper. She even loved spending time with my niece and nephew; taking Mikey to the Natural History Museum and talking about when Ronnie would be old enough to do more things with. She really opened my eyes to the wonders of New York and I found myself falling for the city and for her more and more.

Tonight we were walking to 46th street to meet Gary and his new boyfriend. I was elated when I had run into Gary the week before and was looking forward to catching up with him. So many years had passed since I had last seen him at Jacob's wedding. We had lost touch, even after I moved to New York. But I missed him and seeing him only brought all of that back.

"I think you're really gonna like Gary," I said.

"If you like him, I'm sure I will," she said as she put the collar down on my Polo shirt.

"What?"

"That look went out, hon, a few years ago."

I loved how she looked out for me.

"Does this all seem strange to you?" I asked. "To be meeting my married brother's ex boyfriend?"

"Now come on … you know me better than that. Do you think I would see this as strange?" Naomi said, as she passed through the restaurant door I held open.

"You probably like it you kinky, little freak," I said, swatting her on the behind.

Gary was waiting at a back table and stood when he saw us arrive. He looked well and very happy with Roger, who worked on Wall Street. Introductions were made and the four of us ordered drinks.

"Roger, this man is not the same guy I remember from Tennessee," Gary said. "The North has made you mild, Noah."

Naomi laughed. "Trust me, he's not mild," she said.

"Wall Street, huh?" I asked. "I can't even imagine a job like that."

Roger seemed very comfortable and had no problems carrying his weight in the conversation.

"All those years at Harvard paid off I guess," Roger said, a smug look on his face.

This made me very quiet, until Gary cracked up.

"He's kidding, Noah. He started out doing data entry and worked his way up," Gary said.

Roger broke out in laughter too.

"Thank God. I thought the college drop-out here was going to have to get up and leave the table," I said with a grin.

Gary smiled at me and Naomi, who rested her hand on my arm.

"So what do you do, Naomi?" Gary asked.

"I just live off this one here," she joked.

"Don't let her fool you," I said. "Naomi is her own woman. And just as creative — she's a designer at Gortex Swimwear."

"Maybe you can get us some nice Speedos," Roger said.

"My Speedo days are over, hon," Gary said.

"I make Noah act as my personal model for those," Naomi said, kissing me on the cheek.

"Yeah, no one else needs to see that," I said. "Trust me."

"I've read your work, Noah," Gary said. "There is so much heart and soul and good 'ol southern life in it. I like it."

I was honestly touched by the fact that Gary had read something I'd written.

"Thanks, Gary. I'm sure I must have used something you did somewhere."

"Then I would like my cut of the royalties, please," he said.

"Wait 'til you read some of his new stuff," Naomi said. "Still southern in style, but you'd be surprised how his views are changing on certain things."

"Took a nice Jewish girl to get me to open my eyes," I said.

"Then, honey, I'm buying you another drink," Gary said to Naomi as he flagged down the waiter.

"So, how are things at the salon?" I asked.

"Sold it. You are now looking at a high-paid hair stylist on *One Life to Live*," Gary said.

"I love that soap," Naomi interjected. "Whose hair do you do?"

"Sorry, I can't give away the secrets of the stars," Gary said with a wink. "It's in my contract."

More laughter, followed by more cocktails. The four of us could not stop chattering, as if we had all known each other for life. I was glad to see Gary had let go of the salon, which I'm sure reminded him of Jacob. But even more, I was amazed that the words *Jacob* or *Jake* were never mentioned throughout the entire dinner.

***

The next morning, I got to relish in one of my favorite pastimes, as Naomi walked around in my old George Strait concert t-shirt. The last concert I saw before leaving Nashville. She was sex personified and classy all at once.

"What are you smiling at?" she asked.

She sat like a bird, perched on a chair eating a bowl of cereal, one leg folded under her and one leg bent, holding that delicate arm with the spoon in her hand.

"I'm not allowed to smile at you?" I asked in a playful way.

"You can look at me any way you want."

I noticed her empty juice glass and went to the fridge to get her a refill. I loved waiting on her. Because she never once asked me to. Or expected it.

"I'm going to see my brother today," I said.

"Maybe you need to get a massage first."

Naomi had quite the sense of humor.

"Do I get that tense when I meet with him?" I asked.

She nodded vigorously. "You come back pretty wound up," she said. "Don't let it get to you so much. He's happy. Your friend Gary is happy. Just let it be."

"But I can't understand why he's living this life."

"Look. We've discussed this with Tony and Rich," she said.

Tony and Rich was a gay couple who lived in my building. Naomi and I had enjoyed several get-togethers with them.

"They say there are some gay men that believe they can change, though it's not right for everyone," she continued. "So if it's right for Jake, let him be."

Naomi gave me some balance whenever I tried to make sense of my brother's life. We would have many conversations on that one.

She crossed into my bedroom to get ready for her shower. I watched her silhouette as she undressed.

"Oh … I meant to tell you," she said. "Huge family gathering on the Island this weekend. Are you game?"

This was the way she mentioned meeting the family? As an afterthought?

"I'm supposed to think about your family while you're standing in my bedroom naked?" I asked.

Naomi glided into the bathroom. "As long as you don't think of my family naked."

God she was sexy. When she made love to me, it was as if the world was coming to an end. She could go all night and on some occasions, she did. The previous night had been a particularly long session after all our drinks with Gary and Roger. We had mauled each other the moment we came home and her clothes were all over the floor from the striptease she had performed for me. My dick still ached a little this morning from the way she rode me until the wee hours of the morning, but it was all completely worth it.

Wearing nothing but that beautiful smile, she blew me a kiss and disappeared beyond the bathroom door. One of the things I loved about our sex life was how varied it was. Unlike with previous girlfriends, Naomi could make quiet, soft love or have racy sex and both were just as exciting to me. This girl had me hooked.

I grabbed the New York Times crossword and sat to wait for her to get out of the shower. I felt so calm with her. I had no fears of meeting her family. Nothing could be odder than my own. Even though I would talk with Naomi about my brother, my relationship with Jacob remained the same. Careful caution. We were plenty nice to each other, but I sensed my brother changing more and more.

Six down. A word for domineering person. Thirteen letters.

As I thought of the word to fit into the puzzle, more images of my brother filled my head. Jacob seemed to have gone from sharing God's words to rewriting them and calling them his own. While I had never gone to his church, I had been in Jacob's home when Rachel or someone else from the congregation was around.

I noticed how Jacob would tell "his flock" that God spoke directly to him. Not just what to do in his own life, but about others and how they should live, what they should do. A stranger might easily assume that his heart may have been in the right place … but I knew this was the man who moved to New York to become famous. Perhaps he had gotten too old to continue the life of a model and just maybe that was why he gave up on that life the way that he did. But either on a billboard in Times Square or from a pulpit at Radio City; I knew Jacob would always strive for fame.

As I heard Naomi singing in the shower, I filled the word into the thirteen squares on the puzzle.

Authoritarian.

It was one of those rare moments at my brother's place where Sam was out with the kids and it was just the two of us sitting in the apartment drinking soda.

"My brother. A published author of three books now," Jacob said, sounding like a proud papa.

"With a fourth in the pipeline, but who's counting," I said.

We both laughed, but I had to admit, I was still baffled by the fact that people were buying my words on pieces of paper.

"Maybe I could have a shot in my soda?" I teased, but Jacob knew it was a joke.

"Mama would have been so pleased with you," Jacob said.

"You know, I sometimes think the same thing. As much as we fought, I know she'd be thrilled for me."

"Of course she would be. She only wanted the best for her sons."

I looked around Jacob's apartment. It had seemed so large when Jacob and Gary lived here. Now it seemed cramped and over run with strollers, kid's toys, and mountains of clothes.

"Do you have the best?" I asked.

"I'm very content with my life," he said.

"It's very different from what you had with Gary," I said with a smile.

"Yes. It is satisfying. I haven't heard from Gary, but I'm sure his life is nowhere as fulfilling as mine."

"No. He's doing great with Roger," I said.

Jacob looked at me as if he had been punched in the gut, perhaps an affront that I would know something about the man he had spent so much time with.

I could sense Jacob's disapproval, so I backpedaled.

"I ran into him on the street last week," I said.

I didn't want to mention that we had followed it up with dinner.

Jacob paused for a moment as if he were deep in thought and then said, "Well, I can only hope he has not been hit by that plague that is wiping out that community."

I do think my brother was being sincere with those remarks so I had to share some of the knowledge I had on the subject.

"They say people are already doing well on certain drugs," I said. "That's what my friends tell me."

Jacob gave a nervous laughed, seemingly trying to distract himself from thoughts of Gary.

"Who would have thought that my brother, the one who would tease and taunt me for being gay, would end up with gay friends," he said.

"You can't have an apartment in New York City and not end up with one or two," I said.

And deep down I had a feeling that Gary and Roger would become more a part of my life now as well.

"I love that aging has been able to bring us closer," he said.

I wasn't sure how close Jacob meant. I still sensed a wall, perhaps erected by me because of my brother's life, but a wall nonetheless.

"Let's not discuss that please," I said. "I get enough of that from Naomi. We've only been dating about eight months now and I get the

... when are we going to settle down? We're not getting any younger!"

"You should settle down," he said. "Have some kids. My children are my life."

Odd comment from my brother who didn't seem completely connected to his kids.

"Sam did push out some pretty good ones there," I said.

"Hey ... I think I had a little to do with it," Jacob said with a smile. "At least their good looks."

"I just never thought ..."

"What?" he asked.

Maybe we could talk. Why not? Jacob had always talked to Mama. And I had discovered a different side of myself as writer.

"When did you know you were gay?" I bravely asked.

"Probably junior high," he replied matter-of-factly.

"Do you believe you were born that way?"

"God no. No one is born that way," Jacob said. "It's environment, or a traumatic experience."

I was impressed with the two of us. This was going better than I had thought it might.

"Which was it with you?" I said.

"Remember Uncle Rick?" Jacob asked.

Uncle Rick. An army guy who ran his entire home like he was still in the service, his wife and children on a strict schedule and everything top-notch and spotless in his house. He was also a huge jokester, tried hard to be the funny one in the family, but he tried way too hard.

"I hated that guy," I said.

"Yeah, well … he took a liking to me early on," Jacob said. "There were times when we'd be over their house, and you all would be off playing … he'd always want me to go into his study to help him with things."

"Jacob, you're not saying —"

"I didn't know what was going on," he continued. "I think I knew it was wrong, but I also liked how it made me feel. So I went with it. And there was usually some sort of treat that it ended with. Candy, money … and always the warning … this is just between us. Don't tell anyone. They won't understand."

I felt terrible. How could my brother had gone through this alone and told no one?

"I'm sorry," I said.

"For what?"

"For not being there to protect you."

"You're *my* baby brother," he said. "I was supposed to protect you."

"Still … I could have done something. If he were alive, I'd take the first flight there and kick his ass."

"It's the past, Noah. No big deal. It made me who I am today and I'm grateful for that."

"So … that's why you believe you are gay?" I asked.

"I'm not gay."

"I mean, were … or thought you were … oh hell, I'm all confused with this. Sorry."

Jacob smiled at me in an all knowing, preacher-man way.

"No need to worry about it, Bubba," he said. "I'm fine now. And I'm here to help other people out of that darkness."

So we had done it. We had managed to have a real conversation that did not end in a fight. I guess we were growing up.

"So you gonna read my new book?" I asked.

"If you visit my church," he countered.

"Ouch. Guess fair is fair. I'll come to church, you read my book and give an honest review," I said.

"Deal."

Part of me couldn't believe that my own brother had never read one of my books while his ex-lover already had. But it was obvious that Jacob had issues confronting the past. Even in the cold way he had told me the story of our uncle. He seemed to be a master at removing himself from it, while I was all about embracing it. For a moment, I thought of confronting him about it, but just as I was about to get on one of my soapboxes, the front door opened and a tornado came through it as Samantha walked in with the kids.

"Uncle Noah!" Mikey screamed.

And just like that, I became a human climbing tree with two small rugrats, two kids who would never be here had my brother not gambled with God. Some miracles are worth it.

CHAPTER THIRTY-ONE

NOAH

It was Saturday morning on a chilly fall day at the end of another decade. I don't know how in the world I had allowed my brother to talk me into assisting at a soup kitchen at his church, but here I was in an old timey church kitchen, surrounded by members of his congregation. I refused to attend a service yet, but at least I could show that conservative Republicans had a heart when it came to feeding the homeless. The only person I knew there was Jacob's old manager Rachel — who seemed to get more "Holier than Thou" every time I saw her. There was a young chick named Pamela with her and this pompous character actor named Byron. This guy was a piece of work. One of those actors in New York who believed he knew everything. A single man in his mid 40s, his arrogance preceded him, along with the bad hairline of plugs that never took. He also had a look of a leading man that had been frozen in time, so as never to age. Somewhere there was a picture of him, hidden in a closet like Dorian Gray. Jacob had filled me in that he had been involved with the church since its founding and had known Rachel even longer than that. He and Rachel were two of the deacons as Jacob believed in keeping people "like that" close to watch them. And using the word 'deacon' for this congregation really made me chuckle.

"It's amazing how many people show up for the soup kitchen each week," Byron said in a thunderous voice.

"Byron, it's just one more way for us to be reaching the derelicts in this city," Rachel said. "Jesus himself would be right out there in Straus Park doing the same thing."

I laughed at Rachel's response, which reeked of pomposity.

"You sound like Jacob," I said.

"Sweetie, I've been around that man for many years," Rachel said. "Guess he's rubbed off on me. But there isn't much I could tell you or Pamela. Her father is a preacher too."

"Yes. I was one of those in the church every time the doors opened," Pamela said.

"I grew up the exact same way," I said, counting out plastic spoons to place in the bags we would carry to the park.

Byron continued. "I was never one to find myself in a church. A summer of Shakespeare in the park or Chekov in regional theatre, but not a church."

"Stop trying to impress Pamela and Noah with your resume," Rachel said.

I threw him a bone.

"I am impressed, Byron," I said.

The four of us continued packing up the cart with the huge containers of soup. It meant getting the spoons, cups and plenty of salt packets together. Drug addicts loved their salt.

But Byron just couldn't stop his performance.

"I've always had a love for the classics," he said.

"Which is why he hangs around me," Rachel added.

"You are a classic *and* an original," Byron said.

"I still won't represent you … but thanks for the kudos," she said.

I had been told that Byron had been trying to get Rachel to be his manager from the day he met her; but she always cut him down. I thought I could use this time to learn more about the history of Christ Redeemer and what my brother had planned, so I changed the subject.

"Were you ordained a deacon here?" I asked.

Byron answered first. "We didn't have a ceremony …"

"We have female deacons, which is very progressive," Rachel added.

There wasn't much about this church that reminded me of the church from our childhood. It had been a while since I had even been inside a church, but I still wondered where Jacob was getting his rules from. Just appoint someone a deacon of the church and 'poof' it's done.

"I find it odd that none of you have gone through any training," Pamela said.

I was glad I wasn't the only one finding this place a little strange.

"Someday, I might become a minister like Jacob," Byron said in an unusually low voice, almost speaking to himself.

"That will mean time in seminary and away from the stage," Rachel chided.

"Jacob never finished seminary. I'm sure I can take a crash course as well. Performing on stage or at a pulpit. I was born for it."

Rachel laughed. "You big ham."

I was in awe of how little the two of them knew about organized religion, but now I totally got why Jacob wanted to keep Byron close at hand — to keep an eye on him. When I caught Pamela's eye. She seemed to be thinking the same thing.

"Man, I had a different experience growing up in the church," Pamela said.

"Honey, how do you justify your lifestyle with how you were raised?" Rachel asked.

Jacob had told me that Pamela was a lesbian, but was Rachel really going to attack the poor woman while we were volunteering?

"I don't need to justify it," she said.

Nice comeback.

"Jacob sure would prefer if you weren't living with Jeff and Lauren," Rachel added.

"We've been doing quite alright for a while now," she said.

Byron, of course, needed to interject his two cents as well.

"I've been meaning to bring that up at a church meeting," he said. "It doesn't seem right, especially if Jeff is a leader of the church." Jeff was the music minister, he explained to me.

This church was small with numbers dwindling all the time; which didn't make my brother too happy. Worse than in a small town like Nocona, it felt like everyone was in each other's business and in a big hurry to knock each other down. Building up the love, I thought. That's what Mama had taught us from our church. Not happening here. Suddenly, I wasn't so certain it had been a good idea to volunteer for this; and I was damn sure it would be my last gesture of good will at this place.

"Jeff and I were both raised the same way," Pamela said. "I like that we have similar backgrounds and can help each other as we deal with being gay Christians."

"Pamela, you can't have it both ways. You need to choose," Byron said in a scolding manner.

"Byron is right. Besides, Jacob is really trying to help Jeff turn from that lifestyle," Rachel said.

"I know Jacob is always on him about it, and I wish he'd stop," Pamela said.

"Jacob is doing what God has called him to do," Rachel said.

These people were crazy, I thought.

"You have been around gays your entire life in your business," Pamela said.

"You're right," Rachel said. "I have. And I love each and every one of them … and pray for them all."

"I don't see it as an issue," Pamela said. "I love God. God made me in his own image and yes, I happen to be a lesbian. So what? Does that take away from my faith?"

"The papers are saying lesbians are going to be very chic in the 90s," I said to lighten the mood.

Samantha walked into the church kitchen just at that time, which made us change the subject. I was surprised these people would have this talk right in front of me, but I guess this is how the group went.

"Noah! I'm glad to see you here," Samantha said.

I gave my sister-in-law a kiss and was glad to see a familiar face.

"We were just about to head out with this soup," I said.

"Those people will be really grateful for it on this cold day," Rachel said.

I looked around for the kids.

"Where are Mickey and Ronnie?" I asked.

"Jeff is watching them today," Samantha said. "They love having a guy around who will play all those games with them."

"Yes, Jeff is very good with kids," Pamela said, looking directly at Byron.

So if I could get all this straight, this church had a lesbian with a gay roommate and was led by a man who thought he was no longer gay. Yes, I definitely didn't need to be visiting here on a Sunday anytime soon.

Byron paid no attention to Pamela's remark, and instead went to Samantha's aid loading up a hand basket.

"Here, Sam," he said. "Let me get that for you."

"Oh … thanks, Byron," she said.

I saw something very telling at that moment. Byron smiled at Samantha as he lifted the huge pot onto a pushcart. This guy was flirting with my sister-in-law … the woman married to the leader of their church.

"You smell very nice today, Sam," Byron said, as he finished packing the cart.

Yes, I know flirting. I wondered if it felt good to Samantha. To have an honest-to-God straight man pay attention to her. I knew that Samantha was a woman who always had food stuck in her hair from her children or clothes that were never pressed because she just didn't have time. But someone noticed she had put on perfume today … even if it was this arrogant prick.

"I figured I needed to hide the mother smells that usually make up my scent," Samantha said with a smile.

There. It did feel good for her.

Rachel heard the last part.

"You are amazing, Sam," Rachel said. "You're always on the go and always have a wonderful glow about you."

I sensed embarrassment from Samantha when Byron chimed in.

"I couldn't agree with Rachel more," he said.

I'm sure Sam liked the compliment, but one thing I knew about my sister-in-law was that she hated being the center of attention. That was my brother's place. I decided to put a stop to this.

"Let's get this outside to all those cold hungry people," I said.

We took the soup and walked out into the wintry weather, ready to feed the insides of those that needed it, while some in our group would be reciting to them the word of the Lord at the same time.

***

I had now been with Naomi longer than I had ever been with any girlfriends — without taking breaks or breaking up in between. I loved that she could bring out the young kid in me. She actually traveled with me down to South Carolina when I had to do a book signing and we turned it into a mini-vacation. Or she was great at deciding last minute things. The previous New Year's Eve, we were sitting at home and she decided we'd head down towards Time Square. Before you knew it, we were bundled up watching the ball drop with thousands of people, but I felt like we were the only two there. It was just the effect she had on me. And she always kept me on my toes with new things.

I sat inside the synagogue with her like a frightened child. I wasn't sure what I was afraid of. I mean, I had spent so many years growing up in a church, and this was very similar to that. Perhaps I thought I was going to do something wrong and embarrass Naomi. There was nothing fancy about the place — scrolls with Hebrew lettering hanging on the wall, a small altar at the front for someone to be able to lead the group. I had expected some sort of huge temple with gaudy marble ceilings and ornate sculptures everywhere. But this was just a neighborhood type meeting hall.

I had taken the small cap they had given me and placed it on my head when I came in, like the other men had done. I watched Naomi for guidance on what to do next. The man at the front, who I assumed was the preacher, spoke as he held up some cloth.

"Barukh ata Adonai Eloheinu melekh ha'olam, asher kid'shanu b'mitzvotav v'tzivanu l'hit'atef batzitzit."

I looked at Naomi, who smiled at me in a way that said she knew it was hard for me to be here. But I had wanted to share part of her heritage with her, even though I knew she wasn't stricly observant.

Naomi whispered to me. "He just said a prayer. Blessed is the Lord who commanded us to wrap ourselves."

The man continued.

"Ma yakar hasd'kha Elohim, uvnei adam b'tzel k'nafekha yehesayun. Yirv'yun mideshen beitekha, v'nahal adanekha tashkem. Ki im'kha m'kor hayim, b'or'kha nir'e or. M'shokh hasd'kha l'yod'ekha, v'tzidkat'kha l'yish'rei lev."

I knew this was going to be a long day, listening to the man as he continued speaking in Hebrew which might as well have been Greek to me. Noami leaned in to tell me it was another prayer.

"You can give me a recap when it's all done," I said, not wanting to be a nuisance to her.

Naomi squeezed my hand as the rabbi continued. I stood and sat when everyone else around me did. I started to realize the rituals were no different from rituals that Southern Baptist do. Each Sunday, it was the same for me growing up. The first hymn. The welcome. Sharing of the peace. Accepting the offering. The sermon. The invitation. All religions must be used to their own methods and comfortable with them. I was happy to be sharing something with Naomi, which she had grown up with. While I had not returned to my own religion in years and years, I respected what she had grown up with. Besides, God already had a hold of one Garrett brother and I think he was doing enough for the both of us.

It was a call and response. I jumped in.

"Barukh ata Adonai," I said.

Naomi smiled at my broken Hebrew coming out of this big lug of a cowboy. But I knew my Long Island woman was very happy with this lug, and I was ecstatic to be with her.

CHAPTER THIRTY-TWO

JACOB

Sometimes, I felt that time was working against me as the clock ticked and the days, months, and years kept flying by. I had so many plans I wanted to accomplish with the church while I was still on this earth, but Satan would continue to test me. The city had turned into a nasty jungle that would try and wrap its vines around me. Temptation became a regular visitor whenever something would go wrong during my day. I was pleased that people viewed me as their true pastor. But I was not happy with our membership numbers waning, and with that, the funding for the church taking a nose-dive. Then my old friend Jack Daniels would call out to me from inside a liquor store as I would walk past; but I wouldn't give in. Perhaps it felt stronger in New York because you had to walk everywhere. Had I been in a car, the lure of alcohol and sex wouldn't nag at me as hard, I thought. But it was tantalizing and would cause me to forget my plan, my family, and my well-being.

I was also perplexed by how expensive New York was — something I never really noticed before. Rent. School for my kids. Insurance. Groceries. It all added up. Thank God Samantha's parents continued to send the kids money to help take care of them. It was some peace of mind knowing that she could handle the household while I worked on my career. At times when I felt like a failure or personal issues would start to overwhelm me, I would have to zero in on one thing to concentrate on. And at this moment, it was about certain members of this congregation continuing to do whatever they wanted — paying no attention to the incredible insights I was offering them.

Jeff had been living with Pamela and Lauren for two years; I had been unable to get him to move out or to denounce his homosexuality. The older he got, the less he seemed to need me or listen to me. He seemed to forget the fact that he had ever wanted to change from being gay and had even dated some guys in school. He was whizzing through his college years and coming into his own as a young man. Either figuring it out by himself or with the help of Pamela. As good as she was for the church financially; at times I believed I should cut her loose in order to truly save Jeff. I had already let too much time pass as it was.

Sitting in my office, I had thought long and hard about this phone call and knew that there was no more putting it off. I would use every way I could to get people to do what I knew was right, even if they didn't like my strategy. I knew God agreed with me. I had met Jeff's mother on several occasions when she had come to visit. She reminded me of my own family, so I knew I would be able to talk openly with her.

"Mrs. Golden, I understand you love your son," I said. "And I have loved having him here in my church leading the music, sharing his talents for over two years now. My entire family loves him, but you need to make him go back home to Tennessee."

The voice was strong on the other end.

"Jacob, he is a grown man," she said. "I cannot make him do anything."

"Yes you *can* make him," I insisted. "You are his mother."

"Did you do everything your mother wanted you to do?"

She had me there. I have always done what I wanted. I never thought twice about leaving home. I decided to change the subject, away from my life.

"Jeff told me he came out to you when he went home for a visit," I said.

"Yes, and I told him I loved him and accepted him as my son," she said.

I was getting frustrated now. God did not want her to accept it.

"He's in danger in this city," I said, knowing first hand all the sin this town had to offer. "It is like Sodom and Gomorrah here. He is just asking for trouble."

"My son is smart enough to make his own decisions," she said. "I will not tell him what he should and should not do."

Now I was getting very angry at this woman. Why wasn't she listening to me? Didn't she know that I was trying to save her from a life of misery? Didn't she know that I have the answers for her?

"Well then you obviously do not love your son as much as you profess," I said. "If you did, you'd have him on the next plane home."

"I appreciate your concern, Jacob, but I love and trust my son and have no intentions of interfering in his life," she said.

"I'm sorry to hear you say that, ma'am, but my God does not tell me to let up," I said. "I have been sent to share the truth with you and you just do not want to hear it."

With that, I hung up.

What a stubborn, southern woman she was. Here I was, a southern man who had already lived through it all, and she shuts me off. I knew the heartache and despair of being a gay man. Nothing good could come for her son. Nothing.

I bowed my head in prayer.

"Father, please be with that family as they continue to make terrible mistakes in their lives. Mistakes that will affect their son for the rest of his life."

My watch alarm went off. I opened my drawer, pulled out a pill bottle and took my pills.

My ringing phone interrupted so I swallowed quickly.

"Christ Redeemer Church."

It was Randall. He had gone to Bible Studies at Bill and Judy's years ago, but I hadn't heard from him since he left our church. And now he was calling for advice about if he should buy into his co-op. I had no idea why he was going on the way he was and what my thoughts on the matter really meant to him. But he couldn't stop talking, going in detail into the pros and cons.

"Randall, I appreciate you turning to me as someone who walks with the Lord," I said. "You should always ask God what He wants before making such a large decision."

"That's why I need your help, Jacob," he said.

I didn't really have time to work with Randall now. I was still thinking about Jeff and how to handle his situation.

"Do you have a Bible near you, Randall?"

"Yes."

"Open it. Pray. Point to a verse and you will find everything you need right there to get you through this time."

I described everything to him that he needed to do. He read it to me, and I pontificated on what it meant. How it said he wasn't financially sound to buy into a building at this time. How the country wasn't stable since the stock market crash in '87 and how there was talk of a recession in this year. (I did listen to my brother when he would talk about some things). I fed Randell so many lines just so I could move on to my real problem. We said our goodbyes and I decided to do the same thing for myself.

I opened the Bible and pointed to a verse that I knew proved God wanted me to help Jeff.

If no one else would be honest with the boy, then I would. I was certain I was doing God's work, no matter how difficult the tactics might prove. I had lives to save.

***

It wasn't like the old times at Rachel's house, but when she came over to our place — we sometimes would reminisce about those times. Tonight she was there with Sam and me along with Byron. The four of us were waiting for Pamela and Jeff to arrive.

"You two had some past," Samantha said.

"I can't tell if it was a brother/sister thing or something more," Byron laughed.

"I always had the hots for this man, but he was way into other men back then," Rachel said.

"Everyone used to have the hots for me," I added, as the doorbell rang.

"And on that note, I'll get the door," Samantha said, the other two laughed.

"You were a real pain in my ass," I said to Rachel. "Constantly trying to get me to go back on auditions. And then fighting me on everything when I tried to share with you my plans for the church."

"Some of us are just slower, that's all," she said. "But I'm here, ain't I?"

"Looking a little gray, time to get some more red hair dye," I said with a laugh.

Samantha came back in the room followed by Pamela and Jeff. I had tried to make this as informal a meeting as possible by doing it at my apartment instead of the church. But I still knew exactly what I needed to accomplish.

"Thanks for coming you two," I said, hugging both of them. "Sit down. Sit down. Sam, can you offer our guests something to drink."

"Don't pull that women's stuff with me, Jacob," Pamela said. "Sit down, Sam. We know where your kitchen is."

Everyone laughed at Pamela, which immediately lightened the mood — even if the joke was at my expense.

"We wanted to have a small meeting about some things going on at the church," I said.

"And outside the church," Byron added.

"Byron," I said with a glare that told him to be quiet.

"Is this about our financial issues?" Pamela asked.

"No. What Byron means is the fact that you guys are holding Bible studies in your apartment. We, as the elders of the church, do not feel it is such a good idea."

"Why?" Jeff asked.

"You know why, Jeff," Byron said.

"Byron!" I said.

The man just wouldn't shut up.

"We really thought we were doing something useful for the church," Pamela said. "Adding more time during the week for people to get together."

"We think it's best for people to get the Lord's word inside our church building, instead of at your apartment," I said.

"This from the man who used to meet on a sidewalk in front of Radio City?" Pamela asked.

I let out a small forced laugh, as the others waited for my response. She shouldn't be questioning how I chose to do things.

"I know it must seem odd, but it just makes the most sense for our congregation. You understand."

"Oh … you mean the twenty people that attend the church might be offended? All twenty of them," Pamela said, starting to get hostile.

"But some of them have been in our apartment," Jeff said. "I don't think they have a problem."

"It's not right, Pamela," Byron said. "You are both gay and it seems like we are condoning that lifestyle by having meetings at your place."

"You are kidding me, right?" Jeff said. "Our church has a gay man … sorry … ex-gay man as pastor."

"The important part there is the *ex*," I said, noticing that Jeff was sounding more like Pamela every day.

Why was Pamela being quiet and just staring at me? I was starting to feel uncomfortable in my own home.

"You can't compare that to Jacob's life," Rachel said. "Jacob has a powerful message to share. An incredible story that others want to hear."

Finally Pamela decided to speak.

"Is that why you did it?" Pamela asked.

"What are you talking about?" I asked, not sure I wanted the answer.

"Is that why you made your change — just so you would have a story to tell to everyone later in life?" she said.

Everyone in the room grew very quiet, as I looked into the lesbian's eyes. I wasn't sure if the question was truly from her or if Satan were using her to test me. Did she know how much I still fought daily? Had Jeff broken my promise to me and told her anything about our time together?

"God moved in my life," I said. "I was standing at the very gates of hell and God pulled me back and told me to turn to Him."

Pamela stood up. "I'm not feeling the greatest love coming from this room. I think I need to leave."

I noticed Jeff starting to stand as well. I did not want to see him walk out my door. There was so much potential in that young man. God had so much planned for him.

"Jeff, you can stay," I said. "You do not have to leave."

Jeff looked at Pamela and then around the room to each of us. I could feel his struggle.

I tried to send him a message with my eyes. Pleading for him to sit and stay with us. I did not want to lose him from my life; from the church.

"I think … I think I need to go and pray about this," he slowly said. "Sam, can you tell the kids hello for me? I'll talk to you tomorrow, Jacob. Is that alright?"

I couldn't answer him. I was afraid of saying the wrong thing, so I said nothing. I watched my project walk out of my living room.

Pamela and Jeff walked towards the door, Samantha right behind them to see them out. I didn't know if I was angrier at the two of them or at Samantha for staying so quiet.

"What is wrong with those two?" I said. "Why do they not see the wicked, wicked ways in which they are living?"

"It took us a while," Rachel said, rubbing my arm.

"I understand Pamela may be a lost cause, but Jeff should know I'm just trying to make it easier for him?" I asked. "Why can't he get that?"

"They haven't lived the life you have," Rachel said. "They haven't needed to rely on God in the same way."

Samantha walked back into the room and stared at me. I wasn't sure what her eyes were trying to say — but I didn't feel good about the level of support in this room.

***

Rachel had stopped by our apartment to visit with Sam, which she would do on occasions as she enjoyed mothering us both. I was tired of hearing Rachel badger me about how frail Samantha was looking. She would go on and on about how drawn her face was and how worn down she looked. I knew. I saw the change in both of our faces, but sometimes ignoring things was how I got through the day. I tried not to listen to them in the kitchen, while they had their tea, but

I felt I needed to pay attention to these conversations. I was worried Rachel may give Sam the wrong information about something and I needed to deflect, worried really about anything wrong she might say.

"Rachel, I find I'm tired all the time," Samantha said.

"Sam, it could be from the medicine," Rachel said. "I've been reading about it."

I really didn't appreciate Rachel giving her two cents on this. I stayed in the other room, strategizing when to walk into the kitchen.

"The medicine. A son and a daughter to raise. A house to keep clean. A church that is simply not growing, which means very little income. Health insurance we can barely afford."

Samantha tried to lower her voice when she spoke, and I pretended to be busy in the other room, but I could sense the fear in my wife's voice.

"The congregation should be helping you all more," Rachel said. "Perhaps if they knew what you were going through."

"No! I don't want to be anyone's pity project," Samantha said. "We made this bed, we'll lie in it."

A twinge of guilt shot through my body. I could sense this was not the life my wife thought she'd be living at 39. I had told her things would get better, but she kept waiting for that to happen. I would often remind her that God would not want us to wallow in our misfortunes, but there were times I would wallow in it myself. There were times the past seven years when I wondered what all of this new life had been for. I thought I was doing what God wanted. He had saved me in that bathroom. He had sent Bill to my life to talk me away from my homosexuality and he had sent Samantha to me to love. But I wasn't hearing much love from the other room. It was time for me to join them. I walked into the kitchen in a jovial manner.

"Look at that," I said. "My two favorite women."

I kissed Samantha on the cheek and patted Rachel's shoulder as I went to the sink to get a drink of water.

"I went downtown this morning to meet with a potential funder for the church," I said. "Let's hope something comes of it."

"When you think back to the amount of money you used to make," Rachel said.

"If I stop to think of that, I'd be asking you to send me on an audition right away," I said.

Samantha pointed out the obvious with, "Neither one of us has the looks we used to … sorry, sweetie."

I knew that sentence was laced with blame.

"I spoke to Jeff's mom about getting him out of the city," I said. "She wouldn't listen."

"Well, it's her son," Samantha tried to start.

"But Sam, God has specifically told me to work with that boy," I said.

"He's not really a boy. He's twenty-one," Rachel said.

I didn't like the way Rachel had looked at me. It reminded me of the old days when she would sometimes get judgmental about the guys I had been with behind Gary's back. But I was not sleeping with Jeff.

"Don't you think you've invested enough time in Jeff by now?" Sam asked. "It seems a little obsessive."

It was time for me to let both of them know the decision I had come to, the secret that Rachel had kept from the church and from most people. It was time to let it out.

"I'm going to tell him about us," I said.

"Jake, no. You can't. He could tell others in the church. It could get out," Samantha cried out.

"I want him to know what could be in store for him," I said.

"Sam is right. You don't need to let him know about it," Rachel said, putting her hand on Samantha's arm.

"Rachel, he's not going to tell anyone else. And if I think it's the best thing to do, then it will be done. You both understand?" I said.

Rachel looked at Samantha with a face full of questions and concerns. But it wasn't for her to be concerned about. It was our health, our decision. It was my choice to decide who knew and who didn't.

"Sometimes I see the same man that I witnessed years ago at an audition I was working at," Samantha said.

"What do you mean?" I asked.

"I saw you, Jacob. When you were a nasty person. There may be no drugs now, but at times that same cutting man comes out."

"I'm not trying to be nasty," I said. "I'm just telling you what it is I plan to do."

Samantha stood up walking into the other room and said, "Go ahead, play God with both our lives. It wouldn't be the first time."

I stared at the doorway Samantha had passed through.

"Let her go. She's just having a hard time right now," Rachel said.

"If she wants to be angry, let her be angry at God, not at me. God brought us together," I said.

Now I had confused Rachel, who wasn't sure how to respond to that statement.

"I better get going," she said. "Anything I can do for you now?"

"I'm not an invalid, Rachel. I'm fine," I snapped.

Rachel left without saying anything else. I could hear her walking down the stairs and could hear my wife sniffling in the other room. I knew I should go to her, but I was unsure what to say. Suddenly the last five years were flashing before my eyes.

The fairy tale proposal. The incredible picturesque wedding at the glorious chapel in her home town. The birth of my first son. How it all felt so wonderful, until that summer day. That terrible day. Sam was already pregnant with Veronica when it all unraveled. I had gone to my doctor for a simple test for cholesterol. Aging and all. He had mentioned the new HIV tests they were doing and suggested I get one — *better to know* he said. Stupid, stupid of me to listen to him. But thinking the doctor was right, and since he knew about my past, I went for it. Telling him I wanted to keep this between us. I actually had put the entire thing out of my mind by the time he called me to come see him in his office. I started off with some silly joke and he told me to sit down. I didn't really hear much more after that. I was completely blown away by the news. Never in a million years did I think something like that could happen to me. He talked of medications I could start right away, but I wasn't paying attention. I had to get away from there and left his office.

Life was moving along at home with Samantha planning for a little girl. Choosing clothes, glowing from the fact she was having a daughter — and what did I do? I became more distant towards her, aloof — throwing myself into growing the church. But being my wife, she knew something was wrong and eventually forced the awful news out of me. Why had she pushed me? The fear of telling her was almost unbearable.

"I never wanted to hurt you," I said.

This was never supposed to be part of the plan.

"I'm sure it's not that bad. And we live in a city where many people are dealing with it every day," I continued, trying to make the news less of a trauma.

"How long have you known?" she asked.

I wasn't sure she wanted that answer but I told her, told her as much as I could without completely destroying everything.

"A few months now," I said. "I didn't want to tell you. I don't want you upset while you are pregnant!"

"Good God. What about me and our baby?" she asked.

Terror shot through my veins as I stared at her that day. There was nothing I could say. All I could do was look at her and cry. Cry for her and our unborn child. Cry for what I had done to her because of my inability to let go of my past. Cry for myself. At that moment, her strength took over, and we would need it to get us through the next few months.

She did not want to go to her own doctor to find out. Instead, she went to the free clinic down in Chelsea where she could be tested anonymously. The waiting was brutal on us both. Not telling anyone what we were going through. But she still had to be the mother to Mikey and smile and pretend that everything was okay while at church. Then to hear those dreadful words was more than either of us could bear. Learning about her status was much worse than hearing about my own. But somehow, we got through it. And she proceeded to carry our unborn child to full term and miraculously have a healthy baby girl who was not infected. Nor was our first son. Two positive people had created two lives that were untainted ... by the grace of God. And we had a beautiful family that was complete with the birth of a little girl.

I couldn't continue reliving that horrible scene in my mind and went to the living room and turned on the TV. I tried to watch *The Cosby Show*, sensing Samantha watching me from the bedroom doorway.

"So are you going to try and scare Jeff? Is that your plan?" she asked.

"I'll do whatever it takes," I said. I reached for the water glass.

"Jake, I'm really tired of all this," she said. "I think we should move closer to my folks."

"God wants me here, Sam. How could you ask such a thing of me? This is where He has told me to do my ministry."

"We haven't gotten any new members in over a year, you do know that, right?" she said.

Was that right? Was it time to finally give up on this city that had changed my life in more ways than I could ever imagine? It offered me freedom from Tennessee, riches and fame, a changed life, a wife and kids — and now dealing with a disease eating away at my body. Perhaps moving away from it would be best. But it was now a part of me. And I still had a chance to do one last amazing thing by being known as the man who brought God to this horrible place.

"We're being tested," I said. "God tests His most faithful. We're not the first and we won't be the last."

She walked behind my chair to pick up some of the kids clothes piled on the floor. I knew she was close to tears.

"I don't know how much longer …" she said, not quite able to finish her thought.

I put my hand up in the air to reach for her, but kept my gaze locked on Rudy Huckstable on the television. If I looked up, we would both start to cry.

"We'll take it together," I said. "Till death do us part. That's what we said."

Samantha took the clothes to the kids' bureau upstairs in the loft. I could hear her doing stuff upstairs, but she was through talking to me. I knew that both of us were thinking, "*How long is that gonna be?*"

CHAPTER THIRTY-THREE

NOAH

America was at war in the gulf, but the long war between the Gar-rett brothers seemed to be over or at least under an extended ceasefire. I kept my promises to my brother to come to his church … even if I did let over a year go by. But here I was on a Sunday morning. I decided not to bring Naomi, because I did not want her to think this represented all churches. I dressed in a sports coat and a tie, I guess to make Mama proud or something. I watched as people came in. There were about fifteen to twenty people in all. Some were dressed in Sunday clothes, while others had on jeans and T-shirts. My nephew and niece ran up and down the aisles like little monsters. They were cute though. The people I had met at the soup kitchen were there and the young man I had heard about led the music. There was the sharing of the peace, in which Rachel introduced me to a wonderful couple that I swore I had seen on some TV show.

What was this place? The religion hub for the actors union?

Then a man who had come down from the Abyssinian Baptist Church sat at the piano and sang *It Is Well with My Soul*. I remem-bered the song from my childhood. The lyrics of peace and content-ment touched me. For a moment, listening to the amazing man sing, I realized how content I was in my own life. Finally, after all those years of fighting my family and being unhappy, I had found a place where I could be at peace.

Now this is church, I thought; glad I had picked the day that he was here to sing.

The offering plate was passed during the song and then my brother got up to speak. He didn't look well. He was only three years older than me, yet he looked like he could be my father. I wondered if he had really found peace as well.

Was he doing drugs again and no one knew about it? I was concerned. Jacob addressed the congregation.

"That is one of my favorite hymns of all times. Thank you, Jimmy, for visiting from your own church and sharing your love of God with us through song. Can I get an Amen?" Jacob asked.

The few people responded, letting Jimmy know what a wonderful job he had done. Jacob continued.

"You know. Today is a special day for me. The prodigal son has come home."

I twisted in my seat, the ease I had been feeling slipping away. He better not embarrass me.

"My baby brother is sitting here in the house of the Lord, listening to his brother share a sermon," Jacob said. "Thank you, Bubba, for being here. Thank you for loving God. Thank you for loving me."

I felt my face turning red and thought, *Okay, okay … get on with it.*

"Too many people do not pay attention to what God is saying," Jacob continued. "They do not hear when He speaks. They are waiting for some huge miracle, but sometimes, God speaks to us through the smallest voice. Sometimes, it's not a flood, but a drop of rain.

Sometimes it's your preacher telling you what God wants you to do."

Again, people expressed their consent with Jacob. This was the new Jacob, of which I had already seen plenty. A man who wanted people to do what he told them to do, not just what God wanted. I gazed hard at a notch someone had cut out in the pew in front of me.

"Sometimes you need to walk away from things you feel are right," Jacob said. "You may think you're supposed to be here, in New York, but God may want you to be somewhere else."

This was confusing. Was my brother upset about me being here?

I saw the young kid who had led the music rustle in his pew. Pamela was sitting behind him and leaned forward to touch his shoulder. Jeff. Maybe this was about that kid and not about me.

Jacob continued.

"We all have things we love, but just because we love them, do not mean they are of God. I had an amazing life that I walked away from because it was not *of* God. I was on top of the world, but it was the wrong world. God showed me the way. God set me straight. God can lead each of us if we take the time to listen to Him speak."

Jacob flashed his famous smile at everyone, that toothy smile that had gotten him so far in life, that had given him the advantage in every fight with Gary, that got him to New York, that had been his ticket on many auditions and had made churchgoers follow his every word. But that smile had taken on a different look the past few months: more menacing than friendly. Others didn't seem to notice. They all continued to buy into whatever he was selling.

"And if you can't hear God ... just ask me," Jacob said. "I can hear Him fine. He talks to me about each of you and I have plenty to share."

I wondered when this would be over. While I had originally thought the place reminded me of home, I wished there was someone other than my brother leading the sermon at this point. But I had done what I said I would do. I came here to listen. To support. Now I just couldn't wait to leave.

CHAPTER THIRTY-FOUR

JACOB

Jeff sat in a chair in my office, and I perched myself on the edge of the desk in my usual position when he was in my room. But today had a much different feel to our visit. He couldn't hold back the tears from the story I had just told him. I knew that it was very confusing for him now, but he would grow to understand why I had shared it.

"You don't need to cry, Jeff," I said. "It's not a death sentence."

"I just don't understand how God could do this," he said. "You did what He wanted. You turned your life over to Him … you changed! But it wasn't enough. You still got punished."

"I don't see it as punishment," I said. "It's just a cross I bear, that's all."

"It doesn't make sense. How can you not be angry at God?"

"God didn't do this to me. My actions did."

"What about Sam?" he asked. "Her actions didn't do it to her. Why is she positive?"

"We don't have answers for everything … but one day, we will. And when I get to heaven, I'll ask my Savior for those answers," I said.

I wasn't sure if telling Jeff this news had helped the situation or hurt it. He had more questions about our medicines, how it affected my ability to lead and fear about my children. I tried to tell him that everything was fine. The kids were well, healthy, and negative. I could continue leading the church as always, but that I was using this as a warning to him. He needed to see what was in store for him if he did not turn from his ways.

"I … I need to go," he said, standing up. "I need time to process this."

I stopped him from leaving.

"Jeff, don't you think it's time for you to move back home?" I asked.

"I'm not finished with college yet," he said.

"But you should surround yourself with family, while you work with God on changing your life?"

Jeff paused before he spoke again. Was he thinking about what I had just told him? Had this story finally been the thing to get him to walk away from his lifestyle?

"Jake, I don't plan on changing my life," he said. "I'm happy with who I am. I fought this for so many years, but once I prayed to God and said, *This is who I am. This is who you made me to be. Thank you, God.* I was at peace with myself. A peace like I've never known through all the rough years."

The response made me angry. This young man was so thick-headed! How could he be so accepting of that life? But then again, how was I able to walk away from it so easily? He had found a way to accept being gay and still talk to God. No. It was wrong. I thought I had accepted it, but it would only lead to heartache. Everything I was working towards, the reason I was opening my life up to him, all to help him turn from his wicked ways.

"You are living a lie. It's not what God wants for you," I said as I turned my back on him walking away from the door.

"I am fine with it. I am happy as a gay Christian man. I don't feel I'm the one living a lie," Jeff said following me across the room.

There was the influence of Pamela once again. I had lost Jeff and he would surely be pulling away from me even more. No longer coming to see me for afternoon chats. His circle of friends would grow beyond what I could offer him. I was sad. I was hurt. I felt betrayed. But I still longed to have him in my life.

I reached out to touch the young man's shoulder.

"Would you care to pray with me?" I asked.

Jeff touched my hand on his shoulder.

"I think I better leave you to pray by yourself," he said.

I sat down in my office chair as he started to leave. He stopped for one last thing.

"I love you, Jacob. I do," he said.

Jeff walked over and kissed me on my cheek. My old sunken cheek that could not seem to hold much meat on them due to the drugs. But here was this handsome man showing such compassion for me. I couldn't allow the moment to take on the wrong tone.

"I love you too, Jeff. I can love the sinner without loving the sin," I said.

Jeff left the office and I began to pray.

"Heavenly father, please show that boy how wrong his life is. Shake him to his core so that he will see the true meaning you have for his life."

I was starting to fear that I would never get through to Jeff and save him from his wicked ways. The admission of defeat made me sick. I took out the pack of cigarettes from my coat pocket, opened the window and sat on the ledge. I lit the cigarette and hummed my favorite hymn.

Was all truly well with my soul?

Is this just Satan's way of testing me? Making me question the entire second part of my life, the life that God had not only designed but also facilitated. No, I couldn't think this way.

I finished the cigarette, popped in a breath mint, grabbed my coat and went out the door. My mind was racing with images from my past. So much had happened, but I trusted the Lord. I knew He had great things in store for me and I would prove to everyone that I could do those things.

I walked to the corner with every intention of going home. But something felt uneasy. Like I needed to get away. I went to 86th and Broadway, down the stairs and through the turnstile to the subway. I had no idea where I was going, I just wanted to go.

I got on the number 1 Local heading downtown and found a seat. A man walked from the opposite end of the train and sat across from me. He stared hard into my eyes. Why was he looking at me like this?

I looked at the man, average guy. Nothing exciting about it.

I looked away, out the window at how fast the train was traveling. Why wouldn't Jeff pay attention to what I was trying to tell him? Why would anyone in my congregation question me or my connection to the Lord?

I looked back at the man across from me. I couldn't believe it. The man now looked like a male model. Was this the same guy as before?

It was.

Same clothes, same intense stare at me. He was gorgeous now. How could that be?

The man smiled at me and gave a small wink. I looked down at my shoes and began to pray.

"God, take this temptation away," I prayed.

I looked up again and swore for a split second, the man had a head of a beast. Just as I had thought. This man was Satan tempting me. The beast licked its lips. I lowered my head again and shut my eyes.

"Lord ... I call on you to remove Satan from me. Take him from my sight," I said. "I love you and only you."

I opened my eyes and the man was gone. Anyone else would have assumed that they had imagined the entire thing. But I knew better. Satan was always tempting me. I knew there were forces that did not believe in my plan, my mission for New York.

I also knew I needed to get home to my wife.

I got off the train at 42nd Street, crossed over to the uptown side and waited for the next train, keeping my eyes on the tracks below.

***

Lauren had come to me asking about her living situation with Pamela and Jeff. She had been away on the road performing in a National Tour of a show and was never even in their apartment much. But being home, the two of them had talked to her about my issues of them living together.

"So how do you feel about it?" I asked, not wanting to set her off too quickly.

"I'm surrounded by gay people on the road, so I hadn't thought of it as a problem—"

"But what do you think God thinks of it?"

Lauren got quiet.

"I think He might think it's wrong," she said.

I smiled feeling confident that someone around here understood where I was coming from.

"Absolutely. It is. But you don't have to live in sin with them," I said.

"I just don't know how to get out of it without hurting them."

Part of me wanted to hurt Pamela for the crap she was feeding Jeff, but I couldn't let on that I felt that way.

"You don't have to hurt anyone," I said. "You make decent money on the road and you have to go back out again, correct?'

"Yes."

"Then just tell them you are putting your belongings in storage. It will cost you less money and you can save while you're on the road. An added bonus to doing God's will," I said with a smile.

I knew I had her and I was pleased. So happy that people in my congregation trusted me and believed in what I told them. And that some of them knew the Lord's will and could follow through on it, even if it took a little coaxing on my part. It was still all God's overall plan.

CHAPTER THIRTY-FIVE

NOAH

I missed Naomi every time that I smelled her Trésor perfume and saw remnants she had left around the apartment. She was spending more time out on Long Island, because her father was ill. While she didn't believe in everything that her family did, she knew she needed to be close to her mother and father during this time. I knew what it was like from when Mama was sick, so I thought it was smart of her to be there. Her father seemed to be doing a little better, but one could never be too sure.

Today was a busy day. It started with a meeting with my agent. I just needed to let her know how even these years later, I still felt like the odd man out when we were sitting in a meeting with a publisher and editor. Even though everyone in the room was discussing my baby, this dad could feel like the country bumpkin in front of the city folk. Guess that's what they found appealing about my work though.

Next, I had talked Gary into going with me to meet an old friend in town from Tennessee. It seemed that whenever someone showed up in New York from back home, they assumed they had to call me. But this was different. It was Tricia Reynolds's little sister and I had promised to have lunch with her. Good thing Naomi was not the jealous type. I knew if the roles were reversed, I would have been right by Naomi's side as she went off to lunch. Gary would be playing the part of the doting girlfriend in Naomi's absence.

"I really can't thank you enough for coming with me," I said.

"I think it's cool you are checking out your old girlfriend's sister," he said with a laugh.

"Hey, don't even tease," I said as we walked into the diner on Park and 23rd.

I strained my head, searching for someone who might look like Tricia. There, in the corner, were three beautiful women. Each was more beautiful than the other, long hair, long legs and six of the largest breasts I had ever seen. One of them waved me over.

"Naomi is going to kill you," he said as we joined the ladies.

"Noah! It's so great to see you," said one of the women.

"Suzy?" I asked.

"In the flesh," she said. "And this is Amber and Margi."

"Hello, ladies," I said. "This is my friend, Gary, He also lived back in Nocona years ago."

"Sorry to hear that," Suzy said.

"At least I got out," Gary said as we sat down.

Had I stepped into a porn movie and no one had told me?

"Sit down," Suzy said. "I want to hear all about what it's like living up here."

I was still a little stunned. These three perky women were giggling and talking and had more energy than I could muster.

"It's great," I said. "I've had several books published …"

"That is so cool," Amber said. "A real author."

Gary looked at me with eyes that screamed "oh my God" — so

Amber was playing into the dumb blonde thing a little too easily.

I smiled at her. "It is … it is pretty cool."

"He's actually a very accomplished author," Gary added.

Someone walked over to take our orders. It was an evidently gay waiter and this table was completely lost on him. He was too busy putting all his attention on Gary. I was hoping at least some straight guy would see me with these beautiful women and feel a twinge of jealousy. They each ordered and continued talking about Nocona and New York.

"So what brings you all up here?" I asked.

I didn't realize what I was walking into.

"Well all three of us met in Nashville, at a dance club where we all worked," Suzy said. "We found out we could come up here once a month and make a shit load of money at the Repo Lounge."

The Repo Lounge was a Gentleman's Club that was pretty upscale, despite its name. So my mind had been in the right place when I sat down after all.

"You dance?" I asked.

Suzy started laughing.

"You should see your face," she said.

The girls laughed.

"I've been dancing since I got out of college," she continued. "Amazing money. Five grand in this one weekend."

"That's the way to pay for college," Gary said.

I was in the wrong business.

"Does your mother know?" I asked.

"Let's just say my family knows as much as they want to know,"

Amber said.

"But Suzy ... I was there in your family room when Tricia taught you and your friends moves for your 6th grade dance recital," I said.

Suzy broke out in more uproarious laughter.

"Trust me, it's nothing like that anymore," she said.

"Wow, I'm a little in shock. Sorry," I said.

Margi broke in. "It's no big deal. We're not ashamed of it."

"No, you shouldn't be," I said, trying to make up lost ground.

"You should come watch us," Suzy said.

"Yeah, Noah, we should do that," Gary said, as I hit him on the leg under the table.

Now there was a thought. I would just tell Naomi, while she's out on Long Island with her sick father, "I'm just going to run off to a strip club to watch some old friends dance." Never.

"I have plans all weekend," I said. "Thanks, though."

We continued talking and eating ... and wow, these girls could eat. I guess they got plenty of exercise at work.

"How is Tricia?" I asked.

"She's married with three kids and working at K-Mart," Suzy said.

It was a little shocking to hear that that's what had become of Tricia. Such a different life from mine. Yet I knew I was in a much better place.

"We don't even have a K-Mart in New York," Gary said.

"I know, it is way better here," Amber said.

After everyone finished off a piece of cheesecake and the girls insisted on paying for lunch, leaving a wad of bills on the table, Gary and I said goodbye and headed away from them, out the door. Once outside, Gary broke out in huge laughter.

"What the hell was that?" he said, barely able to control himself.

"I had no idea that was what we were walking into."

"I still say we should go see em dance," he said, as we walked down the street.

"Why don't you go without me," I said.

"They don't have the right parts," he said.

"It's obvious we can't ever go back. I can only assume that Tricia is having a great life as a mother and is content—"

"Her little sister sure is perky," he said.

"It's so great to see you so cheerful," I said. "I'm just so glad your life has worked out so well."

"You said it. We can't ever go back."

We walked in silence for a moment and I knew Gary was thinking of Jacob.

"How is he?" he asked.

"Honestly, Gary — he's completely fucked up."

"That's not what I wanted to hear. I really do want to know he is well."

"So do I," I said.

"Well, gotta get to my volunteer work at GMHC, so I'll catch ya later," he said giving me a hug.

"You're a good man for having your job and still doing volunteer stuff too."

"You can join me anytime you like," he said. "Next time I go to Fire Island to hang posters, you're going with me."

We said our goodbyes and promised to get together with our

other halves when Naomi returned. At least some of us were happy. I know I was. Happy I had left that world where I would have continued being a maintenance man until I was sixty. Happy I had gone into the bookstore on the day I met Naomi. And happy that I had a wonderful woman who did not see a reason to put implants in her chest.

CHAPTER THIRTY-SIX

JACOB

I had invited Rachel and Byron to our apartment, not to corner Samantha, but as deacons of the church. I needed their support in my decision. I wanted to have a representative from the Gay Men's Health Center come to our congregation and answer questions about HIV and AIDS, make them understand that I was really fine and that they were okay by being around me. Get them to stop talking about my health and causing harm and conflict for God's work. Samantha wasn't blind to all the questions being asked. I knew she didn't agree with my reasons for announcing our personal problems to the congregation, so I had to get her to see things my way.

"I just don't understand how telling them is going to help us," Samantha said.

"This is the 90s," I said. "People are not as scared of the words HIV and AIDS."

"That's what you're hoping, Jacob. What if they are? What if they all turn against you?" she said in a panic.

"That won't happen," I said. "God won't let it. And He told me it's time to get this out in the open, so that it is not an issue. It's time to let them all know."

Rachel stepped in to help me.

"Sam, honey, listen to Jake," she said. "He's trying to help you both."

That's the first time I recalled Rachel calling me Jake since my new life. Must have been a slip of the tongue.

Sam wasn't buying it, at all. "Rachel, tell me how this will help."

Rachel continued. "People cannot be afraid of what they know. You will have the support of a broader community. Won't that make you happy?"

Samantha's face looked distant, as if walls were closing in around her.

"Right now, I don't know what will make me happy," she said.

I tried to continue in a soothing voice.

"You're just scared, honey. But I'm telling you, it will be no different than Rachel and Byron knowing."

"This is our lives, Jacob! *Our* lives," she said. "Not the congregation's! Why would God want them to know?"

"To give you solace, sweetie," Rachel said, matching my soothing tones. "To give you peace, knowing that you are not carrying this burden alone."

Samantha tried to hold back tears.

"But it is my burden, Rachel," she said. "I have to carry it. For some unknown reason, God chose me to be the one —"

There it was. My wife's true feelings about our relationship.

"The one to marry me," I finished the sentence for her.

"That's not what I meant," she said. "I'm just very confused right now, so don't twist my words."

I couldn't allow her comments to hurt me. I know I had caused her a lot of pain, and right now, I needed to keep my mind on the task at hand.

Byron put his arms on her shoulders, trying to offer some sort of comfort to her in this trying time.

"I think the four of us should pray on this right now," he said.

"Byron is right," I said, taking control again. "Let's all get on our knees and pray to God."

I was down on my knees, followed by Rachel and Byron who began to pray. I knew Samantha's tears were going to fall at any moment.

"Sam, please!" I called out, lifting my hand to her.

Samantha looked down at me on my knees, pleading with her. There was an unspoken power that I knew I had in our relationship. I wasn't sure why, but she couldn't resist me whenever I made a request, no matter how much she didn't want to. But this time she resisted.

"Dear heavenly father," I said. "We need you in this hour, most precious Lord. Clear our minds. Clear our thoughts. Let us see and hear you."

Samantha stood there, fighting the urge to join us.

"Show Sam that it is your will that we allow others to know about the journey we are on," I said.

Rachel was reaching her hands up to God, while looking at Samantha, also pleading with her.

"Give her a peace in this decision," I continued. "Show her my heart. That I would do nothing to hurt her, that we only want to help her in this most trying time."

Rachel and Byron were adding in Amen's to God and swaying,

showing their support of my words.

Samantha finally fell to her knees and began to cry. She couldn't hold back all the pain, anguish, guilt and concern. Rachel began to cry as well. She and Byron held Samantha in their arms, as I continued my prayer.

"Yes, Lord," I said. "That's it. Bring her to your light."

Samantha started to add to the prayer, reciting one of her favorite hymns.

"*I need you, oh I need you. Every hour I need you …*" she sang.

I continued.

"Lord, I raise my wife to you. She is a pillar in our home, a pillar in our church. A constant to me, oh Lord, that I could never be without. Please open her heart to your words. Let her know of your love and my love and how she can benefit from by the love of others."

There, in front of us all, Samantha broke. There was so much uncertainty about why or how we had gotten here, but she was here. She crawled across the living room floor on her knees to my waiting arms. I looked at her with compassion and thought about the charm that had won her over when we first met. I know she truly loved me, even with all the heartache of our marriage. She clung to me, holding me and sobbing, while Rachel and Byron continued in prayer, circling me as I held my wife in my arms. The woman that God had led to me all those years ago and who still served Him daily, right by my side.

CHAPTER THIRTY-SEVEN

NOAH

Rachel had asked me to stop by her office. I had never really seen Rachel in her own element; I only knew her now around the church people. Jacob had mentioned she was starting to lose clients to other managers, but she stayed in the business. I guess in some strange way, she thought she could be a leader of the Lord's army with the entertainment world.

"It really meant a lot to your brother that you came to church last month," she said.

"I had to, Rachel, for him to read my book."

"Has he read it?"

"Not yet, but a deal's a deal."

"You Garrett boys and your deals," she said.

"He made the largest deal, don't you think?"

"Your brother hasn't been feeling well lately," she admitted up front.

So she had noticed it too. I was worried that maybe Jacob was taking drugs again, but Rachel assured me that wasn't the case. She explained how hard his job was at the church. Everyone seemed to turn to Jacob with every problem and placed all responsibility on his shoulders.

"Wait. If you called me over to get me to agree to become more involved with your church forget it," I said.

She laughed. "You really are as stubborn as your brother says."

"You bet your ass I am."

"Then maybe help at home. Take out your nephew and niece sometime, to give the two of them a break," Rachel said.

I smiled. I loved those kids and promised I would help out more.

"That I can do," I said. "Now let me ask you something. Why do you play the role of the Garrett mother so much?"

She stood up behind her desk indicating the meeting was over.

"Cause someone has to watch after you boys," she said.

We both laughed, and I shook her hand and let myself out the door. As I did, I passed Byron going in.

"Do all of you people hang out together all the time?" I said under my breath as I walked past.

Byron pretended I wasn't even there and went straight into Rachel and shut the door behind him. I could hear him through the door, as he mentioned my brother's name.

"Rachel, it's time for an intervention with Jacob," Byron said.

Something was definitely going on that no one was sharing with me. Rachel had clammed up in our meeting and now I would see if I could get any other information. I put my briefcase down, pretending to look for something in it, so I could listen.

"What are you talking about?" Rachel asked him.

"Jacob. The Church. Samantha. I think it's time to find someone else to step up to be a leader," Byron said.

"Stop right there, Byron Lodi! Jacob Garrett founded this church.

This is his place," she said.

Byron's tone grew immediately subdued. As a classically trained actor, I guess he knew the art of using his voice to get his point across very well.

"It belongs to all of us," he said.

"There isn't one person who will go against Jacob. The church will dissolve first," she said. "I'll be damned if I let his hard work go to waste."

I was beginning to sense some sort of power struggle.

"Do you realize the jeopardy we are in?" Byron asked. "There are too many things happening that could very well be standing in the way of God doing His will here."

"Byron, do you even have any idea what God's will is?" Rachel asked. "And if you did, do you have the first clue how to lead a group?"

Byron became defensive. "I didn't say I wanted to lead."

"I know what you're trying to do, and it's not going to work," she said. "Get out of my office."

Rachel's door opened and I tried to hide myself inside of some papers and my calendar.

"I am going to keep my eye on the situation," he said. "I don't want it turning into a mockery."

"Good bye, Byron. I have work to do," she said. "I have clients out there dying to do real theatre ... and it's up to me to get them jobs."

"Real theatre? What are you saying? Musical theatre is not real theatre," he said pointing to a show poster of the musical *City of Angels* hanging on her wall.

Rachel shut her door and Byron looked down at me sitting there.

I put my papers back into my briefcase and stood to leave.

"Trouble at the altar?" I asked.

"There are some things happening at your brother's church that I just don't approve of," he said.

"Hey guy, there's been things my brother has done for years that I don't approve of," I said, as I walked out in front of him.

I wondered what Byron was referring to. I didn't know Rachel well, but I knew you couldn't make outright demands on that woman. She adored my brother and whatever it was Jacob was doing, she was going to stand behind him, just like our mother had done for so many years. I wasn't sure what it was, but something was going on with my brother. I just wished I could find the right person to give me the information.

CHAPTER THIRTY-EIGHT

NOAH

My visit to see my brother was two-fold. I had known for six weeks that something was wrong, but no one was talking. I noticed how weak Jacob seemed. I had seen his face age considerably. But today, I also needed my older brother. Naomi's father had died and I wanted to talk to Jacob about it.

"I just feel so bad for her," I said. "He's been sick a long time, but to get a call out of the blue that he's gone."

"It's very hard to lose a family member," Jacob said in a solemn voice.

I thought back to Mama's funeral. His absence.

"In the Jewish faith, she has to sit Shiva," I said.

Jacob was suddenly wide awake.

"This could be your time now, Noah."

"What do you mean?" I asked.

"The patriarch of family is gone," he said. "Now is the time for you to marry Naomi and bring her to see Jesus' light."

I was completely thrown by this turn in the conversation.

"I just want to help her with her pain right now, brother," I said.

Jacob stood and started to pace maniacally around the room.

"Noah. God is talking to me. He's telling me to tell you to go to her. Propose to her right now."

"But her father just died," I said.

"And that's why you should do it now," he said.

"That's just crazy!"

"It's God's will. I'm sure of it. He wants you to do it," Jacob said. "To become one with her … finally to be her family."

I was very put off by this. Jacob didn't even seem like himself as he was saying it. I felt like I was in the room with a skinny, aging version of Jim Jones. The man seemed deranged.

"Jake … this is one time I just can't listen to what you're saying," I said.

Jacob looked deep into my eyes.

"It's not me! It's God talking to me … through me … trying to make you understand," he said, his eyes burning with intensity. I was beginning to grow afraid.

"Brother, I think your marbles are a little loose on this one."

"You are to bring her to Christianity," he raised his voice.

"Look. We've discussed marriage," I said. "We've even discussed how we'd raise children. We're both very open, progressive people. Yes, that's what I have become. We'd probably have a dual religious family."

"How can you say that? How can you bring up children in a world where you say Jesus is the son of God and we're still waiting for the Messiah?" Jacob asked, as befuddled as if he himself were a confused child.

I was getting frustrated. I had not meant to get into a religious discussion, not at this moment. I had only wanted to talk to my brother about the pain my girlfriend was feeling.

"Let's pray about this?" Jacob asked.

"No, Jake, I don't want to pray. Look. You can pray for her family … you can pray for God to give her peace during this hard time … but don't be praying that I'll marry her now and win one for the Christ man," I yelled.

I got up and left his office in a huff. It felt like Nocona all over again. Why was Jacob pushing me so much on this? The look in Jacob's eyes was scary. It was as if I had to convert her this instance, or everyone would burn in hell. Who the fuck had my brother become? I tried to put it out of my mind as I ran for the cross-town bus. I needed to decide on my own how to comfort Naomi and to show her that I was there for her during this tough time. Whatever she needed. Space from me or have me close by. She was going to get it. That's how much I loved her.

CHAPTER THIRTY-NINE

JACOB

I stared blankly down the hall as Noah walked out. I could not recall what I had been doing before. What day was it? The phone rang and me back on track.

"Hello, Redeemer Church …"

An annoying voice asked for Pastor Garrett.

"This is Pastor Garrett …"

More annoying questions about where certain promised funds were from Christ Redeemer.

"No. We don't give to that cause … because we are not associated with that ministry. Goodbye," I said, slamming down the phone.

I was tired of hearing from the association about my paper work in the convention. I never quite understood why my church had to be a part of a larger organization. I always managed to do what I wanted to do, without having to answer to anyone. I liked it that way. It's not like I needed a pope to tell me what I could and couldn't do in my own damn church. I was upset. I needed to get out. I looked out the window and noticed the sun was going down.

The sun was going down on me as well. No matter how much I fought, I knew everything was closing in around me. How did I get here? This was never the life I had intended when I left Tennessee.

Gary and I had a great life when we arrived. But my damn drive — that drive to succeed, to derange myself with others — pushed me away from him and doing things I had no business doing outside our relationship.

Thank God that He intervened when he did or I would be dead. But why was my addiction to men included in that tale of surrender to God? As many times as I would proclaim how I was a changed man, Jeff was right. I knew I was still a gay man trapped inside of this fake shell of a body. Living a lie daily that affected so many people around me.

The whole new life snowballed so fast; there was no way for me to get out of it now. If only I had stayed where I was. Then I never would have hurt Samantha in the way that I had. Why did I listen when others said I was to marry a woman? Why did I get caught up in this entire twisted world? That was never my intention. But there I was. Father of two, husband to a woman — and both of us dying. Nothing seemed fair. Nothing seemed right.

But I only had myself to blame.

I would never share any of those thoughts with another soul. They made me weak. They made me a failure. But they were true. No one else did this to me. I had just become so caught up in the life and the façade that I had kept this mask up for too many years now to ever remove it. And the strongest guilt of all hung over me.

I had cheated on Samantha once after we were married.

I thought perhaps if I just had sex with a man, it would jumpstart my sex drive to have sex with my wife. And Jake had reared his head and he won out that night in the struggle in my brain. I had gone into the backroom of a video store, met a stranger and had sex in one of those small, cramped booths in the dark. So the guilt was always there, haunting me daily, questioning if that was the time that I had been infected. Of all the hundreds of men before my marriage — that could have been the one to do it and I'd never know the answer. And to this day I still didn't. For years now, I have wrestled with that thought and have done my best to try and outrun the chastising voice in my head — but there was no let up from it. I was a bad person who had screwed up people's lives. People I loved — and I could not shake that thought. My own fault for pretending to be straight.

I put on my coat, walked out the door and went down the elevator. Instead of turning right out front to go home, I turned left and walked towards Riverside Park. I walked along the edge of the park watching the sunset over the water. This was cooling me down, bringing my temperature back to normal. Dusk looked beautiful as it shimmered on the water. I walked down deeper into the park where evening joggers passed me. I wished I had that kind of energy again. To go out for an evening jog.

And then I found myself in an area I knew all too well, a spot where men cruised for sex.

I knew I should not be here. I should be home preparing dinner with Sam.

But a familiar feeling came over me that felt … well … like home, like when you put on a pair of jeans that are worn in and the fabric knows exactly how to caress your body. I closed my eyes to remember what it used to feel like inside those jeans. That life. What if the last ten years of my life had never happened? What if Gary were waiting home for me right now?

What had become of Gary? Should I find him and let him know about my health? No. Nothing good could come from pulling the scab off of that wound.

I opened my eyes and saw a man standing against a tree. Obviously, he was not a jogger. I walked past the man very slowly, with more trepidation than had I ever had in my previous life. We both stared into each other's eyes and I my heart raced. No words needed. We both knew what the other was looking for.

I walked past him and went towards a bench. It was getting much darker now. What was I doing? Jacob, go home. But I couldn't. The sin had a hold on me and it felt good. I turned and went back towards the man, pulling out a cigarette.

"Light?" I asked.

The man pulled his lighter from his pocket and lit my cigarette.

"Thanks," I said.

Both our eyes pierced into each other. I took a huge drag on the cigarette.

As I exhaled, all of my morals, beliefs, and Christian way of thinking left my body with the smoke. I watched the man turn and walk towards the bushes. All the while, he continued to look back at me.

I looked around.

Was anyone watching? Was there anyone who would know me?

I walked towards the man and disappeared behind the bushes, waiting to see if God would talk to me from the bush, but God was doing no talking tonight.

***

I hadn't seen Jeff since he stopped coming to Christ Redeemer, but he had asked to meet me on this gorgeous spring day. He was just one more person that had dropped off our radar. We had about ten people showing up for church on a Sunday now. I blamed myself. My inability to control Jake from rearing his head and causing me to do things I no longer wanted to do. I was ashamed of my actions in the park the previous week. And I told no one. There was no one that I could tell. Being with that stranger had caused my body to ache for that kind of sex more, but I fought that feeling with every fiber of my weak being. I could not allow temptation to win again.

People could tell I was growing more feeble. Even getting around made it obvious. My children noticed it that Dad couldn't play with them. People on the subway would give up a seat to me. And Byron was trying to force himself on me to take on more responsibilities at church, but I didn't want to allow him to do anything. I started that church and I would see it to the end — no matter what.

I was sitting on the park bench at the carousel in Central Park thinking about how much my own children enjoyed coming there. The world seemed right as I watched them play. I saw Jeff walking towards me. He had grown so much older in the four years I've known him. The smile across his face was huge.

"I did it!" he said. "You are looking at a theatre graduate from Columbia."

I stood and gave him a big hug. It felt good to see him again.

"Congratulations, Jeff. Good for you."

"So now, it's just about getting out there and to start auditioning."

"That's a rough one, trust me," I said.

"They had such crazy rules about us not auditioning while at school — I just can't wait."

He told me all about his graduation. How his family had come up. We talked about everything except for Christ Redeemer Church or where he was attending church now.

"I wanted to see you, because I was sorry you didn't get to see me graduate," he said.

"We've been so busy—"

"No worries," he interrupted. "It's just that I feel there were things I never said to you that I wanted to say."

What was this kid about to say? Declare his undying love for me?

"I think you know what you've always meant to me," he said. "You helped me by just being you. I learned so much about life, God, family."

I didn't know what to say.

"And then you taught me about being angry at God."

What did he mean by that? I don't recall discussing that with him.

"I became so mad after I found out that you were positive," he said. "It didn't seem fair."

"Do you feel like walking?" I asked, wanting to hide any weakness in my body.

We began to walk north, past the bandstand towards the Bethesda fountain. I basically just wanted to change the subject, not talk about my health. Or God. Or so many things going through my head. I began to walk slower, so Jeff put his arm into mine to help hold me up a little. I suddenly felt like a grandfather. Gone was all sexual tension that I had ever felt with him. Instead, here was this man ready to take on the world, while I felt my life was slowly shutting down. Jeff talked all about school and what he had learned. His plans for his future. We walked across the bridge and I glanced over towards the Rambles and swore I saw the old Jake there, smiling that smile and waiting for men. Jeff continued walking me north to the 79th Street exit on the west side.

"I appreciate you calling me, Jeff. For seeing me and filling me in on your life."

"I appreciate you for being such a strong part of my life," he said.

"I better head on home. Sam will be waiting for me," I said.

Jeff reached into his pocket and pulled out a folded up paper.

"I wanted you to have this," he said. "I wrote this to God after you and I had our last talk and I've been holding on to it."

I took the paper, gave him a hug and wished him well. He walked down the street towards the subway and I turned to walk on home. I stopped, leaned against a building and opened up the paper in my hand.

I don't understand,
This cruel trick that you play.
Lives were changed and dreams were made,
But the best laid plans of men go astray.
He did what was asked.
Tried all that he could.
Said his prayers, raised a family
And lived his life the best he thought he should.
Now you tell me that's not good enough.
Now you're saying that there's more.

I know that things happen for a reason,

but what reason is this for?

Now you close your eyes to the problem.

Make believe there's nothing there.

I'm so confused, I don't know which way to turn.

Won't you tell me if you care.

I don't understand,

Why so many have to die.

Is this what you want,

Or is this all just another lie?

Help me understand,

I just give myself to you.

Open my eyes that I might see,

Exactly what you want from me.

Here is the riddle, where is the key?

Open our hearts and let us go free.

What is the reason that this must be?

Is my question Lord, to you.

I couldn't believe that I had meant so much to Jeff. Maybe I had done something for him after all, and I just never knew it. I went home asking God the same question.

What is the reason that this must be?

....

CHAPTER FORTY

NOAH

Talking to Pamela and Jeff was the best thing I could have done. Pamela didn't hold back any punches. As I had suspected, she felt things at Christ Redeemer were very much in line with what happens in a cult — much as I had thought there was some Kool-aid being passed around at that place. Any place where someone tells you what to think, how to feel, what God is saying to them about you — something is wrong. I felt guilty because it was my own brother doing all of this, but there were some in the group who were smart … and I was talking to two of them.

"So that's why we started visiting the church in the Village," Pamela said to me.

I looked around their apartment on the East Side. No signs of Satan. Nothing that seemed ungodly to me, and yet the church hated the fact that this kid lived with her. They were both gay — so it wasn't as if they were sleeping together, but something about it bothered that congregation, or maybe it was just Jacob. We listened to music from a group I never heard of called The Indigo Girls while we sat and chatted.

"You were very wise in moving on from there," I said.

"We don't mean to speak ill of your brother," she said.

"Don't worry. Really. I've had years with this man and not much can surprise me anymore," I said.

"That man lives on a story of a spiritual awakening in New York, this pipedream where he will be preaching at Radio City," she said. "The saddest part is, I saw a sign on the subway for a huge gospel rally happening there next month. First thing I thought was, Jacob's dream is coming true and he's nowhere near it."

My brother had always dreamed big. It brought him to New York and now he was still doing it, only under the guise of leading folks to the Lord.

"Part of my issue is him saying he's changed from being gay … or at least proclaim to have changed," Jeff said.

"Jeff, I never thought he changed," I said. "Even after he married Sam, I still thought he was gay."

"I could feel it. Every time we were in a room together," Jeff said. "He was still gay."

I couldn't help but wonder if my brother had ever made a move on him. Something made me feel bad for this kid. I knew my brother had made it his personal mission to change this guy around. But he was just trying to live his life and I think he enjoyed the work he had done with Jacob.

"I've always said you can be gay and still be a Christian," Pamela said. "And I think Jacob would agree with that, if he wasn't hiding behind a lie."

"Yeah, but Byron doesn't believe that," Jeff added.

"That guy gives me the creeps," I said.

"I think he's Satan," Pamela said in a tone that didn't make it sound like a joke.

"Maybe someone will drop a house on him," Jeff said with a laugh.

These two were good, solid people who could enjoy a joke now and then. They weren't robotic, like many of the others I had encountered at Jacob's church. It was nice talking to normal people about my brother.

"I've noticed my brother becoming more controlling," I said. "He did it to me in his office two weeks ago, trying to control my life with my girlfriend."

"He does it a lot, Noah," Pamela said. "I sometimes get scared when I look into his eyes."

I knew exactly what Pamela meant. I had seen it. It was a desperate need to get people to see things his way. But like Pamela, I also believed my brother was living a lie, since he was a gay man. So while he was trying to get people to believe strongly in what he said, he couldn't believe in it himself.

"I had a great meeting with him last week in the park where I wouldn't let us talk about anything relating to the church," Jeff said.

"It's hard to dictate what Jacob will and won't talk about," I said.

I heard the girls on the stereo sing lyrics that cut through me. *The less I seek my source for some definitive, closer I am to fine.* How true that was. If only all of us could stop looking for the answers so much — me, Jacob, anyone — how much better off we'd be.

"That meeting with the Gay Men's Health Crisis pushed me over the edge," Pamela said.

"I have a friend that volunteers there. What meeting did you have?" I asked.

Pamela and Jeff made eyes back and forth and I could tell they were keeping something from me.

"Come on, you can trust me."

Pamela said there was something more going on, but she didn't feel comfortable sharing it with me. She thought it should come from someone in the family. I had no idea what else could be happening, but thanked them both for spending some time talking with me.

"I want to try that Mexican chicken you make some time, Pamela," I said, walking towards the door.

"We'll have you and your girlfriend over and I promise. I'll cook it for you," she said.

As I was about to leave, Jeff handed me a paper.

"It's a copy of something I wrote about Jacob to God," he said. "I gave it to him, but you can read it sometime too. I just wanted you to see a different side of your brother that someone was able to care about."

"I appreciate people who care about my family," I said.

I took the paper, said goodbye and walked into their hall towards the elevator. Once inside, I opened to read what Jeff had handed me. The entire poem puzzled me.

What did Jeff mean that this was about Jacob? Part of it made sense and part of it troubled me deeply. I began to read between the lines and only hoped that the thoughts going through my head were a misreading of mine. I wasn't sure I would be able to take it if it were not. Closer to fine, Noah. Stop seeking the answers.

CHAPTER FORTY-ONE

JACOB

I had the young married couple from church in my office. They had always come to me for advice. I had shown them my way of using the Bible to get answers. But secretly, I preferred they come directly to me. Even when I was feeling run down as I did today. I now used a cane to help me get around and those closest to me would try and ignore the added appendage that I had. But my mind still worked. And who heard God as well as I did?

"Whether its money problems, sex problems, or other fights, you should always turn to God," I said, through a coughing fit that hit me out of nowhere.

"I told her that, Jacob," the husband said. "Sometimes she's very defiant."

"A man should not allow that to happen," I said. "Leslie, you know God expects you to be submissive to Joe."

"I have a problem with that one," she said.

I knew Leslie could be headstrong, but also knew she was wrong.

"The problems exist because you fight him," I said. "Don't you see that? If you would just submit, you would not continue to have any problems."

I stared at Leslie and she stared right back. But she was outnumbered in this room. I wondered if I was getting through to her.

Leslie spoke. "That statement tells me the problem wouldn't exist because Joe would be getting his own way."

Joe tried to explain to her that she wasn't listening to me, which might have been getting harder and harder to do because of my persistent cough. I talked to her about repenting to God, while I gulped down some water.

Joe spoke up. "Honey, we need to go and let Jacob get home to his own wife so she can care for him."

Leslie leaned into her husband to whisper to him, while I took the moment to look for a cough drop in my coat pocket. But I could hear her.

"I think he needs to get to a doctor. I'm sure this is part of the illness."

I turned to face the young couple again. Who did she think she was, throwing my illness in my face like that?

"God just told me you are hiding a secret, Leslie," I said. "Something you do not wish your husband to know."

Joe looked at Leslie and she glared at me, perplexed.

Try and mess with me, missy.

"Do you wish to share it with us both?" I asked, through another fit of coughing.

"I think … I think …" Leslie looked at both of us.

There was no winning for her tonight. While she usually put up a fight, her compassion for me was going to trump her need to be right.

"Joe, you are the master of our home and I'm sorry for questioning you," she said. "I have secretly longed to be the bread winner, but

I know that is your place."

Had I caused her to share a secret or did I just catch a smirk across her face? In any case, I had to take it as a victory, which were becoming few and far between. I didn't want to continue this talk.

"Leslie, I am proud of you," I said. "Joe, hold your wife. Take her home now and show her how the man can truly love a woman who submits to him whole heartedly."

Joe stood, grabbed his wife and walked out of the door. Even as tired and sick as I was, I had just won another battle, however slight. But as they entered the elevator down the hall, I heard Leslie say once she was home alone with Joe; she was going to beat some sense into his thick skull.

I was failing at my job as a minister. The battle going on inside of me was obviously manifesting itself in my work. My purpose didn't seem as clear to me; my health was getting in the way of what I could accomplish. The rapid growth of the disease had to be in response to my giving into temptation in Riverside Park those months ago. Whenever that was. If God were going to fight Satan on my behalf, I wish he'd hurry up.

CHAPTER FORTY-TWO

NOAH

It seemed as if everyone had been trying to keep this secret from me for as long as they could. But Samantha was tired of fighting Jacob over whether to tell me or not and had to make the call. It was exactly what I had dreaded from Jeff's poem. It was my worst fears come true. My brother was sick. He was not using drugs again. No matter how many other people I knew that had succumbed to this horrible disease, when it hit your family — when it was your flesh and blood — it was a different story all together. The dreaded virus was attacking my brother and his fight would not be an easy one. His medicines had stopped working and he had been in and out of the hospital a few times. Samantha and Jacob had managed to keep it from everyone except Rachel, but now she needed me to know.

I went to Samantha's apartment to pick her up and ride down to St. Vincent's Hospital. Even though they lived on the Upper West Side, Jacob's doctor was associated with the hospital in the Village and she would constantly take the long subway down. I told her that this time she was worth the cab fare.

"How are you, Sam?" I asked, as we rode downtown.

"We pray," she said.

"Sam, I want to know about you," I said. "Don't give me all the church crap right now."

She looked into my eyes.

"I'm exhausted. It's tiring on my body to come down to be with him each time he goes in," she said. "I have the children. Thank God that Mikey is in school all day, but Ronnie's preschool is only half a day."

I felt awful for Samantha. It's not fair that she was handed this lot in her life, but I didn't want to pity her, even though she looked tired and fragile herself.

"Please let me help more," I said. "I can go sit with him. I can pick up the kids. Just call me."

"Thank you, Noah. I appreciate that," she said.

"I can't lie and say I'm not upset with what he has done to you ... to himself. It was a choice he made," I said, looking out the window on my side of the cab.

"I made a choice too," she said.

"How long have you both known?" I asked.

"I hate telling you this. You are family and we've never shared it with you."

"It's fine," I said.

"Four or five years now," she said.

She had found out right before she had Veronica. The thought of what she had gone through made me extremely sad. I pulled her into my arms. I wanted her to feel safe, if only for a short while of riding down 7th Avenue. We didn't speak. She just looked out the window, as we passed Madison Square Garden. I wondered if she was thinking about Jacob, or about herself, if there was a life before

Jacob that had made her happy?

"My whole life has changed," she said. "Christ Redeemer changed everything."

"I'm sure you feel angry and misled by it all," I said.

"I don't ask God for answers anymore," she said. "Just an ending."

The cab went down passed 14th Street and slowed down on the left hand side. I paid the cabbie and offered my hand to help her from the car.

"Noah, your brother is not the same man anymore," she said. "If he says something to you, just go along with it. Dementia has set in, the doctors say."

"I understand," I said. "And I won't hold it against him. Or against you for standing by his side. You are an incredible woman."

Samantha gave me a huge hug and turned to lead me through the front door of the hospital. We walked to the elevator and took it to his floor. I hated walking those hallways, with its sterile smell and noisy monitors. Sickness, death, endings — it all flooded my mind.

There was my older brother, barely taking up much of the bed, looking weaker than I had ever seen him before. There had always been a frailty to him, but only in his build and demeanor. A misconception, for he had always still been strong. But not now, now the illness was ravaging his body like a coyote feeding on its prey.

He looked like a vampire in his gauntness and paleness. I thought the parallel was strange. A vampire feeds on blood and Jacob had a time bomb running through his blood that could eventually kill anyone that came in contact with it.

"Honey, I'm here with your brother," Samantha said. "Are you asleep or just resting your eyes?"

Jacob opened his eyes in a slow and deliberate way.

"I'm asleep," he said.

I decided it was time for a joke.

"I see the hospital hasn't taken your sense of humor," I said.

"Why are you here?" Jacob screamed. "How did you know? Sam?"

I stopped him.

"Don't blame Sam for anything," I said. "You think I don't know when something is wrong with my own brother? I knew something was up. I wanted to see you."

"The walls are green with spaghetti," Jacob said.

I caught Samantha's eyes, which seemed to say *go along with it,* so I didn't miss a beat.

"We'll have to get that cleaned up then," I said. "Nothing worse than green spaghetti."

Samantha sat on one side of the bed wiping Jacob's forehead with a wet cloth. I walked to the other side to my brother and put my hand on top of his.

"You have Dad's hands, bro," I said.

"Funny. I thought I would have Mama's," he said.

We all laughed at his joke.

"Naomi sends her love," I said.

"Are you married yet?" he asked.

"Not yet. Still thinking about it," I said.

I was happy that at least Jacob was making some sense.

Samantha stood and picked up the water jug.

"I'm going to go get some more ice water."

I smiled at her as she walked out of the room. I looked back down at my brother and settled into a chair, sitting right up next to the bed.

"My little Bubba … what am I going to do with you?" Jacob asked.

"With me? I'm not the one in a hospital bed," I said.

"Are you writing anything?" he asked.

"Got a short story going about a boy named Skipper," I said with a smile. I wasn't even sure if Jacob remembered telling me to call him that in a book.

"That sounds like a dog's name," he said.

I guess he had forgotten. Oh well. An attempt at a sentimental moment.

Jacob turned to look out the window.

I wasn't sure if this was a good time to ask, but he had brought up my writing.

"Why have you never wanted to read my work?" I asked. "Are you that afraid of visiting the past?"

Jacob didn't respond. I suppose I may never get an answer to that question. Instead he changed the subject.

"What do you think Mama looks like?" he asked.

I wasn't sure if that was a real question or if it was his dementia.

"I think she's probably just as beautiful now as she ever was," I said.

"I think she is sitting next to God," Jacob said. "Between him and Jesus and holding court."

I smiled. "That would be Mama all right."

"I want to see her," he said.

This made me feel very uneasy.

"You will see her," I said. "Someday. We both will."

"I want to talk to her," he said. "Apologize for everything I did."

"She knows, brother. She knows."

"I messed up my whole life. Sam's life."

I didn't know what to say to him, because I agreed.

"My back hurts," he said.

"It's called bed sores," I said. "You've been in one spot too long."

"My finger wants to fall off and walk across the hall," he said.

His mind was slipping. Is this what would become of the last conversations I would ever get to have with my brother?

"If it does ... I'll go get it and bring it back," I said.

Jacob started singing.

"She's 41 and her daddy still calls her baby. All the folks 'round Brownsville thinks she's crazy."

Suddenly I was back on Peachmont Street in Nocona, sitting in our living room while Mama was in the kitchen cooking something and singing. Jacob and Gary were locked away in his room — Gary. It occurred to me that I needed to let Gary know what was happening with Jacob. It was only right for him to be made aware.

Jacob stared out the window, as I put my head on my big brother's lap. I turned my head outwards as tears flowed down my cheeks. The sounds of my brother singing muffled the sounds of my weeping.

"Delta Dawn, what's that flower you have on ... "

***

As a writer, I had a thing for pens.

I had all colors, all kinds. I had also become much more on the meticulous side once I moved north and had some OCD in me. My apartment had to be kept a certain way. I would walk around shutting doors and turning off lights. The toaster always had to be unplugged after it was used. Those kind of small quirks. But my pens. My pens always had to have their covers on them or if they were a flip tops, they had to be closed. Naomi loved playing the game of walking around the house and flipping each pen to the on position, just to leave a piece of her in my house after she was gone. I found it adorable.

I saw the pen on the counter next to my grocery pad flipped in the on position.

"You think I don't notice," I said with a smile.

"What? I didn't do anything," she said.

"You know, you have quirks too," I said.

"Oh, okay. Let me hear them," she said.

She had several.

She had to make sure both feet touched the floor at the same time when she got out of bed. The soap in the shower had to be her favorite kind and she hated any soap scum in the soap dish. If we got into a cab that was too hot, Naomi always had to lower the window to get air. She also had a thing for cotton swabs and I found them in my wastebasket every time she left my house.

"Nothing. You are perfect," I said.

I didn't want to share her quirks, because I loved them all. They made up who she was.

"Chicken." Naomi went towards the fridge to get herself a diet soda.

I watched her walk towards the kitchen. I loved this woman more than I had ever loved anyone. And I appreciated her trying to make tonight as normal as possible, just to keep my mind off Jacob.

"Do you know how much I love you?" I asked.

"Of course, cowboy. I love you too," she said.

This wasn't one of those tender moments from a movie. It was a night that I had taken off from going to the hospital, pretending it was just another evening of watching television, eating popcorn and drinking soda. The night was not meant to feel special, but to mimic any other night so I could temporarily forget about my brother. Yet, it was then that I realized I wanted to be with this woman forever.

"You know how you've been saying we're not getting any younger. How it's time to live together?" I asked.

"Yes. I'll move in once we get married."

Perhaps it was watching my brother die slowly in the hospital, the fear of being left alone, or maybe it was just the simple fact that I had found the person I wanted to spend my life with.

"Let's do it. What are we waiting on?" I said.

Naomi looked over the counter from the kitchen.

"You want me to move in here? Now?" she asked.

"I want to get married," I said.

Naomi stopped and walked around the corner, back into the living room.

"Noah, what are you talking about?" she said.

"I'm talking about you and me. Forever. Naomi, I'm in love with you and have loved you for so long," I said. "I want to grow old with you. I want to be the new breed of family with a Christian and a Jew."

Naomi laughed. We had talked several times about the joining of the two faiths, what it would mean for us and our children and she was fine with it.

This simple proposal was who we were. She didn't need to be whisked away an exotic, touristy location. She just wanted to be with me — the Long Island Jewish American Princess married to her Southern Cowboy.

"You big goon."

She came to my side and sat by me, tracing the scar on my chin as she did often, just as Mama had done to me before she died.

"In my heart, I'm already married to you," she continued. "I love you too and want nothing more than to be your wife."

I took her in my arms and kissed her. This was home. This was real.

"So where is the ring?" she asked.

And … just like that, the moment was broken.

"Ah, you see, I didn't plan this out correctly," I said. "It just sort of happened as I watched you walk into the kitchen."

"Oh? So I guess I'm picking out my own ring, huh?" she said.

"Would you have it any other way?" I asked.

"Absolutely not."

We laughed at each other.

"I love you, Mrs. Noah Garrett," I said.

"We'll discuss that too. There may need to be a hyphen in there somewhere," she said.

I expected nothing less of my bride to be. As strong a woman as she was, I was certain she'd find a way to keep her maiden name. We curled up on the couch and watched TV as if nothing at all had changed.

CHAPTER FORTY-THREE

NOAH

Two weeks had passed and Jacob was still at St. Vincent's hospital, growing weaker by the day. Samantha paced the halls, full of so many gay men fighting the same thing her husband was fighting. I'm sure those halls were a constant reminder to her of the life she had chosen for herself. A huge sign hung over Jacob's bed that read, *Must Wear Gloves at All Times.* I wonder if Samantha thought about that becoming her fate.

I stood in the hallway before I let them know I was there, as I watched her add a few more pillows to Jacob's back. Each move caused him to grimace with pain.

"They say you are doing a little better today," Samantha said.

"The shingles are unbearable," Jacob said.

"I think that must be part of the cancer," she said.

"Who's preaching on Sundays?" Jacob asked a smirk on his face.

I couldn't understand why he would be thinking of church right now. Why wasn't he asking her about their kids? Curious about their schoolwork?

"Byron," she said, and hastened to add, "Until you are better."

"I should write some sermons for him," Jacob said. "God has been talking to me while I'm here. He feels no one is listening to Him …

only me … and He needs to get His message out."

"Others are listening," she said.

"Not like me."

"Jacob … I'm scared," she said.

I felt I should have made my presence known earlier.

"God would not want you to be scared," he said.

Samantha became angry. "God should have thought of that before He put my husband in a deathbed while I have two small children at home."

Jacob reached out for her hand. "I'll be home soon."

"It's me," she said. "Don't lie to me."

"I'll be home soon," he repeated.

"Fine," she said. "Keep saying that if you think it'll make it true."

I cleared my throat. Jacob saw me over Samantha's shoulder.

"Bubba! Come in," he said.

"How's my favorite sister-in-law?" I asked, kissing her forehead.

"Your *only* sister-in-law is tired," she said.

"Why don't you head home," I said. "I can stay here awhile."

"He could deal with another face to look at besides mine," she quickly agreed.

She kissed Jacob in a loving way that I'm not sure I will ever understand and walked out.

"I'll be back," she said.

"You getting the right kind of food in here?" I asked.

"You know what I could go for," Jacob said.

"What?"

"Granny's chocolate gravy."

At least the man still had an appetite (and the long-term memory was there), even if it were for the sugary breakfast food we would have with biscuits as children. But looking at him, you'd never believe he had an appetite there at all. Jacob was so thin it felt hardly possible that he could lose more weight.

I have some amazing kids, don't I, Bubba?" he asked.

"Yes, you do," I agreed.

"They are the two great things that came out of my life," he said.

Jacob was right. As much as I didn't understand the so-called changes he had gone through, he managed to have a son and a daughter to leave a part of him in the world. And they were regular, crazy little kids. Not yet understanding why their father was in the hospital or what was happening to him. When they visited, they wanted to play with all the machines in the room and would go up and down the halls causing the sick people to smile. Yes, God had a reason for seeing to it that my brother had children. I just wasn't sure why God wanted to take him away from them.

I looked up and saw Jeff standing in the door.

"Hey," I said.

Jeff walked in the room, mesmerized by the spectacle of Jacob's body.

"How is it going?" he asked.

"Fine," Jeff said.

"A little cancer can't get me down."

"Cancer?" Jeff asked.

"Yes, they said it's spread through my body," he said. "But I know I'll be back preaching soon. And just wait until we're filling up that church until it's overflowing ..."

I looked at Jeff as if to say it was ok to go along with it. Everyone in that room knew my brother was dying from AIDS.

"God has called out to me from the burning bush and has said ... take hold, Jacob. Hold onto me," Jacob said.

"God can talk to you in here just as well as at your church," Jeff said.

Jacob became angry and looked at Jeff as if possessed.

"You better be careful you don't end up in hell, Jeff."

"Jeff is a Christian, brother. He knows where he is going," I said.

"I just wanted to see you, I felt I needed to come," Jeff said through a hurt-filled gaze.

Suddenly, Jacob's demeanor changed towards Jeff.

"I'll see you once I'm out," Jacob said with his old smile.

I was heart-broken, knowing Jeff would not be seeing Jacob outside the hospital again. I patted him on the back as he started to leave.

"Yes ... I'll see you then," Jeff said.

Jeff started to leave and then Jacob spoke. "Do you know if it's well with your soul, Jeff?"

Jeff stopped.

"Yes, sir. I do," he said.

Jacob began to sing in a throaty voice.

"*When peace like a river attends my way. When sorrow like sea billows roll. Whatever my lot ...*"

Jeff's eyes filled with tears as he touched my arm on his way out the door. Jacob turned and looked out the window towards the heavens. I knew he didn't mean the nasty things he had said to Jeff.

It was the virus speaking, not my brother.

"Noah, make sure I'm buried in the same place as Mama."

I couldn't believe he was talking like this. That he would want to return to his roots — the man that had spent a lifetime getting away from them. But in a strange way, he had caused me to see my own escape towards freedom and I would see to it that he got what he wanted.

"Absolutely brother," I said.

Without looking at me, he continued to sing.

"*Whatever my lot that has taught me to say …*"

"*It is well with my soul,*" I joined in singing.

***

Some days, Jacob was coherent; others, he was completely out of it. I never knew what to expect when I arrived. Samantha had stopped bringing the kids to visit, since they didn't need to remember their father in this state. I wasn't sure I wanted to remember him that way either. He was as emaciated as Mama was on the days before she died. And like with her, I was here by his side. I guess we all have our roles in the family. Jacob's was to be the brash person in the family, the one that got all the attention. Mine was to come along and clean up the mess.

I was glad that Samantha was home napping the day that Gary showed up. I had warned him what to expect. How gaunt Jacob was at a mere 90 pounds. Gary had lost other friends to this horrible disease and had been volunteering for a while at GMHC, dealing with it all the time, but it wasn't the same as seeing the man you had loved for so long. I was reading a newspaper to Jacob about Jeffrey Dahlmer being arrested for killing over 17 young men, but he wasn't really listening. I looked up and there was Gary standing in the doorway. He immediately started crying. I went over to him and put my arm around his shoulder.

"Hey, buddy. Glad you could come," I said.

I stepped him into the hall for a moment.

"Just breathe," I said.

"God, Noah. I wasn't ready —"

"I know, I know. Just try and pull it together."

"I'm okay. I'm okay."

He wiped his eyes, took a deep breath and walked into the room. He walked over to the side of the bed and leaned down next to Jacob. He took his weak, spotted hand in his own and Jacob looked at him.

"Hey, babe — how ya hanging in here?" he asked, pretending as if the past several years never happened.

Jacob couldn't speak. I knew there must be so much he wanted to say. He tried, but nothing would come out.

"It's ok. Don't try and say anything," Gary said. "I just wanted to come and see you."

Jacob looked over at me.

"Don't blame me, brother. Gary must just know," I said.

Jacob squeezed Gary's hand as tightly as he possibly could and I saw tears form in the corner of his eyes. I guess I had my answer about his fear of addressing the past. Here it was standing in the room right beside him and I just knew that Jacob was full of regrets over his life. He had to be. So much had happened that never had to — but no need to go through that now. Gary leaned down closer to talk to

Jacob and I felt this was something I didn't need to be a part of. No matter if words were to be said or they just wanted to sit in silence, I excused myself to the hallway and left the two men alone to share their final time together.

***

The day he passed was not as gut-wrenching as I would have expected. I had already cried my tears for him. Samantha and I sat on opposite sides of the bed. Rubbing his arms, wiping his brow — talking and singing with him. I grasped my brother's hand tightly as his soul left his body — thinking if I held on strong enough, I could keep him here. But Jacob always got his way. And on that day, he wanted to go. He wanted to be with Mama and Daddy and move on from this world.

When the machine told us he was gone, Samantha stood and walked out of the room. Perhaps it was to go and get a nurse. Perhaps to be alone. But she left me there with the last remaining blood relative I had. As difficult a relationship as I had with Jacob, I loved him. He had taught me so much about who I was — without ever knowing he was teaching. Simply by being my big brother, he was sharing the world with me. He, along with my beautiful fiancée, opened my eyes to things I had never known. My mind had expanded so much beyond my narrow views of the world to a broader understanding of people, what they do, why they choose to live the way they live. I traveled all these miles to end up in the same city as Jacob and now he was gone. Gone but not forgotten.

I thought of him getting to see Mama and Daddy and leaned down and whispered in his ear, "Say hello to them from me."

The funeral service was held in Tennessee just as Jacob had requested. That was where he wanted to be buried. Naomi and I flew down there with Samantha and the kids. While Mama's family was all gone, there were a few cousins and of course, the congregation from Mama's church. These were people who had mocked Jacob's life for so many years — until he had made it big in the modeling world. On the day of his funeral, they all showed to pay their respects to the man who had left Nocona to make his mark on the world. And what a mark it was. At least for me.

The organ played his favorite hymn. In my mind, I could hear Jacob singing along. Our former preacher gave a sermon, which included the plan of salvation for any sinners at the funeral who did not know the Lord. He spoke of all the great things Jacob had done, about his wonderful wife and children, which I'm sure was a pleasant surprise for those who had talked about him being gay for so many years. If they only knew that people don't change. My brother was born gay and died gay.

But there was not one mention of the inhumane disease that was ravishing so many people in the world and that had taken Jacob, the very virus biding its time in Samantha as she sat there with her children next to her, only the mention of cancer taking such a young man. I don't know if I wanted them to say the word or not. I'm not sure how I would have felt. But the entire thing had a feeling of not being truly authentic to whom Jacob was.

Naomi and I stayed by the graveside as people were leaving, many coming up and giving me their condolences and saying how much they loved Jacob. But then a woman approached me I had never seen before. She had driven three hours across Tennessee to be at the service. It was Jeff's mother. Jeff had told me that my own brother had called her, told her she was not a good mother, all in his attempt to save Jeff. But here she was — wanting to pay her respects to the man.

"I met your brother on a few visits to New York and I know deep down he was doing what he believed God wanted him to do," she said to me, as she shook my hand. "God be with you."

And she walked away. Others left the site and Naomi went to make sure Samantha was doing alright, as she and the kids got into the car to head to the hotel. I stood alone by the coffin that would soon be lowered in the ground; and I promised my brother to help Samantha as much as I possibly could. I knew life would not be easy for her. It dawned on me that I did have other blood relatives left in this world — all thanks to Jacob. Michael and Veronica. Sam would need help raising them alone and I wanted to do whatever I could to alleviate her burden. I had no idea what her fate would be, but I knew being there for her was something I needed to do for both myself and for Jacob.

***

I had told Naomi whatever she wanted in a wedding was what I wanted. And true to Naomi's style, it was a beautifully simple, yet elegant ceremony outside on the West Gilgo Beach on the south side of Long Island. Naomi wore an off-white cocktail dress and I wore linen pants and shirt that complimented her outfit to a tee. Neither of us had on shoes, and the sand crept up between our toes. She looked beautiful with her hair long and flowing in the early summer breeze; an angel that God had sent to me.

We kept the guest list small. Naomi's mother, a few family members and some work friends on her side. Samantha came with the kids, but to my disapproval was accompanied by Byron. I invited Pamela and Jeffrey. I had discovered I really liked those two and we had shared a common bond over my brother. My agent and editor were there, plus Tony and Rich from our building, and of course my other 'brother' Gary came with Roger.

My niece was a beautiful flower girl in a lavender sundress dropping rose petals on the beach as she walked towards Naomi and me. Next to my glowing bride was her best friend since high school. And by my side, was a seven year old who would beam as he looked up at me. Mickey was great at standing in the place where his father would have been. He looked like a small clone of his uncle dressed in the very same outfit.

The waves lapped against the beach as the officiate we had paid to oversee our marriage welcomed our guests. There was no religion placed on this union — it wasn't about that. It was about two people who had found love and wanted to share the rest of their lives together. I thought it must have been killing Naomi's mother, not to have a traditional Jewish wedding, but I looked at her sitting on her chair on the beach and she was smiling brightly at her gorgeous daughter.

"I promise to love you, honor you, bring you a drink when you are thirsty and feed your soul when you need nourishment," I said as the people witnessing chuckled.

"I promise to be there for you, when you write a good story and when one bombs," Naomi said causing me to crack up. "I've loved you since I met you and I can't wait to spend the rest of my life with you."

I placed a ring on her finger and could imagine Mama smiling down on me — that I was finally getting married, even if it were in my thirties. It took me longer than most people, but I had found her and I was happy as I possibly could be. I took her in my arms and kissed her until I felt Veronica trying to push between us, bringing everyone to their feet laughing and applauding.

We all retired to the area on the beach that had been set up with food and drink. Naomi had chosen a steel guitar to play for her cowboy as the sun set in the distance. We made our way around to our guests to talk to each of them.

"What is this about some lesbian concert in the park you attended with these two, Noah?" Gary asked has he wrapped his arms around Naomi.

"I didn't say anything," Jeff said with a sheepish grin.

"Just don't mention the brownies that Pamela made," Naomi quietly said with a laugh.

"Just keep drinking, kid, and spill the beans," Gary said as he smacked Jeff on the back.

Naomi kissed him on the cheek and gave Roger a hug. It was great to witness new friendships being made among people in our lives. I sat with Samantha for a while who seemed weaker each time I saw her and we reminisced about her wedding day. Having Sam and Gary at my wedding just seemed to be the right thing to do.

While the small crowd ate and watched the sun go down, I rolled up my pants legs, took my new bride's hand and walked along the beach in the water talking about our future together. Knowing the entire time we were being followed by Mickey and Veronica who were enjoying making fun of their uncle and new aunt.

CHAPTER FORTY-FOUR

NOAH

O ctober. The Toronto Blue Jays won the World Series becoming the first Canadian team ever to win; the Kentucky Supreme Court declared same sex sodomy laws as unconstitutional and a 29 pound meteorite landed in the driveway in Peekskill, New York. But in New York City, a few people had gathered in Jacob's apartment as they had just a little over a year earlier for my brother's memorial service. This time, it was to celebrate Samantha's life. She had succumbed to the disease, not able to maintain her health on the medicines not too long after her husband's death.

Naomi and I had tried to do as much for her as we could the entire year. Even though we had moved to Long Island, we would come in and help every chance we got. But in the past few months, something strange had occurred. In a move that shocked everyone, Samantha married Byron and signed everything over to him. I suppose I should have seen it coming from the way Byron had flirted with Samantha that day at the soup kitchen or how he was trying to take over Jacob's position in the church — but I hadn't done anything to stop it. Once that happened, I notice he started to push Naomi and me away when we offered our help. I couldn't believe that Samantha had married him, but she confided in me that God had told her to do it and allowed

Byron to watch over her children. And now she was gone. Gone like my brother. The new drugs didn't seem to help her much. Or maybe she had simply given up. Whatever the reason, like my brother, she would never be able to witness her children growing up.

Rachel went around the apartment making sure everyone was getting plenty of food. My nephew and niece seemed to stay to themselves up in their loft. Naomi and I tried to play with them as Jeff, Pamela and Jeff's boyfriend, Carlos, were talking in the corner.

"It was a beautiful service," Carlos said, trying to break the silence.

Jeff added, "How many more of these do we have to attend?"

I knew they had attended numerous memorial services the past few years for friends they were losing to the terrible disease.

"The difference is, no one mentions the word AIDS at these," Carlos said.

"Look at Byron over there alone," Pamela said.

"I hate the thought that those kids have to stay with him," Jeff said.

Naomi and I walked down the stairs towards them as Pamela voiced her disdain as well. "It makes me sick to think she married him so fast."

"Join the club," I said.

"Sorry, Noah. Were we being too loud?" Jeff asked.

"Not at all. We just knew what you'd be talking about over here," Naomi answered.

"Notice how Rachel and Byron act as if Christ Redeemer is still operating," Pamela said.

"Did it close?" I asked.

"Oh yeah. They gave up the building and 4 or 5 people were

meeting here in this apartment until Samantha couldn't take it anymore," Jeff said.

Naomi looked at me and decided to change the subject.

"Jeff, Noah and I are so excited to be seeing you on Broadway in *The Will Rogers Follies*."

"Few more weeks of rehearsal and our guy here will be going in," Pamela said grabbing him in her arms.

"You know we'll all be there your opening night," I said, trying to forget all the strangeness in this house — but I found myself staring at Byron.

Pamela looked at him as well. "Marrying her was his way to get this fabulous apartment on the Upper West Side."

I felt my blood start to boil.

"I should take it away from him," I said.

"Noah," Naomi scolded.

"I'll help you," Pamela added. "You guys are like family."

Family. I was beginning to miss that word.

"Excuse me please," I said.

I went into what had been Samantha and Jacob's bedroom. And before that, it had belonged to Jacob and Gary. Rachel walked into the room behind me.

"Have you said anything to Byron?" Rachel asked me.

"About what? All the lies?" I asked.

Rachel was shocked by my candor.

"What?" she said.

"This memorial service here," I said, "the burial of my brother back in Tennessee, no one admitting what actually happened to both of them."

"They both got very sick and their bodies gave out," she said. "Cancer can do that."

"There are other things that can do that too," I said. "I was in that hospital as Jake was dying. I saw the signs on the walls warning people to stay clear of him. They don't treat cancer patients like that."

"Please don't do this here …"

I kept going as I walked around the room looking at photos. I found myself getting very upset.

"This whole service is opening up wounds all over again," I said.

Rachel tried to calm me down.

"Jacob and Sam knew they were here for a higher reason," she said.

"Come on, Rachel. You can stop with the pretending now. They are both gone."

"God had a purpose for their entire lives."

I wondered if she really believed that.

"What purpose?" I asked. "Jake was a selfish bastard."

"Noah! He's dead and gone. Don't speak ill of your brother like that," she said.

"All my life … all his life … he had it all planned out. And always got what he wanted," I said. "Gary. Moving to New York. An incredible career. Then a preacher … and a beautiful woman who loved him dearly. Loved him to death. Two gorgeous kids. Shit … if he could have had it in New York, there would have been a white picket fence."

"Are you jealous?" Rachel asked.

"Hell no," I said. "I've had my life and I am grateful for it. No.

It's not jealousy. It's pain. It's hurt that he could not just stay who he was … who he was meant to be. Then maybe her life would have been spared."

"We can't question why God does the things that He does."

I couldn't believe that Jacob had gotten so under this woman's skin that even now she was going to maintain this crazy charade as a religious fanatic.

"Well maybe it's not God doing it," I said. "Do you really believe a loving God would allow all of this to happen?"

"I knew Jacob Garrett as Jake and as Jacob," she said. "I knew the party animal … I was right there with him. But God moved in his life and mine and many, many people that your brother came in contact with. He was a good man. A just man. And he died as who he was meant to be."

"Then what about that young man out there being who he is meant to be?" I asked.

"You mean Jeff?" she responded.

"Yes. He's gay. He loves the Lord —"

"And his life will be full of heartache," she interjected.

"His life will be full of a lot of things," I said raising my voice. "But not because he's gay. Because that's just how life is."

"He will have to come to terms with his lifestyle at some point, Noah, or he'll never truly be close to God."

"You mean like my brother was?" I asked. "Jeff told me he felt that Jacob was jealous of the peace he had found in himself and you know what, I believe him."

"Jacob found peace as well —" she tried to say.

"The hell he did," I said. "Think back, Rachel. Was your life really that bad off before you met the late, great Jacob Garrett? Before a man, a regular man told you what to think, how to feel, what God wanted you to do?"

Rachel couldn't respond. But I saw her mind working somewhere underneath that tightly wound scarf that had gone out of style years before. Instead, she turned and walked back into the other room where people were looking at a photo album. She called to Byron to come out of his corner and join them as they looked at the photos.

Naomi walked into the bedroom with me.

"You ok?" she asked.

"Just having problems making sense of all of this," I said, turning my back on my wife, fighting back tears. I almost wished that I smoked, so I could grab a cigarette about now.

"I can't stop thinking about your nephew and niece," Naomi said. "Those poor kids. So much in such a little time."

"Living with that freak in the other room."

I turned and knew that Naomi could see the pain, sadness and years of hurt in my eyes.

"Noah, they deserve to grow up in a world where they are able to make choices, make mistakes and above all, know they are loved," she said.

"I don't see how that can happen with that S.O.B."

Naomi did not miss a beat with her response.

"It can happen with us," she said.

I couldn't believe what I had just heard from my remarkable wife.

"You want to raise someone else's children?" I said.

Naomi walked over and took me in her arms.

"I love those two," she said. "Where else can they learn about their parents ... who else can tell them incredible stories? You ... the Long Island Cowboy."

I was able to push back the rest of the tears. "You know this will mean a big fight with Byron," I said to her.

"I think they are worth it," she said.

I kissed her. And as I pulled back, I saw a picture of my brother over Naomi's shoulder still hanging on the wall.

"I think Jacob would like that," I said.

"I think *you* would like that ... and so would I," Naomi said as she started to lead me out of the room.

I stopped her and pulled her to me one more time.

"Mrs. Garrett-Weisman, you are the most amazing woman I've ever met."

Naomi took my hand. "We are here to show our respects. Let's join the others, get through today, and then we will go file papers in court next week."

"I think Jacob will be able to rest in peace ... knowing his children are with family," I said.

There was that word again.

Family.

The history of it had filled my writing — flowing through my veins from my soul. It prompted me years ago to use the pen as a tool to share my stories. It had been a catalyst to bring me to New York in order to connect to someone — something I had tried to do ever since my father had died. And it would be the one thing to hoist me into my future, branching out beyond a world of myself … but including a wife and two small children. Children that would carry on the Garrett name, not only for me and for my brother — but for our entire family, always.

ACKNOWLEDGEMENTS

Having been an actor, director, producer, playwright for most of my adult life, I find writing to be the loneliest of them all. Thank God I have people in my life who are there to support me, lend an ear, or read something I have written and give me brutal honesty. A huge thanks to Ernesto for his thoughtful and engaging edit; making the story all that more moving. Lori Ann, you led me down the right path with your help on POV and structure — I can't say thanks enough. PJM & JBF — you put up with my OCD while I worked on every element of the story and gave more than friends should; reading constant rewrites without yelling at me to stop sending them, offering constructive criticism, praising and encouraging when my spirit was floundering. Actors who read an original stage version of this story and helped shape what it became by bringing my characters to life — I thank you. Countless other friends — too many to mention — who listened while I talked about these characters over lunch or phone calls and let me brainstorm ideas off of them; what would I do without your attentive ears? To those that traveled the 'twenty-plus years' journey that brought me to this novel — what a ride! To my mother who has always encouraged me to dream and my family who are my biggest fans no matter what I do — so much love I send to all of you. And to Anthony who has followed the many creative flights I've taken, yet has always managed to keep me grounded — La Dear.

www.ingramcontent.com/pod-product-compliance
Lightning Source LLC
Chambersburg PA
CBHW032142190626
46814CB00005BA/1799